Death
in an
Ivory Tower

5

Death
in an
Ivory Tower

MARIA HUDGINS

W💀RLDWIDE®

TORONTO • NEW YORK • LONDON
AMSTERDAM • PARIS • SYDNEY • HAMBURG
STOCKHOLM • ATHENS • TOKYO • MILAN
MADRID • WARSAW • BUDAPEST • AUCKLAND

For Elizabeth and Nate Newton

Recycling programs
for this product may
not exist in your area.

Death in an Ivory Tower

A Worldwide Mystery/August 2016

First published by Five Star Publishing.

ISBN-13: 978-0-373-27950-0

Acknowledgments

Many great mysteries have been set in Oxford, UK, in the university or in the town that surrounds it, and like many writers before me, I've taken the liberty of inventing a college that doesn't exist. Oxford University consists of some forty autonomous colleges scattered about the town amid shops, restaurants, and churches such as you'd find in any town.

I call my college St. Ormond's and I've been deliberately vague about exactly where it is. There is, for instance, no Cobbler's Lane and no Sycamore Lane. But the main thoroughfares, such as the High and Broad Street, are real, since any lover of Oxford would cringe at my renaming them. Major landmarks, like the "Emperors' Heads" and Blackwell's Bookshop, are not disguised. If any reader familiar with the town notices a similarity between my fictitious college and Jesus College, Oxford, it may be because I stayed there one summer while attending the St. Hilda's Crime and Mystery Weekend. I chose Jesus College because its oldest halls date to the Elizabethan period, and because it had the atmosphere I was looking for as a setting for this story. I'm grateful to the porters of Jesus College for taking me to some parts of the school normally closed to visitors. But beyond the arrangement of the quads and the incredible flowerbeds, any resemblance between St. Ormond's and Jesus or any other Oxford college is coincidental.

I'd like to thank my friend Brian Smith for his help with the technical aspects of an insulin regimen. I'm also grateful to Dr. Donna Forrest for her plot suggestions and her help with the details of gunshot wound surgery and recovery.

As always, I thank my dogs, Holly and Hamilton, for keeping me company while I wrote this story and my Sisters in Crime friends for their patience and help.

Cast of Characters

Dotsy Lamb—Ancient and medieval history teacher from Staunton, Virginia. At sixtysomething, she's determined to complete her PhD at the University of Virginia.

Lettie Osgood—Dotsy's lifelong best friend from Fredericksburg, Virginia. She's come to Oxford, UK, to babysit her grandchildren while her daughter, a physician, works at a local hospital.

Larry Roberts—European history teacher at the University of Virginia and Dotsy's major professor. He's returned to his alma mater, Oxford, with anticipation and more than a little trepidation.

Bram Fitzwaring—A big, rough-hewn New Ager from Glastonbury. He believes King Arthur was a real person and he's determined to prove it.

Mignon Beaulieu—Bram Fitzwaring's companion, also from Glastonbury. She supports Fitzwaring one hundred percent.

Keith Bunsen—A don of St. Ormond's College, Oxford. His research may improve the lives of those living with diabetes.

Harold Wetmore—Master of St. Ormond's College, he's an authority on early English history but otherwise a stereotypical absentminded professor.

Daphne Wetmore—Harold's wife and the one who does the donkey work at St. Ormond's.

Georgina Wetmore—Harold and Daphne's niece. Beautiful, blond, and twenty years old, she's a third-year student at another Oxford college.

Robin Morris—A director at Oxford's renowned Bodleian Library. Along with Dotsy, Larry, Harold, and others, he's participating in the summer conference at St. Ormond's.

Claudia Moss—From the British Museum in London. She's presenting a paper at the conference and having a bit of extra fun while she's at it.

John Fish—A man of indeterminate age who leads Oxford Ghost Tours at night and prowls the streets by day.

Dr. Lindsey Scoggin—Lettie Osgood's daughter. She lives in Virginia, but she's spending the summer in Oxford on a physician exchange program.

Claire and Caleb Scoggin—Lindsey's children, aged seven and five. In spite of their precarious situation, they steal Dotsy's heart.

Dr. St. Giles Bell—Handsome, sexy neurologist and new boyfriend of Lindsey Scoggin. He's a widower, some say by his own design. His nerve-tissue research involves oysters, mice, and a particularly potent neurotoxin.

Lord and Lady Attwood—Anthea, Lady Attwood, is Daphne Wetmore's sister. The Attwoods spend as much time on the front pages of the tabloids as they do in their Oxfordshire mansion.

Simon McAlister—Owner of The Green Man, a shop catering to the New Agers of Oxford. His large circle of friends includes both town and gown.

Bumps McAlister—An actress and the wife of Simon. Her roles range from Shakespeare to—well—practical jokes.

Chief Inspector Child—Thames Valley Police. Inspector Morse, he ain't.

Detective Sergeant Gunn—Chief Inspector Child's associate.

Pete—Audiovisual man for conference attendees.

Also, various porters, servers, scouts (housekeeping staff), and gardeners of St. Ormond's.

ONE

THE CARD READ, "Six-thirty for seven," the British way of saying, "Drinks between six-thirty and seven. Dinner at seven sharp." My watch said 6:42, and the next eighteen minutes loomed eternal. I studied the shabby but genuine Persian carpet on the oak floor in the Master's Lodgings. Concentrating hard to drown out Larry Roberts's voice, which was blaming me for the presence of two people he thought should not be here, I tried to decide which was older, the carpet or the floor. In Oxford, one is perpetually agape at the antiquity of almost everything.

"Who wrote who first? You or him?" Larry's volume was barely above a whisper, but the force of his breath lifted the hair on my forehead.

I mentally swept his words under the corner of the Persian carpet.

The occasion was a conference for history scholars, among whose numbers I presume to count myself. Entitled "The Lingering Effects of the King Arthur Tales on Life in Elizabethan England," my own connection to the subject of the conference was tenuous at best. My nearly finished dissertation under the tutelage of the aforementioned Larry dealt with the sources available to Shakespeare when he wrote *Macbeth*.

Oh, God. Did I just say *aforementioned*? I've been hanging around these folks too long. In real life, I'm Dotsy Lamb, Virginian, mother of five grown children, divorced wife of the nouveau riche but alcoholic Chet Lamb, teacher of ancient and medieval history at a small Virginia college, and—for the moment at least—doctoral candidate at the University of Virginia. This last position depended on my strength in holding my tongue until I could break free of Larry.

I studied the silhouettes of Bram Fitzwaring and Mignon Beaulieu, hazy in the slanting afternoon light from a tall mullioned window. Bram sported a long single braid, hanging well below his waist. It had to be his real hair and, given that braiding shortens the apparent length of hair, when unbraided must have fallen to his knees. He wore a caftan of rough wool in a sort of mud color, baggy cotton trousers, and sandals. His sandals had thick rubber soles and bungee cord ties. I'd seen similar footwear in the L.L.Bean catalog.

His companion, Mignon, whose name sounded French but who spoke with a Welsh accent, wore her auburn hair in a braid as well, but instead of stretching back from a receding hairline as Bram's did, much of it escaped to form an unruly cloud around her face and neck. Her ankle-length, midnight blue dress of crushed velvet topped a pair of rubber-soled sandals identical to Bram's but a few sizes smaller.

They both held their wine glasses as if they'd be more comfortable with ale mugs. They'd arrived today from Glastonbury, a Cornish town whose ruined abbey was famous for its alleged connections to King Arthur. Some believed Glastonbury was the fabled Isle of Avalon. Glastonbury attracted New Age types and assorted nut cases, as Larry had informed me. I wish I'd known that when I told Bram Fitzwaring, by email, that he should apply to attend the conference. I assured him that his credentials, as listed by him and accepted by me without question, would certainly enhance our understanding of the mythical king. But here he was, sipping Chablis with Oxford scholars, like a dusty thistle in a bed of primroses. A guffaw from Mignon, too loud for the circumstances, cut through Larry's monotonous attack on my left ear.

I tried to remember exactly how the correspondence between Fitzwaring and me had proceeded. I had to get my story straight because I knew Larry would keep harping on it for the duration of the conference. Fitzwaring had emailed Larry's office first, citing his interest in the conference. No, that wasn't it. Larry had asked me to scare up some more attendees, and I had found Bram Fitzwaring's name on a website that dealt with early Arthuriana. I emailed him first. Would I have done that? That doesn't sound like something I'd do. Oh, hell, I was so stressed out all this spring I might have done anything.

I spotted Keith Bunsen, a lecturer in biochemistry and a fellow of St. Ormond's College at which we were now gathered. Keith lived here year round, he had told me, because his long-term research kept him in town when most of the faculty left for the summer. I wondered why he was here at this little gathering, schmoozing with history scholars. Tall and awkward, he tried to brush a wine spill off his tie with his free hand but jostled his glass as well and spilled a bit more. Then I saw the reason.

Georgina, the lovely young niece of our host, weaved delicately through the throng with her tray of hors d'oeuvres. Keith nodded at her, smiled, and lifted a shrimp from her tray with another nod, another smile, and another slosh of wine down his tie. Our servers were dressed as Elizabethan servants. Nice touch, I thought. I imagined the costumes were the brainchild of Daphne, our hostess and the wife of Harold Wetmore, Master of St. Ormond's College, Oxford. Georgina's thin cotton blouse lightly skimmed the tops of her pretty breasts.

I could hear Keith now:

"Wha-wha-what's on tonight, Master? The k-k-kitchen's gone daft."

"Kickoff for that Arthurian Conference."

"Enjoy yourselves while I'm cooking porridge on the g-g-gas ring."

"Feel free to join us for drinks. Six-thirty to seven."

"Thanks. I may j-join you for a bit." Keith Bunsen's blatant wangling for an invitation would have followed his discovery that Georgina would be there, and Harold Wetmore's invitation would have been the obligatory sort not meant to be accepted.

Georgina offered her tray to Larry and me.

"Lovely," I said. "What are these?" I pointed to some circular green-and-white items in the center.

"Steamed scallops on avocado and toast," Georgina said as Larry relieved her tray of a bacon-wrapped broiled mussel. I took one, too, because the scallops looked too large to manage without a fork and saucer.

"You're l-l-looking especially lovely tonight, Georgina," Keith said, swallowing his shrimp with a bob of his Adam's apple.

"Thank you," she said, curtsied, and added, "and thank you for not calling me a serving wench."

While Larry and Keith went on, trying clumsily to amuse Georgina, I looked around the room. Some thirty or forty people were present and I knew only about ten. I wondered how many of them were staying here at the college, as I was. My gaze swerved to an interior doorway where I saw Daphne Wetmore, our hostess, tugging at her husband's sleeve in a vain attempt to pull him away from a circle of academics, their heads bent over a glass display case full of antique guns. Harold had already shown me his prized collection, which included a flintlock musket he called "Brown Bess," and a beautiful pair of eighteenth-century dueling pistols. Sweat dotted Daphne's upper lip. Her face was flushed, and no wonder. This was Harold's party but it was all her doing. She had probably reminded him to shower and laid out his clothes for him, else he would still be sitting in his study, poring over ancient medieval maps. Daphne, barely five feet tall in heels, had to stretch to peer around her husband's bent arm. Still failing to make eye contact, she tugged at his elbow again, then turned toward the open door behind her.

My gaze followed hers, and I think I must have gasped because Keith's and Larry's heads turned as well. A grey figure glided past the doorway in the direction of the staircase. My first thought was, Lady Macbeth! I know it was stupid but that's what I thought. I imagined her climbing the stairs, wringing her hands, crying, "Out, damned spot!"

Larry said, "What the fu—?"

Daphne released her husband's sleeve and dashed through the doorway.

It couldn't have been my imagination because others saw it, too. And the most interesting part of it, for me, was the wide variety of fleeting impressions recalled later by the onlookers.

DINNER WAS IN the great dining hall, a long room with walls lined with oil portraits of past luminaries and ter-

minated by a slightly raised dais, the High Table, behind which hung a gargantuan portrait of the founder.
A morose-looking sixteenth-century bishop in clerical
garb, he stood staring disapprovingly down at the center
row of tables as he had done for several hundred years,
condemning a dozen generations for the sin of gluttony.

I found my name at a place about halfway down the
center row. Glancing around I saw, to my delight, Larry
Roberts pulling out a chair at the table nearest the south
wall and knew I'd have a break from his badgering. But
my heart sank when I spotted Bram Fitzwaring and Mignon Beaulieu. They were seated at the far end of that
row, and no one else sat anywhere near them. Were there
no place cards for them? Had they taken these places because they were unassigned?

Harold Wetmore, standing at the center of the High
Table, clinked his knife against a glass and called on a
man in a clerical collar for the blessing, which the man
delivered in Latin. *How classy! If folks back home could
see me now!* I thought, understanding none of the words
beyond *in nomine Patris, et Filii, et Spiritus Sancti,* and
rather pleased with myself for even catching that.

I sat between a woman from the British Museum and
a man from the Bodleian Library. Directly across from
me, Keith Bunsen seated himself with a bow to each of
us. This really surprised me. I assumed he was only attending the pre-dinner gathering, but my intentional flip
of his place card while reaching for the water pitcher revealed that, indeed, his name was on the card.

The talk was all about the apparition. The Grey Lady.
Some said she was wearing black and some said green.
Some marveled that she had no feet, saying she glided
silently a few inches above the hall floor. Others said she

wore black slippers. A man at the table behind me declared that she must have been a ghost because Daphne Wetmore said there was nowhere for her to have gone but up the stairs and no one was on the stairs when Daphne pursued her through the doorway, seconds after the apparition had passed.

A few people thought it was a man.

"I'm ashamed to confess that the first thing I thought was, Lady Macbeth," I said, leaning to one side so the waiter could place a roll on my bread plate. "I suppose that's because my head has been immersed in the Scottish play for the last year."

The woman from the British Museum laughed and admitted she'd thought of Lady Jane Grey. "The poor girl. She'd be perfectly within her rights to haunt a conference like this." She was referring to the young Tudor woman, beheaded after serving as England's queen for nine days.

The man from the Bodleian Library said he suspected it was the ghost of Prudence Burcote who died of a broken heart when her Cavalier lover left her. "But Prudence normally hangs about on Magpie Lane," he said.

To bring Keith into the conversation, I said, "As a scientist you probably think we're all crazy, talking about ghosts. Did you see it?"

"I must confess that I did, and that I rather thought it might be M-Madame Curie."

That lightened us up. The diners on either side of Keith joined in. The discussion meandered easily from ghosts, to folklore, to the vast differences in the impressions of witnesses to a single event. We all laughed when Keith suggested we were lucky the Grey Lady didn't kill someone out in the hall because the police would have concluded we were all completely potty. I felt my level of anxiety, at a dangerous peak earlier thanks to Larry, returning to a more reasonable level.

Between the pheasant and the dessert, Daphne Wetmore left the High Table and made her way down the aisle behind me. She touched me on the shoulder, leaned over, and whispered, "How are your accommodations? Is your room satisfactory?" A purely perfunctory, good hostess question. I'd already told her I liked the room.

I assured her, again, that it was and that I loved staying in a room that dated back to the Elizabethan period.

"Which staircase is it? Thirteen? You know, some people refuse to stay there. Unlucky, they say."

Unlike the typical dormitory rooms in American colleges, the residence quads at St. Ormond's didn't have long central halls on each floor with rooms leading off left and right. Instead, the three- and four-story stone buildings had numbered staircases winding up, ground floor to top, with only one or two rooms on each level and no communication with other staircases. If your room was on Staircase Thirteen you had to go outside, into the open-air central garden to visit someone in, say, Staircase Ten. Inside my room I felt a profound privacy—an almost eerie sense of isolation.

Isolation. The word reminded me of the interlopers from Glastonbury.

I searched again for Bram and Mignon by craning my neck to see over the shoulder of the man seated next to Keith. There they were, in the same seats as before, but now surrounded by others and actively conversing with them. Bram's face wore a look of rapt fascination at whatever the man seated across from him was talking about. Mignon and the woman on her left inclined their heads toward each other, nodding. I heard Mignon's hearty laugh in response to an exaggerated eye-roll by the other woman. I felt a bit better.

Daphne made polite small talk with others as she worked her way down the aisle. I heard her say, "Pray that Harold doesn't tell one of his naughty jokes. He's had four glasses of Merlot."

As if he'd heard his name, Harold Wetmore stood and clinked his knife against his wine glass for attention. Slowly the room hushed. He ran one hand in his pants pocket, exposing the green suspenders bracketing his red bow tie. Harold looked like an albino orangutan with a fringe of uncombed white hair framing a great expanse of forehead and small eyes beneath overgrown eyebrows. From his rumpled linen jacket to his unbelted pot belly, Harold was every inch the absentminded professor. He cleared his throat and began:

"I confess that the ghost of Lady Tanfield crossed my mind earlier this evening. Though her fiery chariot normally confines itself to the night skies above Burford, it is rumored that a black cloud sometimes follows her and if this cloud surrounds you it sucks out your mind—a fate one might suspect has already befallen much of Oxford."

This produced a wave of laughter all around the room.

"I'm so terribly pleased to welcome you to St. Ormond's College. We are delighted to have a distinguished group of scholars from three continents, and I am sure we will all find much food for thought as we exchange our ideas over the next few days. It is the Elizabethan period that concerns us here. Not the medieval. Not the rule of the Anglo-Saxons or the Normans or the Celts. I'm sure we're all keenly aware of the tremendous influence of the Arthur myths on social mores in England and France as these stories were invented and popularized in those distant years, but did they die out with the coming of the early modern period? To what extent had they already shaped this island's psyche? And to what extent were they exported to the rest of the world as England embarked upon a great age of exploration?

"That's what we're here to talk about.

"If there are any here who wish to turn this into a treasure hunt for the Holy Grail or Arthur's bones, or Excalibur, for God's sake, let him forever hold his peace and depart forthwith by the down train. Or, as a certain don would have said, 'by the town drain.'"

Amid laughter from the locals and blank stares from most of the foreign guests, Wetmore nodded to his audience and sat down. I had read a lot about Oxford University over the past year and knew that his closing remark referred to William Spooner of New College, famous for his "Spoonerisms." It was said that he once proposed a toast to "our queer dean."

"Well!" said Claudia, the woman from the British Museum, fishing for her purse under the table. "That was rather sharp, don't you think? What was he talking about?"

Keith pulled the wayward purse from the floor near his feet and handed it across the table. "That's Harold for you. He's a stickler for insisting people remember King Arthur is a myth. Don't ever suggest there might really have been such a king. Not around Harold."

"I'll remember that," I said.

"What now? Is this it?" asked the man from the Bodleian.

"There will be c-c-coffee in the Senior Common Room, for those who wish to relax and chat a bit before retiring."

All Oxford colleges kept a Junior Common Room for undergraduates and a Senior Common Room for faculty and grads. In the United States we'd call them lounges. I wasn't sure where St. Ormond's Senior Common Room was, but figured I could find it by following the crowd. Stepping out into the arched corridor that connected East Quad to Middle Quad, I felt a cool breeze in my hair. The night was lovely, high sixties, maybe low seventies, and crisp. I decided to sit on one of the benches in the East Quad for a minute.

My own room was in a corner of this quad but not visible from my seat on the bench because the room's only window, a tiny, leaded-glass one, opened over Sycamore Lane, which ran parallel to this part of the college. An arched passage on the opposite side, leading to faculty offices, was lit now by one small carriage lantern casting a long beam across the grass. In its pale yellow glow the texture of the Cotswold sandstone stood out in bold relief. The flowers bordering all four walls of the quad were now darkened to shades of blue. Drops of water on the hostas sparkled as they swayed in the passing breeze. A hint of grape-scented heliotrope drifted by. All around the edges, expertly tended flowerbeds seemed to have been planned for maximum impact this very week, but I suspected they always looked their best. The only position at an Oxford college harder to acquire than that of Master was that of Gardener, a post some said required a great deal more knowledge. The English love their gardens, and nowhere was this more obvious than in Oxford.

A few lights still burned in the porter's office at the main entrance. A couple, most likely members of our group, tapped the electric eye beside the massive nail-studded door with one of the magic entry buttons the college issued each of us and slipped out into the city night. High heels clicked on a flagstone walk behind me. City traffic noises, damped by the walls around me, seemed farther off than they were. I thought of a line from Dorothy L. Sayers's *Gaudy Night*. "If only one could come back to this quiet place, where only intellectual achievement mattered…"

The cell phone in my purse chattered against the wooden seat. I fished it out and fumbled for the talk button. Not surprisingly, it was from my friend Lettie Osgood, and she was calling from across town.

"Dotsy? I'm not coming back to the college tonight. I'm staying here. Lindsey and what's-his-name are out and they won't be home till the wee hours, I'm sure, so I have to stay with the children."

Lettie rented a room on the same staircase as mine. She was staying here on a B and B basis, not attending the conference but helping her daughter, Lindsey, a doctor who was working at the Radcliffe Hospital in a summer exchange program. Lindsey's two children were here because leaving them with her ex back in Virginia was not an option. Lettie hadn't told me why. Something was going on there, and it wasn't good, I felt. Who was this man Lindsey was going out with? A new boyfriend? Ah well. Lindsey was in her late thirties and divorced. Naturally she'd be dating again but thank heavens Lettie was here. The children were staying in a strange apartment, in a strange country, and their mother was away most of the time—day and night—not good for the little ones' sense of security. They were seven and five, the age when children's fear of strangers, the bogeyman, loomed large and unreasoning.

Conversation over, I switched my phone back to the

ring tone and stuffed it in my purse. A dark form flicked through the lamplight spilling across the grass. I jumped. Silly. Just someone walking through the archway toward the college's north gate.

"Fancy meeting you here." The voice came from behind my bench.

I turned. It was Bram Fitzwaring. "We must stop meeting like this," I said. "Have a seat."

Bram did as I suggested. "Going out on the town tonight? It's still early."

"For the young, maybe, but not for me."

"Oh, come on. How about a pizza? Let's go for a pizza." He leaned his shoulder against mine and gave my arm a nudge.

"We just ate! Are you telling me you could eat another meal?"

"Not on, eh? Ah well, I'll probably pack it in, as well." He straightened his legs, crossed his sandal-clad feet at the ankles, and dropped his head back, looking up at a hazy dark sky. His wooly caftan smelled of incense. "I don't think they want me here."

From nonsense straight to the gut. This man was making my stomach churn. I said nothing.

"Eh? Did you hear me?"

"I heard you. Who is *they*? Who doesn't want you here?"

"Harold Wetmore. Harold Wet Fish. Harold-Head-Up-His-Ass-World's-Foremost-Authority-on-English-History, thinks I should go home." Bram glanced toward me as if to see how I was reacting. I diverted my gaze to the lawn. "Seems I'm sullying the purity of his precious ivory tower. That comment he made at dinner about 'if you're here on a treasure hunt for the Holy Grail or what-ever, you need to leave.' That was for me."

"Does he think you're here on a treasure hunt? I don't get it." Actually I did get it, but I didn't want to say so.

"No. But this bullshit about the *myth* of Arthur—the Arthur *legend*—it's bullshit. I've read all the stories, too, you know. I've read *Le Morte d'Arthur,* I've read Geof-frey of Monmouth, I've read Tennyson. But Grand Mas-ter Wetmore—Lord Wetmore—Lord High Ruler of St. Ormond's—goes bloody nuts if you mention that Arthur was also *a real king.*"

"His opinion is in the majority, you know."

"Majority. Majority of what? Majority of poncing pin-heads who think history is counting pigs in fourteen eighty-two? Who never think about what life was like for the Britons when the Romans pulled out?" Bram's beefy arms flew skyward and a board in our bench cracked under his weight. "They think the Romans left and the Brits just stood there for a couple hundred years wait-ing for someone else to come and tell them what to do!"

"This is Oxford, you know." I stood, grabbed my purse, and started walking toward Staircase Thirteen. Bram's voice was rising several decibels with every com-ment and I didn't want a scene. "It's been a long day. I'll see you tomorrow."

Bram stood and followed me, shouting at the back of my neck. "Just you wait! I'm going to blow the doors off this place! Just you wait. When I get my turn, I'm going to blow the doors off this place!"

I took the shortest route, straight across the grass.

"He'll come a cropper, ol' Harry, ol' Harvey, ol'…" His voice trailed off to an inarticulate mumble.

Climbing the first flight of stairs, I heard Bram's rubber soles squeaking on the stone steps behind me. *Oh, no, he's following me to my room! How can I get rid of him without...* Fortunately, before I said anything I remembered his room was also on this staircase.

When I reached my own door, I saw that he was gone.

TWO

MY LITTLE ROOM on the top floor felt like the garret of a starving artist. All funny angles and slants, with a tiny single bed, desk, bookcase, sink, wardrobe, and a low table, probably from IKEA, for the tea-making facilities. Every day the scout, their term for housekeeper, tidied my room and left me two bourbon cream biscuits on the saucer beside the cup. Every day I ate them.

A large stone fireplace, now blocked up, stood on one end of the room, its surround bearing the graffiti of generations of students. Some were in Latin and some looked more like runes but were probably just idle scratchings.

My room was number six.

Standing at my door I couldn't see the doors of any other rooms because the narrow hall extended a few feet, plunged down four steps, made a forty-five-degree right turn, then descended another four steps. Here stood the doors marked four and five. Down two more flights, now turning left, you hit a landing with the bathroom (shower and toilet) on one end and a bifurcated extension on the other, where the two ends terminated in doors marked two and three. There was no room number one, but another flight down, on ground level, stood a blackened wood door with a brass plaque that read, "Bursar's Office." I'd never seen it unlocked.

Lettie Osgood stayed in room five whenever she did stay here, which, in the five days since my arrival, had

only been twice. Bram Fitzwaring and Mignon Beaulieu had two of the others, but I didn't know which two.
I hadn't noticed exactly when Bram, climbing the stairs
behind me, had peeled off and entered his own room.

I stood on my bed to open the little window beneath a
gabled roof and let in the night air. A neatly printed sign
on one pane of glass read, "No exit." I laughed every time
I saw it. Nowhere but in a college would it be necessary to
stick such a warning. The window was fifty feet above the
pavement and, fully open, produced a hole no more than
a foot wide, but some thin and agile undergraduate would
try it. I set my iPad on my little nightstand, brushed my
teeth at the sink, then paused. I heard something. Drums?
Rhythmic taps. Thirteen taps, then a pause, then thirteen
more. Where was it coming from? I hopped back up on the
bed and turned an ear to the open window. The drumming
noises continued but they weren't coming from outside.

I decided to take a shower before turning in. I grabbed
my towel, face cloth, soap dish, and robe. *Don't forget
the room key.* Thanks to Lettie's earlier mistake, I knew
that forgetting your key meant a trip to the Porter's Lodge
dressed however one was when heading to the loo in the
middle of the night. Fortunately the lodge stayed open all
night, but Lettie had been horribly embarrassed.

On the way down, I listened for the drumming sounds
but they seemed to have stopped. Inside the toilet niche, I
thought I heard footsteps coming from outside. The bathroom window was half open, and I stepped over close
to it. Some ten feet above the walk that ran the length of
the south wall of the quad, the windowsill hit me slightly
below my shoulders. The window itself was the sort that
cranks out in two tall vertical segments. I stuck my head
out and looked down.

I still heard footsteps but I saw no one. My view from the window was of the grassy quad bathed in shades of blue and a faint yellow glow from the carriage lantern under the archway on the opposite side. A fog was drifting in.

I heard something hit the walkway below the window. Something small, possibly metallic. Keys? A huge shadow grazed the stones on the opposite side of the quad. A head and shoulders, but they ended in a pencil-thin shadow that extended all across the lawn and ended, I supposed, on the walkway beneath my window. I raised myself to tiptoes and craned my neck down as far as possible. I could see almost straight down. I could see a strip of the flagstone walk but the wisteria vine clinging to the stone wall kept me from seeing straight down. I saw no one. This was spooky.

Checking the bathroom door to make sure it was locked, I paused until my racing pulse slowed down, then stripped naked and hopped into the shower. Now I was hearing noises everywhere. Clunks. Could be the pipes. A cough? Could be Bram or Mignon inside their own rooms, but could I hear a cough through two doors and a stairwell? Someone outside? An eerie wail sent the soap in my hands flying toward the showerhead. Okay. I *must* have imagined that. I was happy to bundle myself back into my own little room and check my email on my tablet. This little cyber-connection to home, a message from my granddaughter telling me she had won a medal in swimming, comforted me.

I HAD DRIFTED OFF, my iPad on my chest, when a loud *thunk* woke me with a start. I couldn't possibly have imagined it, because, eyes open, I heard another.

My stomach hurt. In fact, I felt as if I might throw up. How long would it take me to get to the bathroom? Grab robe, grab key, down four winding sets of steps, and pray the room wasn't already occupied. Suddenly I wished I'd asked for one of the en suite rooms in the new hall. I'd insisted on this quad because of its ambience. *Screw ambience,* I thought, and pulled the plastic trashcan close to my bed. I heard another thunk. Coming from below, it sounded like a dresser turning over, or a body slamming into a wall.

I jumped up and ran out into the hall. I remembered, just in time, to keep one foot in the doorway so the door couldn't close, as it automatically did, and lock me out. My key was on the opposite side of my room, on the tea tray. Calling out, but not too loudly, "Is there a problem? Does someone need help?" netted me no response. I retreated to my nightstand and checked my watch. Two-thirty in the morning.

Dropping my room key into the pocket of my robe, I traipsed down, past Lettie's vacant room, and knocked on the door of room four. No response. I knocked again. Nothing. Down two more flights with my stomach still churning, I came to the Y-shaped hall and knocked on the doors at each end. Nothing. Nothing at all from room two but after the third knock on number three, a frowzled Mignon Beaulieu opened the door.

"I heard a loud noise from down this way. Are you all right?"

Her eyes were puffy slits and she didn't seem to understand me. She was wearing footie pajamas with teddy bears all over.

"Just checking," I said, nodding and stepping backwards. "Sorry."

I WAS UP at five-thirty, too early for breakfast but wide awake. Breakfast, in fact, sounded good, so the nausea of last night must have passed. I tested my blood sugar and stuck a straw in a little carton of orange juice from the unrefrigerated six-pack I always keep handy. I've been diabetic all my life. I started the kettle for tea and sat down to study the printed program. This was the first official day of the conference and we had a full one ahead of us.

St. Ormond's College
Oxford
The Lingering Effects of the King Arthur Tales
on Life in Elizabethan England

Saturday, July 7

Breakfast 7:30 to 9 am—Dining Hall

Lecture 9:30–10:30—Smythson Hall

Larry Roberts: "Malory's *Le Morte d'Arthur*"

Tea 10:30–11—West Quad Lawn
(weather permitting)

Lecture 11–12—Smythson Hall

Harold Wetmore: "Courtly Love and the Tudor Court: Elizabeth, Raleigh, and Leicester"

Lunch 12–1:30—Dining Hall

Lecture 2–3—Smythson Hall

Claudia Moss: "*Arthur's Tale* and the Players of Mile End Green"

Tea 3–3:30—West Quad Lawn
(weather permitting)

Lecture 4–5—Smythson Hall

Bram Fitzwaring: "The Dissolution of the Monasteries: A Case History"

Dinner at 7—Dining Hall

Note: In inclement weather, outdoor events will be held in the SCR.

I knew the first lecture by heart. With me as his audience, Larry had delivered it in its entirety a dozen times back in Charlottesville, Virginia, and emailed me a hundred alterations to a paragraph, a sentence, or even a single word when I wasn't physically present to hear the whole thing. The time I spent in Charlottesville, an hour's drive from my home near Staunton, I was supposed to be ironing out kinks in my dissertation, with Larry's help. After all, he was my major professor. But every time I brought up the subject of my dissertation, his eyes glazed over. He'd fidget until I paused long enough to change the subject to the only one on his mind: This speech.

In Larry's mind, Oxford scholars stood between God and the angels in the Great Chain of Being. His invitation to deliver the opening paper of this conference was, to him, the pinnacle of his career. I wondered if he'd be able to eat any breakfast this morning.

The big surprise was the fourth speaker. They'd actually put Bram Fitzwaring on the schedule for day one. How had he managed to swing that? I was scheduled to conduct one of the breakout sessions on Monday right after lunch when people were most likely to skip out and go shopping. Bram's topic, however, "The Dissolution of the Monasteries" under King Henry VIII, was apropos of the conference goal and sounded relatively uncontroversial.

I dressed as I drank my tea. This being the first day of the conference, I donned my best black slacks with a black tank top under my new, printed silk, chiffon tunic. I checked myself in the mirror, thinking about Smythson Hall and how I could take off the tunic if the room was too hot and how that would leave my arms bare. The tank top was sleeveless. There are those who think a woman of my age should never show her upper arms. My upper arms looked all right to me. Shoes? I'd only brought three pairs so it would have to be the black pumps because the other two pairs were tennis shoes and brown sandals.

I stopped at the door of room four on my way down and listened but didn't knock because it was only a bit past six. Silence. Down two flights. Silence again at door two and at door three, Mignon's room.

Outside, the morning air felt brisk. The perfect carpet of grass in the quad glistened with dew. I checked the walkway beneath the bathroom window, but found nothing that might have caused that small metallic noise I'd heard last night.

I waved to the porter on duty behind the glass wall of his office as I tapped the electronic pad by the main entrance with my magic button. Shift change for the porters was at seven a.m., I knew, so this man had been on duty since eleven o'clock last night and his replacement would arrive shortly.

The smell of frying sausage, probably from one of the stalls in the Covered Market, floated on the morning air. A short walk took me to the High Street where I decided to head east. It felt like west, but I had studied my map and knew it was east, a fact bolstered by the rising sun in my eyes. Having been born and raised in rural western Virginia, I tend to navigate more by compass directions than by the "two blocks down, left at the corner of Thirty-three and Oak" sort of directions you get from city folk. When I'm turned around, as I was in Oxford, my internal gyroscope feels wobbly. Everyone has a body clock, but we country folk also have a body compass. It was rather like having jet lag squared after flying across six time zones and landing in a town that seemed to me to have been built in reverse.

A red and yellow sightseeing bus barreled past, farting diesel fumes, on what still seemed to me like the wrong side of the street. Cyclists were already filling up the bike lanes. I turned left on Catte Street, passed the Radcliffe Camera, and paused before stepping out into Broad Street. In front of the Sheldonian Theatre, the university's ceremonial center, stood a semicircle of thirteen soot-streaked, morose-looking busts, each atop its own column. Locals called them the "Emperors' Heads" but no one knew who or what they were supposed to represent. Almost certainly not emperors.

A man I knew poked about at the base of one of these columns and kicked at a pile of blown leaves. At first I didn't recognize him because I'd never seen him dressed in anything but a long black jacket and stovepipe hat. His name was John Fish. John led the "Haunted Oxford" tour each evening, squiring groups around town on ninety-minute walks designed to scare the pants off those who wanted to be scared, but still offering a pleasant and informative walk to those who, like myself, don't believe in ghosts.

"John." I greeted him and gave him a minute to recall who I was—the woman who'd talked to him a couple of times while he waited at his assigned spot for his next group to assemble. I knew he wouldn't remember my name. "Dotsy Lamb. From the United States."

"Right-o." Today he wore a light blue T-shirt that said "BU," jeans, and flip-flops. He looked as if he'd had a hard night. Unshaven, hair greasy, and eyes bloodshot. John Fish, I decided, looked better after dark. His teeth were in terrible condition. I suspected he might have a drug problem. He had the prematurely aged, sallow skin that often marks the face of the addict. His hands looked thirty but his face looked sixty.

"A woman in my group last night lost her keys," he said. "Thought I'd sort of retrace the route this morning and see if I could find them. No luck last night in the dark, were it?"

"You're just the man I need to talk to." I followed him to the next column, where he poked about, shifting the debris collected at its base with his skull-topped ebony cane. "We had a ghost at St. Ormond's last night."

"Didja now?" He kept poking.

I expected a bigger reaction, given that ghosts were John's livelihood. Maybe he didn't believe in ghosts himself. Maybe his entertaining spiel was just that. A spiel.

"The Grey Lady, we called her. Know anything about a Grey Lady ghost in Oxford?"

He snorted. "A Grey Lady? There's grey ladies everywhere. There's a Grey Lady at Glamis Castle, a Grey Lady at Denbigh Castle, grey ladies all over Bishop's Stortford, at Rutherford Hall, in Harry Potter, in France," he paused for breath. "There's a Grey Lady in Evansville, Indiana. You know Indiana?"

I laughed. "I had no idea."

"I think it's because, if it's a ghost it tends to be grey. They're not normally solid enough to be in full color, innit?" He leaned toward me, so close I smelled his morning breath, his hands shaping an imaginary ghost. "If they're all white, or all black, how you gonna see 'em, eh? That's why they're grey. So you can see 'em…but not too much."

I loved his reasoning. I told him about our shared experience at the cocktail party the previous evening in the Master's Lodgings.

John nodded vigorously as I described the wide range of impressions it had left on various attendees. "Everyone tryin' to sort it out, eh? Lady Macbeth? Who said that about Prudence Burcote?"

"I think it was the man from the Bodleian Library. Man named Morris, I believe."

"Makes sense it was a local man. I always talk about Prudence Burcote when I take 'em down to Magpie Lane."

"So what do you think? What was it?"

"A ghost, innit?"

"Oh, come on."

"Why ask me? I wasn't there. Did everyone see it?"

John had inexplicably reverted to the cultured British he used for guiding tours.

"Not everyone. Only those who happened to be looking toward the door to the hallway."

"And it was the talk of the dinner table, eh?"

John Fish was obviously delighted we'd seen a ghost. Such things were good for his business. I don't know why I'd even asked him about it. Did I expect him to produce a natural explanation? If he had one, it wouldn't have been in his best interest to tell me.

I found a clean spot on the concrete steps between two of the columns and sat. John sat beside me, tucking his cane between his knees. We faced Broad Street, so named because it's broader than the other streets. Across Broad was Blackwell's Bookshop, where I'd spent many hours and quite a few British pounds over the past five days.

"Daphne Wetmore, the Master's wife. Do you know her?" I asked.

John nodded.

"Daphne followed the…the whatever it was, out into the hall but she said it simply wasn't there anymore."

"Her husband's a right bloody-minded prat."

"What do you mean?"

"Tries to get me shut down, don't he? Any way he can. And naturally he knows people on city council, from the mayor on down. Stood up in front of city council, didn't he?" John raised his skull-topped cane and bellowed, "'Our town is known the world over for academic rigor! For its commitment to *truth*! And yet we allow these fantasy-mongers to ply our streets and fill our visitors' heads with their ghosts and goblins and glowing blobs.'"

I looked all around, concerned that John's outburst

would bring on a chorus of complaints, but it seemed we were alone and the emperors with their droopy beards looked as if they couldn't care less. "He really did that?"

"He did, but so far, touch wood, nothing's come of it." He looked around for something made of wood, spotted his ebony cane, and tapped it.

"What about his wife? Was she there?"

"Daphne? Oh, sure. Sitting there on the front row, she was."

"Do you think she was on his side?"

"Daphne's a good woman. Do anything to help you, won't she? But she won't go against her husband. She'll back Harold one hundred percent, and don't expect her to do aught else."

"You know them pretty well then?"

"This is my fifth year doing the ghost tours. Harold Wetmore's been master of St. Ormond's longer than that. Our paths have crossed. Many times." Under his breath he muttered, "Little troll."

I had a feeling Harold and John may have crossed swords as well.

THREE

BREAKFAST AT ST. ORMOND'S was always buffet-style, with all the elements of a Full English arrayed along the back wall in the dining hall. They also stocked yogurts, Weetabix, and fruits for the health-conscious. My head makes me stick to this end of the line but my heart wants to wallow in the poached eggs, blood sausage, toast and jam.

Larry Roberts waved me over with a vigor I couldn't pretend I didn't see. He rose and pulled out a chair for me, spilling a bit of orange juice on his trousers in the process. "Damn!"

I handed him a napkin.

He brushed frantically at the spot, wrapped the napkin around his finger, and dipped it into his water glass. This action sent the water glass tumbling onto his toast plate. Larry's face flushed. He was so nervous I figured he'd be better off taking his breakfast intravenously. His hands shook as he daubed at the toast plate. I took the plate and the napkin away from him and pushed his water-splashed chair aside.

"Get yourself another chair, Larry." I turned and signaled a server for help. Larry was so keyed up, I didn't think he could handle a sippy cup right now. I asked the server to bring him some dry toast.

Larry, although flushed and with a yellowish wet spot in an embarrassing place, was a distinguished-looking man. I've often told him he could be a model for Perry

Ellis. He always acts insulted and mutters something profane under his breath, but he likes it.

"Where were you last night?" he asked. "I looked for you after dinner. I needed you to listen to my address one more time. I've made a couple of changes."

"I went to bed early."

"I know you're sick of hearing my paper, but I want it to be right."

"I know. It will be. Don't worry."

"Easy for you to say." He let the server place a dry plate with dry toast and a foil-wrapped pat of butter in front of him. "What am I going to do about these pants? I don't have another pair that go with this jacket and tie."

"Don't worry about it. That spot will be dry before your speech."

"Think so?"

"If not, you'll be behind a lectern so it won't matter."

With great difficulty, Larry managed to unwrap the butter and spread a bit of it on his toast.

I looked around the room and spotted two of my dinner companions from the night before, but where was Keith Bunsen? I'd sat with him at breakfast every morning so far, but he wasn't here now. Bram Fitzwaring and Mignon Beaulieu weren't here either. I kept watching the doors whenever someone new entered. I wanted, keenly, to ask them both about last night's noises on Staircase Thirteen.

On the way back to my room to brush my teeth before the day's scheduled activities began, I ran into Georgina. I couldn't recall her last name. She'd been one of our servers at the cocktail party last night and, I knew, she was Harold Wetmore's niece. She was carrying the white cotton coif she'd worn on her head at the party and her blond hair was pulled back into a shaggy ponytail. She was still wearing the blue cotton shift. Her white apron hung over one arm. She nodded at me and, head lowered, hurried past.

I knocked on Mignon's and Bram's doors again, and again got no answer.

I SWEATED THROUGH Larry's speech like a new mother at a kindergarten play. Silly, of course, because this was a grown man with a PhD in medieval European history and I certainly didn't love him like a child. But the majority of sentences he delivered from the stage in the Smythson Lecture Hall were sentences I had tweaked myself. I had a stake in his success.

His topic was *Le Morte d'Arthur*, a compilation of tales about King Arthur, written by Thomas Malory in the fifteenth century and written in Middle English. Larry was conversant in both Middle French and Middle English, as those dialects were spoken back then. When he referenced Chaucer's *Wife of Bath's Tale*, written about the same time, I knew he would launch into a bombastic rendition of the Prologue to *The Canterbury Tales*. In Middle English. *Wan that Aprille with his sures sothe...* I knew it by heart myself, now. I'd tried to talk him out of it because I felt it wandered too far from the topic, but he'd been adamant.

What I hadn't anticipated was the audience's laughter. Not really guffaws; these were scholars after all, but it started with grins, then chuffs disguised as small coughs, then notepads lifted to mouths. Eyes darting toward seat companions. Elbows nudging. And then, from the balcony, an outright hoot.

Why were they laughing?

A whisper from behind clued me in. I heard some-one say, "Wan that Aprille, y'all." This audience was fa-miliar with the sounds of Middle English, but it was the first time they'd heard them delivered with a southern (American) accent.

Now I really felt like a kindergarten mother. I wanted to rush onstage, bundle Larry Roberts in my arms, and lead him away to some nice milk and cookies or a strong bourbon and soda.

SERVERS, ALL IN green polo shirts with St. Ormond's coat of arms on the breast pockets, waited for us outside at linen-covered tables. I skipped the line at the teapot table and dashed off in search of Larry. I wasn't sure he'd caught the reaction to his Prologue recitation. From the stage, the footlights may have obscured individual faces. Plus, Larry wasn't the most perceptive man in the world when it came to reading faces, and the audience had re-warded him with polite applause at the end. I looked through all three quads but didn't find him.

On my way across West Quad I spotted Mignon Beau-lieu heading for the main gate. Calling to her, I scurried to catch up and apologized for waking her up last night.

"You did? I have no memory of that."

"Good. I could tell you had obviously been asleep."

"I'm a sound sleeper. I'm surprised I heard your knock."

"I'm afraid I pounded on the door," I said, donning my humblest face. "But I was hearing horrible loud noises, and I thought they were coming from down below. My room's on the top floor and I didn't know which room was yours and which was Bram's so I knocked on all the doors."

"What time was this?"

"It must have been about two a.m."

"I didn't hear a thing. I was up until after midnight. I must have eaten something bad, because I got deathly ill. I threw up, in fact. Then I went to sleep and I don't think I woke up again until an hour ago."

"You were sick, too? How odd. I thought I was going to barf, too, but I didn't." I caught Mignon's arm as she turned toward the exit. "Have you seen Bram this morning?"

"No, but he's a terrible late sleeper. I didn't try to wake him because his speech isn't until this afternoon, and I thought he might have been out late. Doesn't like to be knocked up if he's having a lie-in."

I stifled the laugh an American always feels when he hears "knocked up" used in the British way. "I don't think he was out late. I ran into him outside after dinner and he was right behind me when I went up to my room, about nine-thirty or ten." I recalled the encounter, and added, "It was weird. He asked me if I wanted to go out for pizza and I said, 'Huh? We just ate!'"

"Oh, dear. This is not good." Mignon's chubby ring-spangled hand flew to her mouth. "He was acting weird, was he?"

"I thought so."

"This is not good. Bram is diabetic. When his blood sugar is low he gets weird."

"But we'd just eaten! Hey, I'm diabetic, too. Blood sugar doesn't run low after a meal. Only before."

Mignon paused and stared at the ancient stone floor of the entrance. "Bram hardly ate anything. He was so keyed up. The couple we sat with at dinner knew so much about pre-Norman history, Bram couldn't stop talking. He must have asked a million questions."

"Maybe that explains it."

"Oh, dear. I'm on my way out to meet up with some friends in town, but perhaps I'd best make sure Bram's all right before I go." She turned back toward the open quad, then paused. "But I don't have a key to his room. What if he doesn't answer? What do I do then?"

"I suggest you go up first. If there's no answer, come back here. The porter has a key."

I started after her, but when I looked through the passage on the opposite side of the quad, I saw a steady stream of people heading in the direction of the lecture hall. I didn't want to be late for Harold's speech, so I let Mignon pursue her mission alone.

I wondered why Harold had chosen "Courtly Love and the Tudor Court" as his topic when his expertise lay, not in the sixteenth century, when the Tudors were on the throne, but in the much earlier Anglo-Saxon period. Upon reaching the lectern he paused, settled his rimless glasses on his bulbous nose, and straightened his notes. He lifted a sheet or two and grimaced, as if he didn't recognize what they were. Of course, Daphne would've made sure his papers were in order already, so the straightening and lifting were purely for show. His bow tie this morning was brown with greenish spots, but his rumpled jacket and trousers looked the same as those he'd worn last night. I wondered if he'd slept in them.

He began by reminding us that the term "Courtly Love," when used as a sort of cliché to describe affairs of the heart among the nobility, wasn't used until about 1900, and would never have been used in the Tudor Court. Nevertheless, the Tudor Court behaved as if they had invented it. He went into some detail about the original idea as set forth in "The Art of Courtly Love" written by a French cleric and discussed in the salons of Marie of Champlain way back in the twelfth century. Love was at its best, its most ennobling, when it was secret, extramarital, and, usually, unconsummated. Marriage was for children; it had nothing to do with true love.

I tried to see how Daphne was taking this, but spotted her sitting on the front row so I could only see the back of her head.

Harold went on to recount, in the most scholarly terms, the relationship of Queen Elizabeth I to the Earl of Leicester, of Elizabeth to Sir Walter Raleigh, and of her father, Henry VIII, to half the women in England. Somehow, I thought, Harold's dry description of these unseemly affairs made them sound all the more salacious. Exciting. Even titillating. The woman sitting next to me began fanning herself when he got to the part about Mary, Queen of Scots, Bothwell, and David Rizzio.

But at no point in his speech did Harold mention Arthur, Guinevere, Lancelot, or a round table.

LARRY GRABBED ME on my way out of the lecture and steered me toward the dining hall. He had a way of latching onto my arm with one hand just above my elbow that actually hurt. I wrenched away, but he still stood slightly behind me on one side, effectively steering me with his body. He smiled and nodded at whoever looked our way as we all headed more or less in the same direction.

Harold Wetmore stood in the arched passage to the Middle Quad, nodding meekly at the many kudos for his fine speech. *Perfect place to stand, Harold. Everyone has to file through this passage and they can't help see-*

ing you. I chided myself for my excessive and possibly baseless cynicism.

As we passed by, Harold shook Larry's hand and the two men congratulated each other on their insightful and thought-provoking lectures. Harold added, "Would you and your…would the two of you join me at High Table for lunch?"

Larry fell all over himself accepting with pleasure. I nodded my acceptance while mentally licking the wound inflicted by that awkward pause. Harold couldn't remember my name. In the dining hall, Larry and I stepped onto the slight rise at the far end where the High Table stood perpendicular to three long rows of tables stretching the length of the room. "Where should we sit?" Larry asked me. I'd hoped Daphne would be there to tell us what to do. Fortunately Claudia Moss, our first speaker of the afternoon and one of my dinner companions last night, was also standing by and wondering the same thing. I recalled that she was from the British Museum in London.

"Golly. I don't want to take someone else's place, but there are no place cards, so what should we do?" she asked.

I introduced Larry to Claudia, and then had an idea. "Let's ask one of the servers." Several green-shirted young people were standing idle along the walls. That done, a handsome young man told us to sit anywhere but in the two centermost places because they were for Master and his wife. Larry took the chair closest the center—I knew he would—I took the next, and Claudia sat next to me.

"Well? You haven't given me your assessment of my speech, Dotsy. How do you think it went?"

"It went well, of course. Although I already knew the

whole thing practically by heart." This answer deftly avoided any mention of the audience reaction, which is what he really wanted to hear.

"How do you think the others liked it?"

What could I say? I paused and craned my neck toward one of the entry doors as if searching for someone, but actually buying time.

Larry filled the gap. "I think they all liked it." He leaned closer to me and muttered, "Did you hear that applause at the end?"

"I did."

"I was nearly thrown off my game when some guy in the back had that coughing fit. And it *would* have to be at the best part of my prologue recitation."

Coughing fit? Those weren't coughs, they were hoots! Poor Larry. He had no idea. Maybe it was a good thing, though. As long as he didn't go around bragging about it, who cared if he went through the rest of his life thinking he took Oxford by storm? "Yes I heard that, too," I said. "And you know what else I've noticed?" I sat back, bringing Claudia Moss into the conversation. "How very self-effacing Oxford people are. They never refer to their own accomplishments. Their attention is always on others. Have you noticed that as well?" I turned to Claudia.

"I suppose it's that Oxford reticence," she said. "A bit of pretense, really. But don't let it fool you. Their apparent humility is only skin deep."

"Aha. Sounds like a Cambridge graduate talking," I teased.

"Oh, dear. Is it so obvious?"

We both laughed.

Larry rose as Harold Wetmore sidestepped along between the chairs and the wall and took his seat.

A server hurried over to fill our wine glasses. Claudia passed on the wine because her turn to speak was up next and she wanted to keep a clear head. Daphne's seat remained empty throughout the meal. The table talk centered on the Bodleian Library's upcoming changes to the History Faculty Library services.

At a lull in the conversation I asked Harold, "Where is Daphne?" Her seat was still empty.

"I imagine she's taking care of the hundred and one things—those pesky little details—that always come up at a conference like this." He turned toward me and his glasses fell into his plate. He picked them up and wiped them with his napkin before stretching them back around his ears. "I don't know what I'd do without her. I'm no good at details. Pesky little things. But someone has to do it."

FOUR

I MISSED CLAUDIA MOSS's lecture.

Instead, I tried to return to my room on Staircase Thirteen to brush my teeth but got no farther than the ground level. A woman in the uniform of an emergency medical technician stopped me with an outstretched palm and said. "Sorry. They're bringing a man down on a stretcher. You'll have to wait."

My heart flipped. It had to be Bram. To my knowledge, he was the only man staying on this staircase. There was another room, number two, which was, as far as I knew, vacant. Lettie's room, of course, hadn't been slept in last night. Then a horrid thought. Could it be Lettie? Might she have come back to her room this morning while I was out?

"Are you sure it's a man?"

The tech looked at me as if debating whether I had a right to an answer, then nodded. "It's a man, and a big man, too. They'll have a right job bringing him down these stairs without dropping him."

"How long do you think they'll be?" That sounded selfish and it didn't matter how long anyway, so I added, "Is he going to be all right, do you think? Is he conscious?"

"Not conscious. Dead, I'd say, but I'm not supposed to be giving out all this information. Is he...?" She stopped. Her face flushed. "Oh, I'm sorry. Is he a relative of yours?"

"No, but I know him. We're both attending the conference here. I talked to him just last night and he seemed fine." *But he didn't, did he?* Mignon thought he might have been going hypoglycemic. "Is anyone else up there with him? He has a companion, a Miss Beaulieu, who's staying in room three."

"Big woman?" The EMT's arms spread out, indicating the woman was overweight rather than tall. "Long braid?"

"That's her."

"She's up there and the Master's wife is up there as well. It's a tiny room, though, what with the three techs working on him, I'm surprised the women haven't been told to leave."

I backed out and headed for the front gate. Several college staffers stood behind the plate-glass window of the porter's station, peering out. The big front door was open. Beyond the door, the blue lights of an ambulance bounced off the stone façade of the college across the street in staccato pulses. One of the staffers stuck out his head and asked me for an update on the problem in Staircase Thirteen.

"I'm assuming it's Bram Fitzwaring in room four. They won't let me go up."

"We know it's Mr. Fitzwaring, but did they say how he is? Did they make it here in time?"

"The EMT at the bottom of the stairs seemed to be of the opinion that they didn't. She thinks he's dead."

"So sad. So sad," the man said, sounding genuinely sorry.

"Who found him? Who called the EMTs?"

Looking back at his compatriots, as if for guidance on what he could and couldn't say, he got a couple of quizzical looks. "The heavyset woman, Miss Beaulieu, she came running down. Said, 'Mr. Fitzwaring! Something's wrong with him. I can't wake him up and I think he's dead!' Said, 'Call for help.' Then, while I was calling nine-nine-nine, Master's wife, she came in and they both went back up the stairs together. I heard her say, Miss Beaulieu that is, I heard her say, 'He's lying on the floor and the furniture's all turned over.' Then the EMTs ran in and I sent them up straight away."

With nothing more to be learned from them, I retreated to the bench in the quad, the same one that Bram and I had shared last night. From here I could see the back end of the ambulance through the open front doors beyond the porter's station. This was the first time I'd seen those doors open. Normally we entered and left through a normal-sized door that was cut into the left half of the huge arched and nail-studded doors whose age I could only guess at. I had wondered if those doors opened at all. Obviously they did, in a case like this.

Conference attendees started to gather in the quad. Everyone who walked by asked me what was going on. Why was the ambulance at the gate? I decided to downplay the situation, because the one thing the EMTs wouldn't need as they were taking Bram out was a crowd of rubberneckers. I told the curious that Bram Fitzwaring had apparently had a diabetic problem and he'd be right as rain as soon as they got some glucose in him.

Furniture turned over. That didn't sound like hypoglycemia. I was fairly well acquainted with the problem of low blood sugar. You get spacey, confused, your vision gets blurry, and your heart goes a mile a minute. If you don't do something quickly, you may lose consciousness as I have done on a couple of occasions I'm determined not to repeat. But why would he have turned over the furniture? Might he have realized he needed help and, in his confusion, tried desperately to leave the room but couldn't find the door? Flailed around blindly, knocking things over? It could have been like that.

But if he was showing symptoms of hypoglycemia as early as nine-thirty or ten, when I saw him, he'd have passed out long before the noises from down below woke me up. That was about two a.m. And after passing out, nothing would have awakened him. He would have simply died in his sleep.

The quad heated up in the midday sun and I slipped off my tunic, baring my arms to a couple of wrens who were now my only companions. My watch said five after two, so Claudia Moss's lecture would have started. That's why the quad was deserted.

At two-fifteen I heard noises coming from Staircase Thirteen and I stepped over until I stood in front of it, but far enough back to be out of their way. A couple of bumps and swear words, then an EMT muscling the leading end of the stretcher down the steep, narrow stairs backed out, his head swiveling rapidly forward and back to avoid tripping off the threshold or dumping the stretcher's burden.

The form on the stretcher was completely wrapped in a sheet, no head exposed. So he was dead. The woman who had talked to me at the foot of the stairs came out last, then ran around the stretcher and out the front to open the back doors of the ambulance.

When I turned back to the stairwell, I saw Daphne Wetmore and Mignon Beaulieu standing on its threshold. Mignon's face was red and swollen, loose strands of her long hair were wet and plastered to her cheeks. Daphne's arms hung at her sides awkwardly, as if they didn't know what they should be doing.

Approaching Mignon, I said, "I'm so sorry!" I hesitated to hug her because I hardly knew her, but she extended her arms to me and buried her wet face against my shoulder. Her hot breath on my neck, she sobbed. I couldn't understand her muffled words, but it didn't matter anyway.

Daphne Wetmore said, "Dr. Lamb, can you help me see her back to her own room?"

"Sure." I ignored the unearned title she had awarded me. In this group, almost everyone had a title, and doctor was the most common one.

Daphne led us up the staircase to room three, then turned and asked Mignon if she had her room key with her.

Mignon, now standing on her own but shakily, looked at the door and said, "I'd like to go back to Bram's room first."

"It's locked," Daphne said. She looked at the keys in her own hand. "Never mind. I have a master key." She led us up two more short flights and opened the door to room four with trembling hands. "I really have to go back to our guests. Do you mind? They'll be in the lecture hall and…oh, dear! The next speaker is Mr. Fitzwaring!" Her eyes bulged. "We have no speaker! What now?"

Before answering, I glanced into the room. Mignon had headed immediately for the student-style writing desk. I saw clothing scattered about, and, on the floor, a mattress and a wall-mounted mirror, smashed. Shards of glass and various papers littered the floor in the vicinity of the broken mirror. I said, "I'll stay with Miss Beaulieu."

Thinking that Daphne might, in her excited state, need someone to point her in the right direction, I said, "You need to find your husband. Get him out of the lecture hall and tell him what's happened."

"But he'll want me to tell him what to do next. He's like that."

"What to do next?"

"What are we to do with all these people for the rest of the afternoon?"

"Why not simply announce what has happened? Either at the end of this lecture or during the tea break, just tell them. There's no need to keep it secret. They can do whatever they want until evening. They don't have to be constantly entertained, you know. They're grown-ups."

Daphne looked at me as if I had introduced a revolutionary new concept. Truth. "I suppose you're right. I'll ask Harold to make the announcement." She fiddled with the keys in her hands, then added, as much to herself as to me, "Perhaps a tour. An afternoon tour of the castle. I wonder if I could find John Fish. He could walk them over to the castle and… I'd have to warn him to stay off the paranormal stuff. These aren't the sort of people you'd…oh, dear. I'd better be going. I'll figure it out on my way over." With that, she turned and disappeared around the bend in the staircase.

"I was right," I said, as much to myself as to Mignon, "Those noises I heard last night were coming from here. Look at the mattress!"

Mignon turned from her search of the top desk drawer and looked at the mattress on the floor. "Oh. That was already there. Bram was afraid the bed frame wouldn't hold him so he pulled the mattress off and slept on the floor."

"But what about the clothes all over the floor? What about the mirror?"

"I don't know. One of the EMTs suggested he might have had convulsions."

"I see. Do you think it was hypoglycemia?"

"I'm sure of it."

Mignon picked up a cell phone from the back of the desk and slipped it into a pocket of her shapeless shift, then extracted some papers from the open desk drawer.

"Is that Bram's cell phone?" I asked.

"Right. It'll have numbers for his nearest and dearest." She heaved a big sigh. "I need to start making calls," she said, her voice quavering. "This is going to be hard."

"What about family? Did he have any?"

"His mother and a couple of brothers, I believe. Live somewhere up near Newcastle, I think. Bram didn't talk much about family. His nearest and dearest are our friends in Glastonbury. We have a lot of friends there. A lovely circle of lovely people." She paused and took a deep breath. When she spoke again, it was barely a whisper, "Lovely like Bram. Lovely like Bram."

"Were you and Bram…?" I didn't know how to phrase it.

"Lovers?" Her eyes caught mine. "Sometimes. Sometimes not. I loved him though, and he loved me."

"How long have you known him?"

"Oh, years? About five." She rolled a few sheets of paper into a fist-size cylinder and glanced around the room. "Would you mind if I left now and went to my room alone?"

"Will you be okay?"

"Sure. Close the door when you leave," she said, and then stepped out.

It felt strange being alone in the room where a man had died such a short time ago, but I reminded myself this wasn't a crime scene so there was no need to worry about fingerprints or whatever. But how sure was I of that? This room was needling me. It didn't feel right. It didn't feel like a room in which someone had drifted off into death by hypoglycemia, but I couldn't think why not.

The tea tray was like the one in my room. Same electric pot, same bowl with sugar in little packets, cream in little tubs, tea bags, and a couple of long paper tubes filled with granulated coffee. Bram had placed his trashcan close to the mattress on the floor, just as I had placed mine near the head of my bed last night. I shivered at the similarity. Had he been nauseated, too? I peered into the trashcan and found three cellophane biscuit wrappers, but these said Chocolate Kreams. The ones the scout had been leaving me were Bourbon Kreams. Same logo and same brand. A couple of soggy tea bags and several empty sugar packs, a disposable razor, some used tissues, a couple of cash register receipts. I pushed the trash around with a pencil from the desk and then dropped the pencil in with the rest.

A blood glucose meter similar to my own lay on the table near the tea tray, along with a couple of used test strips, cotton swabs, and used syringes. These last stood inside a plastic water bottle. I kept a travel-sized sharps container on the back of my sink. I had already noticed his insulin was, like mine, stored in the tiny fridge on the landing outside the loo.

A Celtic cross hung from the gooseneck lamp on the desk. In a metal incense burner, a couple of spent sticks

stuck up at odd angles. I spotted one of Bram's huge rubber-soled sandals atop the bare wooden bed frame, the
other one lay under the sink in the far corner.

I scratched through my purse for my cell phone and
snapped a few shots of the room from various angles.
You never know what will come in handy.

I paused at Mignon's door on my way down, but decided not to knock. She said she wanted to be alone. I
could check on her later. I completed my descent and
headed for Smythson Hall, thinking I could slip into the
back and hear the last of Claudia Moss's paper, but I met
Daphne coming out as I was going in.

"I told Harold."

"How did he react?"

"At first he said we shouldn't tell anyone until after
the day's lectures, but I reminded him that the next lecturer is not going to be there because he's dead. Oh, I'm
sorry. That sounded crass, didn't it?"

"So what did he decide?"

"Harold? He said he'd tell them what happened and
say that he'd have more news at dinner tonight. Until then
they were on their own, and he'd make a few suggestions
for how they could spend their afternoon."

"Is there anything I can do?"

"Aren't you nice to offer?" Daphne took my arm and
looked up at me. She was a good half-foot shorter than
me. I'm five-five, so she was under five feet. "I'm going
to see if poor Miss Beaulieu is all right, then I'll sort out
what to do next."

"Actually? I don't think you should. She told me she
wants to be alone in her room for a while."

"Oh!" Daphne seemed taken aback. We had walked
through the archway and into the East Quad but weren't,

as far as I knew, headed anywhere in particular. "Okay, perhaps I'll wait a bit. Meanwhile…" She didn't seem to have an end for that sentence.

She turned, stopped in front of the bench I had recently vacated, swiped at the seat with her bare hand, and sat. I sat down beside her. This was a pretty good vantage point, I thought, from which to watch comings or goings on Staircase Thirteen and, if a call came into the Porter's Lodge, they could easily find us.

My bench mate heaved a huge sigh.

I asked, "Did you and Harold know Bram Fitzwaring before this conference?"

Daphne's neck muscles tensed. "No. I've never seen either of them before. They're from Glastonbury." She looked at me as if I should know what that meant. "I believe it was your mentor, wasn't it—Dr. Roberts—who suggested Fitzwaring as a speaker?"

Uh-oh. It might have been me who actually made the suggestion. I chose my next words carefully. "We, that is, Dr. Roberts and I, did receive email from him in the early spring. I was staying on campus at the University of Virginia while we collaborated on my dissertation topic, and I ended up handling much of his email for him. I remember corresponding with Bram Fitzwaring, but I rather thought he'd already been invited to speak by someone here."

"Did you know he was from Glastonbury?"

"I don't recall even being curious about exactly where he lived. I assumed he lived in England."

Daphne wrung her hands nervously, but said nothing for a minute.

"How did your husband react when you told him Bram was dead?"

"Harold takes things like this in stride. He said, 'Heart attack?' and I said, 'They think it was low blood sugar.'" Daphne's hands worked constantly with the folds in her dress. "Harold is an academic, Dr. Lamb. His head is always busy with things the rest of us will never understand. My sister calls him a genius."

"Can you call me Dotsy? I don't have my PhD yet."

"All right." But she didn't say call me Daphne, so what was I to do? The British are more formal than we are, but I truly would have felt strange calling this woman who was about ten years younger and six inches shorter than I, Mrs. Wetmore.

"How long have you and Dr. Wetmore been married?" I realized calling him Dr. Wetmore was laying the groundwork for further confusion.

"Three years," she said. "Harold and I were both what you might call late bloomers. Up until the time we met, Harold was totally immersed in his research. He's written more than thirty papers, and published four books." Daphne paused while I reacted appropriately to these impressive statistics. "He works closely with archaeologists in this part of the country, because his field is the early kings of Wessex, and so much of what we're learning now comes from the archaeologists."

"Yes. I was a bit surprised at his choice of topic this morning. The Tudor period? But he handled it beautifully."

Daphne blushed. "Harold can speak on any period of British history. He's amazing. My sister calls him Einstein. I'm continually in awe of that brain of his."

The porter on duty emerged from his office beside the front gate and trudged toward Staircase Thirteen. I stood as he disappeared into its dark interior. "I bet he's going up to Mignon's room. I think I'll follow him."

"Me too," said Daphne, hurrying to catch up.

FIVE

THE PORTER DID go to Mignon's room, but shook his head at Daphne and closed the door behind him. We kept climbing. When we arrived at the landing between rooms four and five, I saw the door to five, Lettie's door, was open. Lettie sat on the side of her bed, kicking her sandals off with a flourish that sent one of them spinning across the room. Her shirt was partially unbuttoned. "You can come in, but you can't stay," she said. "I haven't had a wink of sleep and I need to take a nap."

"Are you all right, Mrs. Osgood?" Daphne's question was perfunctory. The sort of thing she always asked guests, expecting an affirmative answer. The good hostess. She turned toward Bram's room, looked down the stairwell, then back at the door to room four, as if she didn't know where to go or why. "Will you excuse me? I have a million things to do."

She disappeared down the stairs.

"Who's with the children?" I asked, knowing that Lettie's daughter worked at the hospital most days while Lettie babysat. I stepped into Lettie's room and closed the door behind me.

Lettie Osgood is my oldest and dearest friend. We grew up together, but we now live a hundred miles apart so we see each other only a few times a year. One of those times, for the past several years, has been when we go on vacation together. Lettie's husband, Ollie, is a building contractor in northern Virginia and he's busiest in the summer so he can't take those months off from work. Lettie and I, on the other hand, can. The courses I teach at a small college in Virginia don't extend through summer session. Lettie is a librarian, and she also finds her summers the easiest time to leave town. We sometimes take a tour or a cruise, but this summer was different.

I had known since March that I was to accompany Larry Roberts to Oxford for this conference. Lettie had no plans to come with me until her daughter, Lindsey, accepted an offer to work at Oxford's highly respected Radcliffe Hospital in a doctor exchange program with her own hospital back home. Lindsey and her husband are separated, soon to be divorced, and the battle between them has been bitter the last few months. Lettie has called me nearly every night to unload her burden. She takes on her children's troubles as if they were her own. Her main concern in this matter—and my own, too—is that the young ones be spared the ugliness. Claire, seven, and Caleb, five, obviously had to come to Oxford with Lindsey, but Taylor, the soon-to-be-ex, raised a stink, claiming she couldn't take them out of the country. Their lawyers went toe-to-toe, and Lindsey won when her lawyer produced photos showing details of the lifestyle to which the children would be exposed if they stayed with their father.

This presented another problem: What to do with the kids while Lindsey was working at the hospital? She knew nothing about sitters or day care here, and was reluctant to leave them with strangers. Lettie came to her rescue by offering to come over and babysit. As luck would have it, I had already booked a room at St. Ormond's for this conference and knew that they rented vacant dorm rooms in the summer on a B&B basis as well.

Lettie had been here for two weeks before Larry and I arrived so she was already an old hand at getting around in Oxford. She usually took a bus, sometimes a cab, between the college and Lindsey's flat. I told her she'd be better off to lease a car, but she reminded me that, since her unfortunate entanglement with a yield sign in Scotland, she'd sworn off driving in any country that drove on the left side of the road.

Lettie was breathing loudly as she undressed, the way she does when there's something on her mind and she needs to talk about it. I had something I needed to talk about as well but I decided to let her unload first, as my news would probably take longer.

Lettie answered my question about the children. "Lindsey's taking the day off so she's with the kids. She got home at five-thirty this morning." My friend looked at me with her head lowered, the way she would do if she were looking over the tops of her glasses but she didn't wear glasses.

"Out with her new friend?"

"Right. I spent most of the night planning what I was going to say to her, but when she finally came wandering in, sneaking in, like she didn't think I'd hear her—I lost my nerve. I didn't say anything."

"Why the hell not?"

"Because there's something wrong."

"What?"

"I don't know, but I got the feeling that if I said anything it would be the wrong thing. You know what I mean?"

"Are you hungry? Have you eaten today?"

"I've done nothing but eat. Nervous snacking. I ate a whole box of yogurt-covered pretzels. What I need is sleep."

"I'll let you sleep, but first I have to tell you what happened to the man in room four."

"The big man with the long braid?"

"You saw him?"

"He and this woman—girl—heavy," Lettie said, puffing her cheeks out, "were carrying their bags in yesterday as I was leaving. We nodded to each other, but I didn't really meet them."

"What was your first impression?"

"They looked like escapees from Woodstock, nineteen sixty-nine."

I laughed, and then told her my story. Meanwhile Lettie donned her nightshirt, smeared green goo all over her face, crawled between the covers of her little bed, and propped her pillow behind her head. At first she was aiming to get rid of me, but became engrossed as I gabbed on, telling her about the state of Bram's room and about my misgivings. As I wrapped up my story, Lettie was sitting, cross-legged and wide-eyed, with the pillow scrunched in her lap.

"But why, Dotsy? Why do you think there's something else to it?"

"Why do you think there's something wrong with Lindsey?"

"Okay, okay. But hypoglycemia sounds reasonable, considering how you say he was acting last night."

"I agree. But the timing's wrong and there's something else. Something I saw. Maybe something someone—Daphne or Mignon—said."

"Woman's intuition?"

"I don't believe in woman's intuition. You know that."

"Do you know about Daphne Wetmore's sister?" Lettie said in an abrupt change of subject.

"Her sister? I've heard her mention a sister, but no. What about her?"

"She's like royalty or something. She's married to a lord, so that makes her a lady."

"That's not royalty. That's nobility. Royalty means you're related to the queen."

"Whatever. Lindsey was talking about her. Daphne's sister, Lady Whoever." Lettie put her hand up alongside her mouth as if she were whispering a secret to me but she wasn't whispering. "Lindsey told me she was always in the news. There was a huge horse-racing scandal. She owns horses. And her husband, the lord, bought an island in the Caribbean somewhere, but there's a problem with his taxes and the government and all. And some girl who was staying with him on the island drowned. And there are those who say it wasn't an accident."

"Hold on! What sort of horse-racing scandal?"

"Lindsey didn't say."

"What sort of tax problem?"

She shrugged.

"Who was this girl? Was she like a mistress or just a friend?"

"I'm just telling you what Lindsey told me. She didn't go into any details."

This sounded fascinating, but Lettie needed to sleep and I needed to see how my fellow conferees were reacting to the death of their afternoon speaker.

PEOPLE WERE MILLING around the West Quad lawn when I got there. Claudia's speech was over and tea was being served. Heads turned as I stepped through the archway, and several hands caught my arms as I walked across the grass searching for Claudia. I wanted to tell her I was sorry I'd missed her talk. Apparently it was obvious I'd come from the area where, they'd just learned, Bram Fitzwaring had died.

"What happened?"

"Were you there?"

"Who called the ambulance?"

"Is the, er, the ambulance still here?"

I answered all their questions because there seemed no reason to be obscure about it. Nothing was amiss, at least as far as I or anyone else actually knew. Bram, an overweight diabetic, had died in his sleep. Everyone's assumption, including my own, was that there would be an autopsy and we might or might not learn what it revealed. How sad it was that a human being's death so often elicited a few gasps of surprise, a few kind but perfunctory remarks like, *I feel so bad for his family* and *he's in a better place now,* followed quickly by a return to business as usual. In this case business as usual was, "Milk please. No sugar."

I couldn't find Claudia Moss but I did find Larry Roberts, who grabbed my elbow and pinched it between his thumb and middle finger. He pulled me away from the knot of people in front of the tea table. His hand on my arm felt shaky.

"Tell me what happened."

I pulled his hand off my elbow with my free hand. "Mignon—his companion, you know—found him. She went to his room because it was noon and she thought he was still asleep, but he wasn't. He was dead." I repeated the whole story much as I had told it to Lettie.

"Bummer. Are they sure it was low blood sugar? Did he take insulin?"

"Yes. In fact, I saw his used syringes in an old plastic water bottle."

"Have you had…? Of course, you haven't had tea yet." He glanced down at my empty hands. "Hey. I'd rather have tea at the Randolph. Come with me. We can talk."

Larry, rather than staying in one of the college rooms, was staying at the swanky Randolph Hotel, across the street from the Ashmolean Museum. I'd walked past the hotel several times and longed to see what it looked like inside but had been afraid to go in without a legitimate reason. I'd heard they had a Morse Bar, themed on the Inspector Morse TV shows starring the late, great, actor, John Thaw. I'd also been told the author, Colin Dexter, still lived in Oxford. The series had been filmed in Oxford. The Randolph was within easy walking distance, so I told Larry I'd go with him.

Once there, I got a quick glimpse of the lobby—a tasteful, business-like space quite unlike the glitzy caverns you see in most of the newer hotels—before Larry nudged me toward the tea room. The menu had a bewildering variety of teas, all described in flowery prose, so I chose the most expensive one. I assumed this was going on Larry's bill. The tea came with a pretty arrangement of little sandwiches and cakes.

"So. You didn't hear anything last night? Do they know when he died?"

"I heard a commotion about two this morning. It woke me up and I went down and knocked on his door, but I got no answer. I knocked on Mignon's door as well. She was there, but it was pretty obvious I'd woken her up."

"What makes you so sure you woke her up?"

"She had that gravelly voice people have when they first wake up."

"She could have been faking."

"What?" This statement sort of shocked me. "Are you suggesting she was upstairs, on the next floor up, battling Bram, knocking over furniture, killing him in some way that left no marks, then, while I'm running down from fourth floor to third, she's running from third to second, into her own room, closing the door and calmly opening it for me?"

"Could be, if she heard you coming."

"Who commits murder in footie pajamas with teddy bears?"

Larry grinned, slipped some more sugar into his tea. "Really? Teddy bears?" Larry wanted to know more about the strange noises I heard before I went to sleep. "I told you not to stay in that spooky old building. You should be staying here, where it's not haunted."

"Oh, really? I rather feel like it is, by the ghost of Inspector Morse."

"Too bad, isn't it? Did he have a family?"

"He wasn't married, and as far as Mignon told me, no children either. He had a mother and a couple of siblings."

Larry raised an eyebrow at the last little cake on our shared plate. I'd eaten all but one of the little sandwiches and he'd eaten all but one of the cakes.

I said, "Go ahead. I don't want it."

"Very sad. In the prime of life." He popped the little cake in his mouth all at once and sucked icing from his manicured thumb. "To be taken so suddenly. I'm very sorry it happened."

"Come *on*, Larry. Sorry? He was a thorn in your side!

Get real." I could hardly believe I was talking to my major professor this way.

Larry stared at me a minute. "I may have felt he didn't have the stature to participate in a conference like this one, but I certainly did not want him to die." He signaled our waiter for the check and signed it. "I was looking forward to a good old debate with the guy. I would have crushed him beneath my chariot wheels!" With a twinkle in his eyes, he folded his napkin and placed it on the table.

I had no answer for that. Or, more accurately, I had no answer that wouldn't have eliminated any chance I had of getting my PhD.

I LEFT THE Randolph Hotel alone and hiked a couple of blocks to Waterstone's bookstore. I automatically headed for the history section, then had another thought. Mignon Beaulieu had mentioned going out to see some friends today. Where might they be? Where might I find someone who might know someone who knew her? I was still thinking about Larry's comment that Mignon could have been faking. That she might not have been asleep at all, but rather, engaged in combat with Bram Fitzwaring. It was a stretch, but still, I had nothing better to do this afternoon, and it occurred to me that owners of an occult bookstore or a shop that sold the sort of esoterica Mignon and Bram went in for might know them. They might have connections to the Glastonbury New Agers.

I talked to a man at Waterstone's checkout counter.

"Right you are," he said. "Are you walking or driving?" When I told him, he gazed out one of the big plate-glass windows for a minute, and then said, "You might want to try The Green Man, just down the High, a bit past Logic Lane. All sorts of incense and things of that nature."

I followed his directions and walked eastward down the High. My watch said ten minutes to five. Most stores on the High closed around five-thirty or six, so it was getting near closing time. I found The Green Man and smelled the aroma of burning incense through the open door. I stepped inside.

No one was minding the store apparently, but I heard chatter from a back room. It sounded as if a half-dozen or more people were talking, gaily, like a party. The little shop was claustrophobic, with glass cases and racks of the sort of thing I expected to find in a place like this: A wicker basket full of pagan posters in rolls, a rack of greeting cards with fairies and pentagrams all done in a pre-Raphaelite style. Jewelry with spiders. Shelves full of oils and essences. A purple skirt with sewn-on spangles and tiny bells had fallen to the floor under a circular stand of black T-shirts with air-brushed designs.

I strained to hear what was being said in the back room. All I caught was a woman's voice saying something like "holy thorn tree." I detected both male and female voices. A gaunt, slightly stooped man slipped past the velvet curtain separating the back room from the front of the shop.

"Ehh. Didn't know anyone was out here. May I help you?"

"Just browsing," I said. That sounded inadequate. "I'm looking for a card for a sick friend." *Couldn't you come up with something better than that, Dotsy?* "These are so nice." I turned to the card display and picked up a random one.

"Indeed," the man crept behind the jewelry case and began fiddling with the earrings, positioning himself to make it impossible for me to shoplift any of their more expensive items.

I found myself actually searching for a card that would make a sick friend feel better. *Aha. This is a good way to introduce the real reason I'm here.* "This is so difficult," I began. "A couple of friends of mine—acquaintances actually, but we're staying on the same staircase at St. Ormond's College—well, the man died this…"

A raucous belly laugh shook the curtain to the back room.

I stopped in mid-sentence, forgetting all about what I was trying to say. It was Mignon Beaulieu's laugh. No doubt about it.

SIX

I RUSHED BACK to St. Ormond's in time to shower and change clothes before dinner, aiming to be ready for cocktails at six-thirty but failing to notice our schedule said nothing about pre-dinner drinks. It said dinner at seven. I stood outside the garden door of the Master's Lodgings, hearing nothing but silence from within. No light peeked through the curtained window beside the door. When I realized my mistake I wished I could take back my knock, fearing Harold Wetmore would open the door, wrapped in a towel and straight from the shower.

I turned and hurried back toward the East Quad, now wondering what to do with the extra thirty minutes before dinner. Lettie was still asleep, and I assumed she'd set her alarm for whatever time she wanted to wake up. After the night she'd had, I didn't want to wake her.

Keith Bunsen turned into the archway as I was leaving it. "Aren't you staying for drinks this evening?" he asked. He was making the same mistake I'd made.

I set him straight.

"Well! What to do? I certainly c-c-can't go back to my work. My brain has shut down for the day."

"You work here? I thought your research was at a lab outside of town."

"It is. I use the facilities at the Radcliffe Hospital. My laboratory is there but I do most of my paperwork here." Keith's head bobbed like a pigeon's, with a rocking motion, when he walked. He paused when we reached the middle of the quad.

This was a logical place for us to part, me to my staircase and him to wherever his rooms were, but I remembered a question I wanted to ask him. "Your research deals with diabetes, doesn't it?"

"Yes."

Over breakfast on a couple of mornings, we had discussed the fascinating work he was doing on diabetes and I'd told him I was type one diabetic, having dealt with the condition since childhood. "Did you know Bram Fitzwaring, the man who died today, was diabetic?"

"Was he now?" Bunsen tilted his head and looked toward Staircase Thirteen. "I think I m-m-may have known it, but until you mentioned it just now, I hadn't made a link between that fact and the man who died today."

This confused me. "Did you know Bram? I don't understand." How could Bunsen know Bram without knowing his name, or alternatively how could he have heard about the death without hearing Bram's name?

"Bram Fitzwaring may have been a part of the study I'm conducting. I say, 'may have been,' because I don't have a list of my subjects by name."

"I don't understand."

"It'll take a while to explain." He looked at his wristwatch. "We have twenty minutes before dinner. Let's go to my rooms." Those rooms turned out to be across the way on Staircase Ten, where he had an office and a couple of rooms. We sat in his cozy book-lined office, but I could see through a doorway to a small sitting room beyond. I didn't ask for a tour. It would have seemed too bold and besides, we only had a few minutes to talk. Bunsen indicated a brown leather wing chair for me and took the swiveling office chair for himself. *So this is what an Oxford don's office is like.* I quickly scanned a few book spines and found they were medical books, chemistry books, and weighty tomes on statistics.

The room was also cluttered with models of human insides, mouse insides, cell insides, and colorful DNA models. I realized this must be the office Bunsen used during the school term when he was teaching undergraduates. Obviously he kept his visual aids here between lectures. A scientist of his stature would hardly need a plastic model to tell him what was inside a cell.

"I told you the other morning that my research deals with a promising new compound I believe will help to reset the biological clock of diabetics, and regulate the liver's glucose production." He plopped one thin ankle on the opposite knee and leaned back in his chair. "The liver is responsible for the production of glucose and, therefore, the amount of glucose present in the blood at any given time. The livers of diabetics get signals to produce glucose all the time, not just when it's low. So when the production line should be shut down, it keeps cranking out more and more glucose.

"We've already run tests in live mice and using human liver cells in vitro. The data is very promising. So now we've advanced to testing on human subjects."

"How exciting," I said. "Can I be one of your subjects?" I was only half kidding. I knew I couldn't, because I don't live in England and the study, I assumed, was already underway.

"Sorry, no. But with luck you may be able to benefit from the results." He shifted in his chair. "A few years down the road."

I made the appropriate happy face.

"You asked me if...wh-what was his name? Bram Fitz-waring? You asked me if I knew him or if I knew he was diabetic, and I said I didn't know. Let me explain. I have two groups of subjects. A test group and a control group. The subjects in both groups are diabetic, all volunteers. The subjects come to our facilities at the Radcliffe Hospital at regular intervals. They get a battery of tests and a fresh supply of medicine, all administered by my assistants. Normally I don't see them. Each has a coded number and my assistants have access to the database containing the names and codes. The test subjects get the real medication and the members of the control group get a placebo."

So far Bunsen hadn't said anything I didn't understand, but I hoped it wouldn't get any deeper than this. "So you don't know if Fitzwaring was in your study or not?"

"Correct. It's a double-blind study. They don't know if they're getting the real medicine or not and I don't know either. My assistants match the patient's number with a number on a bottle of pills.

"I have actually examined and interviewed each of the subjects at the beginning of the study, but since then, I haven't seen most of them. We're talking about a hundred people, nearly a year ago, and I can't recall what they all looked like. I'm not especially good with faces anyway. As for their names, we have them in our files out at the hospital, but I don't personally have them."

"Oh, look at the time!" I said. It was seven o'clock exactly. I wasn't sure what would happen to late arrivals at dinner. I imagined walking up and down, looking for my name on a place card while everyone else was seated and muttering disapprovingly under their breaths.

As we raced across the lawn to the dining hall, I asked Keith, "Did you, by any chance, have an upset tummy last night after dinner? Several people, including me, did."

"Upset tummy?" Keith grinned at the expression. "No, I didn't, but I have a cast-iron tummy."

WE HAD NO place cards this night so we could sit wherever we wanted. Keith and I, being among the last to arrive, took seats near the entrance on the far end of the room from the High Table. Mignon Beaulieu walked in as Harold Wetmore was calling for the invocation. Fortunately I had an empty seat beside me and I waved her over, saving her the embarrassment of searching for one.

She wore the same midnight blue, crushed-velvet dress she'd worn the night before. Her auburn hair was piled up in a twist and held by a Celtic knot clasp like one I'd seen in the jewelry case at The Green Man. She took her seat quietly, but every head in the room turned toward her anyway. Whispers. I couldn't hear what anyone said but obviously they were saying, "That's the woman. The one who was with Mr. Fitzwaring."

I clasped her pudgy hand under the table.

This was awkward. The handclasp was automatic. Nothing more than I would do to console anyone. But that laugh I'd heard earlier still rang in my head. Was she sad or glad Bram was dead?

The starter was a cold sweet potato soup. Wine, which had been free at last night's dinner, was not free tonight. I ordered a bottle of Chablis and shared with Mignon and Keith. The conversation was stilted and going nowhere so I introduced the topic of Keith's research, partly to loosen things up and partly to see Mignon's reactions.

"Keith has been telling me about his study of a new—what should I call it—a new medication for diabetics. It sounds so promising, I wish I could get in on it, but I can't because it's already started and plus, I live in America."

"Is it the one Bram was in?" Mignon's Welsh accent made questions and statements sound, to my ear, the same. But this answered the question on my mind.

"Mrs. Lamb asked me the same question," Keith said, "and I had to tell her I don't really know." He explained how the study was organized.

"It sounds like the same one," Mignon said. "Bram took a bus to Oxford once every six weeks. They asked him some questions about how he was feeling, checked him out, and gave him a bottle of pills."

"Small world," I said, and turned to Keith. "How many people do you have in your study?" I already knew, but I asked for Mignon's benefit.

"About a hundred. That is to say, I started with a hundred but the numbers invariably dwindle as time goes on." The tip of Keith's tie had crept onto the edge of the table and was taking aim at his soup bowl.

I pointed to the problem. "Why do they invariably dwindle?"

"With that number of adults, even healthy adults, some may die, unfortunately."

Mignon's hand flew to her mouth.

Keith, possibly realizing the effect of his innocent remark on Mignon, quickly added, "Some may move away, some may simply decide to drop out. You have to delete all their data when they do. As if they'd never been in the study to begin with."

"But if they die, isn't that significant? Isn't that what the study is all about?" I asked.

"I didn't explain myself well," Keith said. "If someone in the study dies, you do include it, regardless of the reason for the death. If they get hit by a truck, in the data it's simply recorded as 'deceased,' and the rest of their line is left blank."

"Oh, dear. I can see how that might skew the results," I said.

"Exactly. It does happen. And if it happens more than a few times in a study as small as mine, you run into the old chi-square dilemma."

"What's that?" My own research, thank goodness, didn't involve statistics, although I had heard of the chi-square test for significance. Other graduate students at UVa bandied such terms about much to the chagrin of the mathematically challenged, like myself.

"It's a f-f-formula we use that tells us whether our results are meaningful or totally worthless. If your numbers dwindle too far, it can mean that one more person dropping out can render your whole study worthless even if the results so far are pure gold."

"Let me get this straight." I sat back to let the server remove my soup plate. "The people you're treating may be getting better, even getting well, but if one gets hit by a truck, the whole study can go down the drain."

"Right. Particularly in a study that starts with only fifty test and fifty control subjects."

Mignon had hardly touched her soup. Her question came out in a whisper. "Was Bram in your test group or your control group?"

Keith Bunsen looked at me, then down at the table. "As I told Mrs. Lamb earlier, I don't know. My assistants have that information."

Mignon's implication was clear. If someone wanted

to sabotage Keith's research, killing one of his test subjects might do the job. Or perhaps she was thinking, *if Keith's research is going badly, if too many in the* test *group have died, Keith would have a motive for killing a member of the* control *group.* I wondered if Mignon knew Keith lived only a few yards from our own rooms.

While the wait staff was pouring coffee, making their way around the tables in pairs, one with a pot of decaf and one with regular, Harold Wetmore rose to introduce the evening's speaker. "But first, we all extend our most heartfelt sympathy to the family and friends of Bram Fitzwaring, who passed away peacefully last night in his room. Especially to his friend, Mignon Beaulieu, who accompanied him here from their home in Glastonbury and who, like all of us, was looking forward to his lecture this afternoon."

I wasn't sure if Wetmore knew Mignon was in the room or not. Most of the diners in our part of the room turned toward her and nodded solemnly.

Our speaker was Robin Morris, a director of the Bodleian Library and one of my dinner companions last night. I remembered his remark about Prudence Burcote, his nominee for the Grey Lady of the night before. In light of today's happenings, everyone seemed to have forgotten about that mysterious event. Morris spoke to us about the history of the Bodleian Library and described how visiting scholars, such as we were, could go about gaining entry to one their reading rooms. The Bodleian was not a lending library, and its mission to protect hundreds of rare and ancient documents meant that permission to even sit and read was fraught with red tape. He recited the oral declaration required of all visiting scholars promising not to mark, damage, or remove any document from the premises and to bring in nothing that might start a fire.

MIGNON AND I walked back to Staircase Thirteen together.

"Have you talked to Bram's family yet?" I asked, slowing my pace to let Mignon catch up with me. She was wheezing, and I wondered if this slight exertion was all it took to wind her.

"I talked to his mother," she said. "So awful, having to tell her over the phone, but what was I to do? I couldn't actually go to Newcastle to tell her. That's a whole day's trip." She stopped a moment to catch her breath. "I offered to tell his brothers as well if she would give me their phone numbers, but she said she had to do it herself."

"I understand."

"Bram was a bit estranged from his family."

"A bit estranged?"

"It wasn't like a family feud or anything. It was just that his family didn't approve of his lifestyle or his beliefs. They're all very conventional, the Fitzwarings. You know. Grow up, get a job, get married, have children, go to church on Sunday." She shook her head as she walked along the concrete border around East Quad. "It was weird, though. When I told her, it was almost like she expected it. Like, 'Okay, what else is new?'" Mignon stopped when we reached the entrance to our staircase and turned. "I need to go back to Bram's room. Do you think they'd let me have a key?"

"We can ask," I said. I turned toward the porter's station where lights still burned inside.

The porter handed the key to Mignon. "I was on duty last night, you know, when Mr. Fitzwaring..." He allowed his voice to trail off rather than use the word *died*. His face tightened into a picture of sorrow. "I'm so sorry, Miss. So sorry about what happened. I didn't learn about it until I came back this afternoon."

"You work three to eleven, don't you?" I asked him.

"That's right."

"Then I don't think you were on duty when he died. The EMTs seemed to think it was more like two in the morning." I saw no reason to go into the noises I heard in the wee hours because this porter wouldn't have heard them. However, I did want to talk to the porter who was on duty and find out if he heard anything or saw anyone out at or around the critical time.

We turned back, sticking to the walkway that skirted the east and south wings of the building. "Mignon, was Bram conscientious about watching his blood sugar?"

"Absolutely!" The fat under her chin shook for emphasis.

"I know he took insulin, because his supply is in the same little refrigerator where I keep mine." I responded to her next question, the obvious one, with, "Yes. Type one. I've been dealing with it my whole life."

"Bram was only diagnosed about five years ago, I think. That would be type two?" Climbing the stairs ahead of me she wheezed, "Bram always tested his blood sugar first thing every morning, then he ate breakfast, then he gave himself a shot of insulin." She paused on the first landing and caught her breath. "He tested again before lunch, and after lunch he'd do another injection." She forged ahead, up the next flight. "Before dinner he tested again but after he ate he didn't take more insulin unless his numbers were too high."

We had reached the door to room four. Mignon inserted the key and opened the door. "Before bedtime he always tested again. Always."

"And if the number was too high?"

"He'd take more insulin, I guess, but that never happened. If it was low, he'd eat a snack."

I recalled the Chocolate Kream Biscuit wrappers, the used tea bags, and the empty sugar packets I'd seen in Bram's room earlier. It made sense that he would have tested his blood, found his number too low, and eaten something to raise his sugar level before he went to sleep.

Bram's room had been cleaned. The mattress was back where it belonged, with pillow and covers on top. The floor, the sink, the trashcan, and the desk top were all clean and shiny. New supplies lay on the tea tray.

"Oh, bollocks." Mignon's pudgy hand slapped her own forehead. She stepped across to the cabinet that housed a short clothes rack on one side, drawers on the other, and opened its doors. "Where are his clothes? His clothes are gone."

I had no answer.

Pulling the long drawer under the writing desk open, she added, "Everything is gone. When we came in here before, I took his phone and thumb drive out of this drawer but there were some other things in here. Papers. Chewing gum. Keys. They're gone." She walked around the rest of the room, going, "Clean as a whistle. Gone."

"You should ask at the porter's station."

She stood in the middle of the floor a long moment, and then nodded. "I'll do that."

"I love your barrette," I said. "Did you get it at The Green Man today?"

Her head jerked back and her eyes widened. She touched her piled-up auburn hair and felt for the barrette. "Uh, no. I've had it for years." She turned to the mirror over the sink as if to see which barrette she was wearing tonight.

"How do you know I was at The Green Man today?"

"I was there, too. I took a walk down the High and I saw some things I liked in their window. I went in, but all I bought was a card."

"How do you know I was there?"

"You were in the back room. I heard you laugh. You have a nice laugh."

"I do?"

"It's musical." Actually, *loud* would have been a better word, but Mignon took this choice of words as a compliment.

"It sounded like there was a party going on in the back room."

"No, no." Mignon's face clouded. She turned the desk chair around and sat, sending yards of midnight blue velvet spilling onto the floor on either side of the chair. "I told them about Bram. They all knew him. We started talking about some of the good times we'd shared with him, and…" Her voice quivered. "You have to understand where we're coming from—me and our friends. We believe only the thinnest veil separates this life and the next. We pass back and forth. Sometimes we return to this world in a different form, sometimes we return in the same form. We've all met and talked to wonderful people that others say are long dead. It doesn't matter to us what other people say, we know better."

"You mean your friends in Glastonbury?"

"Friends everywhere." Mignon leaned forward and smiled at me. "Bram will be with us again, as soon as he completes his passage through the Star Gate."

While Mignon was talking, I spotted a piece of paper on the floor of the otherwise empty closet. I wanted it. I stood and announced, "I need to get back to my room. Long day tomorrow." While saying this, I let my room key slip from my hand.

"Me too."

I let her close the door and started up the next flight toward my room. "Oh wait!" I called her back. "My room key must have fallen out in there. Let me have the key and I'll return it to the porter's station when I'm finished." I took it from her and quickly turned away. "And I'll find out what's happened to Bram's luggage while I'm there."

"I can go with you."

"No, no. You go along, now. It's late. Big day tomorrow."

IT TOOK ME only a second to retrieve my key from Bram's bed, grab the slip of paper from the floor of his closet, and return to the stairwell in time to hand the key back to Mignon, still standing on the third step down.

SEVEN

A THIN FILM of light spread across the floor beneath Lettie Osgood's door. That meant she was up. I knocked. Lettie opened the door with a hair dryer, unplugged, in one hand and a brush in the other. Her feet were bare and her short, red hair was wet.

"Are you in for the night?" I said.

"I wish! I got a call from Lindsey a few minutes ago." Lettie shifted her tone to petulant. "'Can you come over right away? St. Giles wants me to go somewhere with him.'"

St. Giles was apparently the name of Lindsey's latest love interest. A slightly pretentious name, I thought, but perhaps not in England. "Isn't it a bit late for a date?"

"Indeed it is, and I told her so, but what am I to do? Leave the kids alone in that apartment?"

"It would be Lindsey, not you, who was leaving them alone."

"Alone is alone."

"Have you eaten anything today?"

"No, but when I get to Lindsey's place, I can fix myself something. As long as I'm giving her free babysitting, she can at least feed me."

"This guy. St. Giles. What do you know about him?"

"He's extremely handsome, he's a neurologist, and Lindsey's so smitten with him she's letting him walk all over her."

"Her divorce problems aren't making her any more cautious? I'd think she'd be a bit gun-shy right now."

"Lindsey's hitting the big four-oh in April. That's part of it."

Lettie plugged in the hair dryer, bent forward, and shook her head so the hair dryer and brush could work on the hair in back. We couldn't hear each other over the dryer noise, so I pulled the slip of paper from Bram's closet out of my pocket and looked at it.

It appeared to be a list. In a man's scratchy hand and in ballpoint, it said:

1. Tor
2. bone 51.9 (x 2.6 + 65) = 2m
3. Sharpham Cromwell
4. TVRA 450 ce.

At first blush, this meant nothing to me, but I love a good mystery. Although the words *bone, Sharpham,* and *Cromwell* were written in cursive, TVRA was printed, as if those four letters might be an acronym rather than a word.

Now looking for her sandals, Lettie said, "I have to hurry. The bus stops outside at nine forty-five, and I think it's the last one." Sliding the heel strap of one sandal to its proper place, she grabbed the edge of her bed for balance. "What's happening with the man in room four? Any new developments?"

"I went with Mignon, who's Bram's companion— *was* Bram's companion—to room four a few minutes ago. Someone's already cleaned the room. They took his body to the morgue and they're supposed to do an autopsy tomorrow."

"Where's the morgue?"

"I don't know. Does it matter?"

"You said there was something strange about his death. Knowing you, you've already figured out a way to sneak in when they're doing the autopsy. With all that stuff they have to wear, you wouldn't need a disguise."

"Really!" I feigned resentment. "Now that you mention it..." Something occurred to me. "Do you think Lindsey could get me into the Radcliffe Hospital?"

Lettie blinked, then stared at me, wide-eyed.

"Not as a patient. I mean could she give me a tour or something?"

"And just happen to take you past the morgue where she silently slips away?" Lettie fluttered her fingers at me.

"No. What I want is to see where Keith Bunsen does his research. I have the idea it's a lab on site but not actually in the part where the patients are." I had to backtrack and tell Lettie who Keith Bunsen was and why I was interested in his research. Meanwhile Lettie finished dressing, shouldered her purse, and inched toward the door.

"I don't know. Lindsey's not exactly in the in-crowd at the hospital, you know. She's a visiting physician."

"I know, but could you ask?"

"So you can find a way to sneak into this lab and go through their files?"

"I just want to see where it is."

"Gotta go. I'll ask, I'll ask!"

WHERE DID THAT come from? I stood in the middle of my room and wondered why I had just asked Lettie to get me a tour of the Radcliffe Hospital. Until I heard myself asking, I'd had no thought of going to the hospital for any reason. I must have had a reason; what was it?

Bram Fitzwaring might or might not have been a part of Keith Bunsen's study, but I'd bet almost anything that he was. Keith might or might not have been telling the truth when he said he didn't know. But Bram was dead, and I didn't believe hypoglycemia had killed him. I've dealt with the problem myself, and the timing was wrong. The overturned furniture was wrong. The cookie wrappers and the empty sugar packets in his trashcan meant that he had consumed a good bit of sugar at some point. The scout on our staircase cleaned our rooms in late afternoon. She always emptied the trashcans, so Bram had consumed the cookies and tea after the scout cleaned the room. Had he realized he needed some quick carbs when he returned to his room after dinner? Did he realize he was acting strangely when he talked to me?

And like Mignon, Larry, and me, he'd had a stomachache after dinner as was shown by the position of his trashcan—right next to his mattress. But he hadn't actually thrown up, had he? I recalled going through the contents of the trashcan, and if there had been any upchuck in it, I certainly would've noticed.

If it had been hypoglycemia, I think he would have died long before two a.m., the approximate time I was awakened by the noises that must have come from his room. Had the cookies and sweet tea staved off the sugar crisis until two a.m.? Then why did he wake up and start trashing the furniture? I needed to think about this some more, but it didn't make sense. I felt sure Fitzwaring had entered the next world or, as Mignon would have it, passed through the Star Gate, with help.

When the results of the autopsy came out, would the

police start looking for the helper? Who would be a suspect? I came up with four names and one of them was
mine.

I GATHERED MY shower supplies and placed the note from
the floor of Bram Fitzwaring's closet on my desk, anchor-
ing it with my phone as if it were so important I mustn't
let it fall on the floor. Actually, I had a feeling it *was*
important. Yanking my robe and nightshift off the peg
on my closet door, I decided to wait and change clothes
in the bathroom. A mental image of myself climbing up
the stairs in a short robe and black heels convinced me
to take my flip-flops in the unlikely event I'd run into
someone on my return.

Walking down the hall outside my room, I heard the
drums again. Thirteen beats then pause, I remembered
from last night. I counted and found that tonight's beat
was different. It was seven beats, pause, four beats pause,
then seven again. I descended to Mignon's room and listened at her door. The drumming was louder here. It was
obviously coming from within Mignon's room. From
this distance I heard another, higher-pitched, drum tap-
ping out a rhythm between the slower beats. What I'd
heard from above had been only the bass part of a more
complex beat.

I descended another flight to the bathroom and tossed
my towel over the shower curtain rod. A large bug had
found its way into the shower enclosure and was now
on its back, buzzing around in frantic circles near the
drain. It couldn't turn itself over or fly away. Probably
the natural end of its short life.

I stepped into the toilet nook and grabbed a wad of
paper, picked up the still-buzzing insect, cranked open

the room's only window, stuck out my arm, and released the bug. I didn't notice whether the bug flew away or not because a figure, gliding smoothly through the gloom on the far wall of the quad, caught my eye.

It was the Grey Lady again.

Draped in a dark, hooded cape, she moved as if pulled by an invisible string. My next move depended on whether or not I had already shed my shoes. I looked down and found they were still on my feet, so I ran. Careening off the far wall of the staircase in my haste to make a ninety-degree turn, I flew out and into the quad.

She was headed for the arched passage that led to the north gate. She. How did I know it was a woman?

I ran straight across the grass, now starting to gather dew. I shouted, "Hey!" as the heel of my left shoe came down on something hard. The shoe turned on its side and my ankle bent painfully outward.

The figure stopped for a split second, then, without turning to face me, took off in a more human-like sprint, her cape billowing out behind her.

I ran, too. My ankle screaming in protest, I dashed through the archway after her, tripping again on the uneven flagstone. This space was lit by one small carriage light that, if anything, made the path more confusing by casting odd shadows. She could only have gone left, because a right turn led to the garden entrance of the Master's Lodgings. No escape that way.

I turned left. Ahead of me lay three solid walls, none with doors, and another archway on the right. I crept toward it, now wary, because I was certain I'd meet the Grey Lady attempting to open the door that I knew opened into Cobbler's Lane. What I didn't know was *how* it opened. I assumed it, like the front gate, had a touch pad that required a magic button. There was no illumination at all in this space except for a tiny bit of reflected college lights slipping in from behind me. I shut my eyes for a moment, to help them adapt to the dark more quickly.

This is not a good time to be standing here with your eyes closed, Dotsy.

I opened them and found—nothing. Nothing but two stone walls and the third with a giant, black, arched gate. Closed. A smaller door cut into the wooden gate was also shut. I pushed on it. No good. I felt around on both sides of the door until I found the touch pad. I couldn't open the door because my magic button was on the ring with my room key—in the shower.

Heading back, now genuinely confused and aghast at my own recklessness, I wondered if it was possible that the Grey Lady had gone into the Master's Lodgings. If so, that rather narrowed down the field of suspects to Daphne Wetmore or someone known by, and in collusion with, the Wetmores.

My ankle was killing me.

I turned and hobbled back through the archway, turned right this time, and gazed through the Master's Garden. Lights were on inside the Wetmores' den. The curtains were open, and inside a half-dozen people in evening dress sat, chatting and drinking what I assumed was decaf from china cups.

I STOPPED IN at the porter's station and asked for some ice to use on my ankle. I reminded them that the refrigerator on Staircase Thirteen had no freezer compartment. The porter on duty pulled a plastic ice cube tray from his fridge in a little nook behind a folding screen, cracked the cubes loose, and dumped them into a Starbucks coffee cup.

"By the way, have you seen a strange woman wandering around?"

The porter raised his eyebrows at me. "The mysterious Grey Lady again?"

"I think so."

He grinned and shook his head. "You professors have great imaginations, I'll give you that!"

"Oh, that's right. You didn't see her last night, did you?"

"No. But if you all say there was a woman who disappeared before you could catch her, I'll believe you. Who am I to say aught else?"

"I thought I saw her again tonight, over there." I pointed to the north wall of the quad, visible from the door to the porter's station, but only partly so from where I stood. "Ah well. I suppose when you have a place that's been standing since Elizabethan times, you're bound to collect a few ghosts." I thanked him for the ice and hobbled back to the shower on Staircase Thirteen.

BACK IN MY own room, I dumped the ice cubes into the quart-sized plastic bag I'd used to move my liquids through airport security. Pressing it against my throbbing ankle, I jammed my pillow into the space between my back and the wall at the head of the bed and trained the light from the bedside lamp on Bram Fitzwaring's note. His last will and testament? No, but it might be the last thing he ever wrote.

Why had it been lying on the floor of his closet? Was this what Mignon had been looking for? I doubted it. It was more likely that she simply wanted to gather up his clothes and other personal effects. The paper had been torn from a notepad. I could see traces of glue along the top edge. It had been folded twice. To fit in his pocket? This seemed likely. He wrote the note, tore it off the pad, and stuck it in his pants pocket. Draped his pants over a hanger and the note fell out in the closet.

When would they do the autopsy? Had it already been done? Who would be told the results? His mother? Mignon? Would Mignon tell the rest of us? If it was hypoglycemia, would the autopsy prove it? My common sense told me there would be no physical evidence of it. The heart, liver, stomach, and brain would look normal. They might well find evidence of his diabetes, but that in itself wouldn't be the immediate cause of death.

They'd take a blood sample. They'd send it off to a lab. The glucose level would be very low if it was hypoglycemia. That's probably what the medical examiner would suspect if he knew Bram was diabetic. How long would it take to get the lab results back?

All this was useless musing on my part. What I needed to do was wring every bit of information I could from the few words on this little piece of paper, and wringing information was my special talent.

This might have been a memo to himself of things to do. A trip to Oxford would be a logical time for research into whatever interested him, and that would be anything to do with King Arthur or the history of Glastonbury. Since, according to Mignon, he had friends here, this might be a list of things to ask them about, or tell them about, or look for books about. Lists are made to remind oneself. The careless way this one had been written in a combination of printing and cursive letters told me it wasn't meant for any eyes but his own. In fact, the numbers inside the parenthesis in item two were in pencil, whereas the rest was in ballpoint. So it hadn't all been written at the same time.

The whole thing was in a tiny, cramped hand. It reminded me of my son Brian's handwriting. This was a funny thing I'd noticed before. The biggest men write the smallest hand as if the instrument in their hand is too small and will only produce letters of a similar size. Or maybe it's a subconscious desire to *be* smaller. I doubted that. Brian Lamb, at least, used his hefty proportions to great advantage.

I started with the first item, Tor. A tor is a pile of rocks or a rocky outcrop. The area around Dartmoor in southwestern England was especially known for its tors. But the only tor I knew by name was Glastonbury Tor. Coincidence? I thought not. I flipped the magnetic cover off my iPad and pulled up a map of southwestern England. Glastonbury lay some seventy-five miles northeast of Dartmoor. So a man from Glastonbury would most likely have been referring to Glastonbury Tor in his notes. Still, I needed to bear in mind that England has many tors, and Bram's list had only that one word.

Next: Bone. Or was that bore? His writing was so small it was hard to tell. Bone seemed more likely somehow. 51.9. A dimension? A length? A diameter? What were the units? If bone was the correct word, it could be length. If length, 51.9 inches would be far longer than any human bone, but might be reasonable for a dinosaur. I can always remember Lettie's height by the song, "five foot two" and "only sixty inches high." A 51.9-inch bone would be up to Lettie's shoulders.

Maybe centimeters? I used an online metric converter and found that 51.9 centimeters would be about twenty inches. But what about these other numbers inside the parenthesis? I multiplied it out, using the rule I learned in school: perform the operations inside the parenthesis first. That gave me 8,771 centimeters, almost the length of a football field. This was getting me nowhere.

Item Three. Now this was more like it. History. Cromwell, of course, was easy. Oliver Cromwell, military leader in the English Civil War and Lord Protector of the Commonwealth in the mid-1600s, was instrumental in relieving King Charles I of his head. Hero to some and an archvillain to others. The preceding word, Sharpham, had me stumped. I googled it and found that Sharpham was a small town near Glastonbury, and also a vineyard on the river Dart south of Dartmoor. Was there a reason why both these names were on the same line? How were they connected?

Finally, item four. TVRA 450 ce. The first four letters were printed so I thought they could be an acronym or possibly a foreign word. 450 ce. A year? ce was the new, politically correct, way of writing a.d. a.d., *anno domini*, in the year of our Lord, had a definite Christian connotation as did b.c., before Christ. Recently most historians had switched to writing bce, Before the Common Era, instead of b.c., and ce—Common Era? It still sounded awkward to me. What's so common about the era we live in?

I googled TVRA and got a number of suggestions, none of which seemed to have anything to do with Bram Fitzwaring, Glastonbury, the Elizabethans, or King Arthur.

EIGHT

MY PHONE RANG at midnight and woke me up. It was Lettie, still at her daughter's apartment. "Lindsey says she can show you around the hospital tomorrow morning about ten if you can meet her in the front lobby."

This made no sense mixed in with the dream the call had interrupted. I sat up and paused a minute to get my bearings. Lettie's voice. Lindsey. Her daughter. Hospital? Slowly the pieces came together.

"Are you still there, Dotsy?"

"Right," I croaked. "That's good. Why did you have to call me so late?"

"It's not late. You're just in bed early. I have to get an answer now because Lindsey's getting ready for bed and I'm getting ready to go back to St. Ormond's. She needs to know tonight so she can clear you for a visit tomorrow morning."

"Ten o'clock. I'll be there."

It took me a few minutes to go back to sleep, and meanwhile I heard thunking noises from my window. Standing on the foot of my bed, I cranked the window open and listened. I heard scrapes and metallic clangs that seemed to be coming from my right, down Sycamore Lane. I knew there was a narrow alley on this side of the lane, some twenty yards down. It was full of trashcans. Why would anyone be taking out trash at this hour? Probably a dog or something.

I dropped to my pillow and my knee flattened the plastic bag I'd used on my twisted ankle. The ice had melted and cold water squirted across the covers.

THE NEXT MORNING as I dressed, I studied the conference program for the day. It was Sunday and nothing was scheduled until one-thirty so people could attend church if they wanted to. Oxford abounded with historic churches, and I'd intended to go to services at the Church of St. Mary the Virgin on the High Street because it had been the site of so many pivotal events in its thousand-year history. I'd taken a quick walk through a few days ago.

But I had made plans, sometime in the wee hours, to meet Lindsey at the Radcliffe Hospital at ten o'clock. I wondered if Lettie was in her room, but decided against "knocking her up" since she may have come in very late. Instead, I went to breakfast alone and found very few people there. The only one I recognized was Claudia Moss, the young woman from the British Museum in London, whose lecture I had missed yesterday. She waved me over to join her.

"You're on Staircase Thirteen, aren't you?" she said. "That's why you weren't there for my lecture yesterday. I looked for you in the audience because you told me you had a keen interest in Shakespeare."

"I was so looking forward to it. But unfortunately…"

She cut me off. "Oh, golly! Was it you who found him?" Claudia tucked her long brown hair behind her ear and leaned forward, her shirt just missing the rim of her plate. She was wearing a brushed cotton shirt that exactly matched the green of her eyes. Her makeup was nothing more than a bit of blush to highlight her cheekbones, and an artful sweep of mascara. She was a head turner of the modest sort.

I recounted yesterday's scene as briefly as I could. "I suppose we have to wait for the results of the autopsy to find out for sure why he died."

"How well do you know Mignon? His companion. Isn't that her name?"

"I only just met her."

"Were they a couple?"

"That's hard to say. I asked her and she said they were lovers—sometimes. Whatever that means."

"So that's where Daphne Wetmore was yesterday when we were eating lunch." Claudia added a drop of milk to her tea and took a tiny sip. "Do you remember? You asked Dr. Wetmore where she was."

"Right. That was when she and Mignon would've been waiting for the EMTs. By the time we finished lunch, the ambulance was already here." I recalled looking at my watch as I sat on the bench in the quad. It was two-fifteen when they emerged with Bram's body on a stretcher.

"It was odd, though." Claudia muttered this into her teacup, as if she didn't mean for me to hear.

"What was odd?"

She paused a moment. She gazed out one of the tall stained-glass windows, and I had decided she wasn't going to answer me at all, when she said, "Before my speech, I was sitting on the dais waiting for Dr. Wetmore to go to the microphone and introduce me. He and Dr. Roberts, your friend, were standing by the side door just off the stage. Dr. Wetmore said something like, 'Got your loins girded?' and Dr. Roberts said, 'Personally, I'd rather be in the Bahamas.'"

"Then what?"

"That's all I heard, but I thought to myself, 'What are they talking about? They both delivered their papers this morning. They can relax. If anyone should be nervous, it's me and Bram Fitzwaring.'"

I TOOK A taxi to the Radcliffe Hospital, a giant megaplex of glass and steel that seemed a world away from the mellow Cotswold limestone of the university in the town's center, and told my driver where to let me off. Lettie had given me her daughter's cell phone number so Lindsey and I stayed connected as my cab approached the entrance. She was waiting for me inside the automatic doors, a visitor's pass for me already in hand. I hadn't seen Lindsey for several years and wasn't prepared for the mature woman in a white lab coat and comfortable-looking shoes. Tall and slender, with her long dark hair pulled back in a ponytail, her blue eyes had sunk deep into their sockets. She looked tired, with dark, puffy half-moons under her eyes.

I hid my surprise and hugged her.

"Where do you want to go? It's a huge place as you can see." She peeled the backing from a visitor's name card and stuck it on my shirt. "Would you like to see the floor where I work?"

I said I would, but I intended to steer our path toward the research area as soon as I could. I was not here to see the sick people. I was here to see where Keith Bunsen conducted his diabetes study and to assess my chances of discovering whether Bram Fitzwaring was one of his test subjects. I had asked Keith twice and both times he said he didn't know. Maybe, I thought, I'd have more luck with one of his assistants, but I knew it would take finesse and a bit of trickery on my part. After fifteen minutes walking up and down the hall where Lindsey worked, glimpsing pulmonary patients in beds left and right, "Oxygen in Use" signs on many of the doors, I asked about research. Lindsey looked disappointed. About halfway down the hall, a little clutch of hospital personnel—I couldn't tell if they were nurses or what—stood eyeing us, none too subtly.

"Are these your co-workers?" I nodded and smiled in their direction.

"Would you mind meeting them?"

"I'd like to." I toyed with excuses to cut this meeting short while Lindsey introduced me as her mother's best friend from America, and they responded with polite questions about what I was doing here. "I'm attending a conference at the university but if you're asking why I'm here at your hospital, it's because a professor at St. Ormond's has told me about some fascinating work on diabetes that's being done here. I'm diabetic so, of course, the research interests me. I'm hoping Dr."—I couldn't remember Lindsey's married name and had no idea if she had returned to using her maiden name or not—"that is, Lindsey, will show me where the labs are."

Lindsey looked a bit surprised and stared at her feet for a second as if revising her tour plans. "We'd better be going then," she said. "The research wing is a right long hike from here." She led me back to the first floor by elevator, then along a glassed-in corridor, around several personnel stations, and through a number of automatic doors. "This is it," she said.

We stood in a brightly lit hall with a gleaming white floor. The rooms on either side were clear glass from waist height to ceiling so I could see into the labs. I love labs. There's something about flasks with brightly colored liquids and rows of test tubes and stainless steel panels and dials with red needles that I find exciting. Neat. Orderly. Precise. But the lab on my right wasn't quite so neat. The beakers closest to the window were filled with something that looked more like pond scum and spoiled milk. A clipboard hanging from a string held a chart scribbled with several colors of ink.

"On the right, we have our genetic research and diabetes research."

I stepped closer to the glass and saw a couple of workers in white lab coats, but they were women. No Keith Bunsen anywhere in sight. While I peered in, studying as much of the room as I could, I noticed Lindsey eyeing the lab on the other side of the hall.

She touched my arm. "On this side we have neurology and nervous tissue studies."

"Can we go in?"

"Not without clearance." She looked through the sheet of glass fronting the neurology lab and waved, then pointed to herself and me. "We just got clearance."

I followed her into a room that smelled of ozone, like the aftermath of an electrical storm. A wall of stacked cages ranged along one wall contained inverted water bottles and mice, one on its back legs with its little front feet hooked over the wire of its cage. They were curious, I supposed, to find out who the visitors were. Lindsey introduced me to a rather short but handsome man who reminded me of Hugh Grant, with a shock of thick hair expertly cut to look messy.

"St. Giles Bell," Lindsey told me.

We shook hands. He had a charming smile. *What do you call a man when his first name is St. Giles?* Did he have a nickname? I said, "Nice to meet you, Dr. Bell."

We exchanged small talk for a minute while Lindsey shuffled her feet and played with her ponytail. This was her new boyfriend, I felt certain. When I got a second chance to look around the room, I spotted a large shallow pan full of oysters in a thin brownish liquid. Oysters? I had to ask.

"My work on nervous disorders involves sodium channel blockers," said St. Giles Bell, "and the best one I've found is called saxitoxin. It's produced by certain marine algae and concentrated in the tissues of filter-feeding animals, like oysters. That's the reason for the oysters. They are happily gorging themselves on a certain kind of algae that I have procured for them at great risk to my own well-being."

"He means snorkeling in the North Sea," Lindsey said, rolling her eyes.

"Well, hey. That water is cold. I could have suffered cardiac arrest." He pressed his hand against his chest.

I found his self-effacing manner charming. The look on Lindsey's face said she did, too. I said, "A toxin, did you say?"

"Right, and an extremely potent one. In fact, it's a Schedule One Chemical Warfare Agent."

I didn't need to ask what that meant. What I didn't get was how it could possibly help cure diseases. I started to ask, but Lindsey and St. Giles Bell had moved away from me and put their heads together, his hand cupping her white-coated elbow. I slipped out into the hall and across to the window of the genetics and diabetes lab. I could see that it wasn't a single room, but a series of spaces that communicated with one another and were connected to the hall at intervals by white-painted doors.

I spotted Keith Bunsen. Damn! There went any chance

I may have had to talk with one of his assistants without his knowledge. He had just walked through from an unseen adjoining room and was carrying a clipboard. Like everyone else, he was wearing a white lab coat. I waved, but he didn't see me. *No need to pretend I'm not here.* I watched while he conferred with a young woman seated in front of a microscope. He seemed to be giving her instructions. When he straightened his tall, bony frame and turned my way, I waved again. This time he saw me and loped to the door.

"Dotsy, w-w-what are you doing here?"

I pointed to the neurology lab across the hall and explained, but omitted mentioning that the real reason I was here was to locate his lab. I made it sound as if my friend Lettie had been anxious for me to see where her daughter, the doctor, worked. Keith invited me in. This lab was full of chemistry apparatus, and the walls were papered with charts: Flow sheets, chemical equations, and a key-shaped diagram I recognized as the Krebs cycle. I'd seen plenty of these while waiting for blood to be drawn.

Keith took me around a partition to a small room where a young woman sat at a wall of filing cabinets. Two built-in desks, both with laptops centered above the kneeholes and printouts scattered about, stood on the opposite wall. "This is where we keep the data. We try to keep the paperwork apart from the stuff that can possibly explode."

I laughed. Suddenly, the direct approach didn't seem unreasonable. "By the way, have you found out whether Bram Fitzwaring was part of your study?"

Both workers sat up straight and I got the feeling I'd said something I shouldn't. Uh-oh. Double-blind study.

Keith isn't supposed to know who is in which group. For a minute, I was afraid I'd ruined his project.

But Keith relieved my mind with, "I have, actually. In light of the fact that he's no longer participating, I asked Katie to check for me." The worker I assumed was Katie looked up from her work and nodded. "Fitzwaring was a part of our study, but he was in the control group."

"So he didn't get the real medicine, right? He was getting a placebo," I said.

"Right. And I thank God he wasn't in the test group. If we lose one more person in that group, we'll have to battle with the old chi-square monster." I must have had a horrified look on my face, because he quickly added, "I don't mean I'm not sorry he died. I o-o-only meant it's a matter of numbers. My test group is doing very well medically. It's just that they keep getting hit by trucks."

"Pardon?"

Keith ran a finger under his collar and his Adam's apple bobbed nervously. "Not literally, of course, but one member of the group has moved to Scotland, one dropped out due to unrelated medical problems, things like that."

After following me out into the hall, Keith closed the door behind himself. I felt as if I was being ushered out. "This phase of the study should be completed in less than a year," he said. "After that, if all looks good, we'll do a broader study. Would you like to be a part of it?"

"Would I be in the test group or the control group?"

"You know I can't tell you that."

"How would I handle the evaluations? I couldn't come here once a month."

"In the next stage, the consultations could be done with your local doctor."

"I see."

"We'll stay in touch after you fly back across the pond, eh?"

I wondered if Keith would put up with all the questions I'd ask before I joined a clinical trial. I turned and found Lindsey standing behind me.

She didn't ask me what Keith and I had been talking about, but looked at her watch and said, "I need to be back upstairs in twenty-five minutes. We've run over into my lunch break, I'm afraid. Would you like to come to the cafeteria with me?"

I said I would.

In the cafeteria line Lindsey chose a ready-made salad and I did likewise. After we found a table and settled in, I poured blue cheese dressing all over my salad and noticed that Lindsey had added no dressing at all. I had a large roll and butter. She had one little cellophane pack of crackers.

"I see how you stay so nice and slim," I said.

"Mom's always on my back to eat more." She pushed lettuce around with her fork but didn't actually pick up a forkful. "You know how she is."

"She's doing you a huge favor this summer, coming over here."

"That she is." Lindsey's tone told me she'd taken my comment as criticism.

"But she loves the time she has with her grandchildren. To her, it's not a job. She enjoys it." I wasn't making things any better, so I tried to think of another topic.

Lindsey's husband, according to Lettie, was a jerk. He was a very successful corporate lawyer in Northern Virginia and until they split, they'd lived in a multimillion-dollar home in Alexandria. Lindsey had married him for his reputation, his well-toned body, and his bank balance rather than for any personal qualities—like empathy or flexibility. Lettie and I had talked about it a lot and in Lettie's opinion, it all started when she and Ollie insisted Lindsey go to a private high school rather than the public school she'd attended in grades K through eight. Until then, Lindsey had never thought about social class one way or the other.

The Osgoods had plenty of money, but they were still an ordinary middle-class family. Ollie, Lettie's husband and Lindsey's father, had succeeded wildly in the construction business but took his beer and football with him as they "moved on up." He was the sort of guy whose motto was "Git 'er done." Lettie and Ollie both thought the public school was exposing their daughter to the seamy side of life too early so they enrolled her in the exclusive private school where she encountered snobbery for the first time in her life and, rather than rebel against it, internalized it. Longing for acceptance, she tried to change herself to be like them. Whenever Ollie picked her up in his old cement-spattered truck, Lindsey ducked into the footwell until they drove out the school gate. She tossed Lettie's artificial flower arrangements into the trash because, "*Nobody* uses fake flowers. It just proves you have *no class*!" Lettie laughed when she told me this, but I think it really hurt her.

Lindsey went off to college after that, and then med school, but the damage was already done. Lettie and I talked about how children never get over their first steps out of the nest and into the big world—the teen world of sex and competition and alliances and self-doubt. When even the bullies are afraid. Lindsey stayed in contact with her high school crowd as they progressed through their various prestigious universities. There she found

Taylor Scoggin, a man who turned the old crowd green
with envy.

They had two beautiful children, and their careers
flourished while Taylor chipped away at Lindsey's self-
esteem. Slowly, she accepted the fact that to Taylor she
was nothing more than an educated arm piece, and that
was too bad, because that's also why she'd chosen him.
At least that was my take on it. After ten years of marriage, one day she asked him if he knew the name of her
childhood dog. The instrument she played in the high
school band. Her favorite color. He went O for three.
Taylor got into cocaine, which he considered nothing
more than a necessary part of his alleged high-pressure
job, and then he became abusive. Lindsey packed up the
children and moved out.

I changed the subject. "Did your mom tell you about
the man on our staircase who died yesterday?"

"Yes. What happened to him?"

"They're saying it was hypoglycemia but I'm not so
sure. He was diabetic like me, but the timing is wrong, I
think. By the way. Where do they do autopsies?"

"I don't know. Why?"

"Will they do an autopsy on him?"

"Was anyone with him when he died?"

"No."

"It was an unattended death. They should do one."

"At the police station, do you think?"

"Why there? Are the police involved?"

"Not that I know of."

"Then I suppose it would be done in a hospital
morgue."

"You mean here."

"This is the largest hospital around here, but I really

don't know. Why?" Lindsey picked at her salad. She looked up, grinning at me. "You want to sit in on it?"

"No. I was just wondering. I'd like to know what they find."

"Good luck with that. They probably won't share their findings with the general public, and, to a medical examiner, that's all you are. General public."

ON THE CAB ride back to the center of town, I sat on the right side of the back seat so I could elevate my left ankle by resting it on the seat. In spite of the ice I'd applied last night, it was still swollen and not the right color. The scenery between the hospital and the center of town was mainly residential, the homes mainly the type the English called "semi-detached," with two residences built to look like one house, each having its own small but carefully tended yard in front.

I reviewed my short tour of the diabetes research lab and decided I'd been lucky. I hadn't wanted to run into Keith, but since I had, I found out what I wanted to know anyway. I found out that Bram Fitzwaring was part of his study. What were the odds that a subject in a study, from a town a hundred miles away, would die only a few yards from the residence of the man who heads the study? What was I thinking? What possible reason could Keith Bunsen have for wanting to bump off any of his subjects, especially when he was worried about having too few, not too many? And if Bram was in the control group, his death couldn't be attributed to anything Keith had done. Bram had been receiving nothing but a placebo from him.

I recalled the smell of the neurology lab on the other side of the hall—a mixture of ozone and ocean. Not exactly ocean. Sea bed. Shellfish. Oysters. In my mind's eye I saw the pan of live oysters happily sucking up the foul-looking soup St. Giles Bell had them bathing in. What did he call it? Saxitoxin? A poison.

I rested my head against the seat back. Scotland! It popped into my head so suddenly I almost said it out loud. But why was I thinking about Scotland? A few years ago Lettie and I had spent part of a summer there. We stayed in a drafty old castle near Loch Ness and became almost a part of the Sinclair family, the castle's owners. Lettie and I had both loved Scotland.

I almost drifted off while the taxi purred its way down the A420 toward town, my mind wandering across the gentle rolling hills of central Scotland. Mushrooms! There was the connection! Almost against my own will, I forced myself to review a horrible time when a half-dozen people's lives were put at risk so one person could be murdered. The sheer evil of it boggled my mind at the time, and now, years later, it still boggled my mind. I could only think it took a special kind of stupidity to come up with such a scheme. Surely if one thought it through to the end, one couldn't possibly go through with it. Any normal person would go back to the drawing board and try to come up with a better idea.

Poison mushrooms and poison shellfish. I recalled the tray of canapés Georgina had offered around at the cocktail party in the Master's Lodgings. Scallops and mussels—I had eaten one of the mussels. I couldn't remember seeing oysters, but I hadn't paid that much attention. I had been sick later that evening and Mignon had, too. Bram Fitzwaring had died with a trashcan on the floor beside his mattress.

Surely any toxin taken up by oysters would also be

taken up by mussels or clams and concentrated in their tissues as time passed. All were filter-feeders in coastal waters. I had a sickening feeling of déjà vu. Bram Fitzwaring had been murdered. I was sure of it.

"Excuse me?" I lowered my swollen ankle to the floor and leaned forward. "I've changed my mind. Take me to the police station."

"Which one?"

"Whichever one is closest to St. Ormond's College."

The cabbie let me off on St. Aldate's Street in front of the Thames Valley Police Station. A bronze plaque donated by the Inspector Morse Society proclaimed the building as a site seen in many episodes of that wonderful BBC series.

Once inside, I lost my nerve. *What the hell am I doing here?* I had expected a large lobby with a desk manned by uniformed cops. I had vaguely imagined myself hobbling bravely across a polished floor, up to the desk, and announcing I was here to report a murder. But the room I found myself in was no more than a wide spot in the hall. Two uniformed officers stood behind a desk five feet from the door and there was no way I could turn and leave without being noticed. Both put down their work and looked up when I opened the door.

"Yes?" one of the officers, a small black woman with her hair pulled back in a bun, asked me.

"I'm… I'm…oh, dear, you're going to think I'm crazy." I know my face was red. I felt like melting into the floor.

"I doubt it, madam," the other uniform said. "We see crazy every day and you don't look like it."

Bless his heart. That helped. "I'm from America and I'm here attending a history conference where one of our members has died under circumstances that I'm sure aren't entirely natural."

"You're suggesting that someone had a hand in it?"

"I am. That is, I think so, but no one will believe me, I'm sure."

"Let us have a go at it."

"Okay." I took a breath. "This is all happening at St. Ormond's College on Staircase Thirteen. I'm staying there, and so is the deceased, a Mr. Bram Fitzwaring— was, that is. From Glastonbury."

"Wait. Before you go further, can we take care of the formalities?" The woman officer had grabbed a notepad and pencil. "Your name and address? Local address and home address, please."

The formalities took a couple of minutes, after which there was absolutely no chance I could make a fool of myself anonymously. I forged bravely on, telling the whole story as succinctly as I could and with a concerted effort to appear sane. It was useless. I heard myself talking as if through a tunnel. My real self stood safely at the other end, disconnected from that crazy woman.

They took notes and asked a few questions politely, no trace of a grin on either of their faces, but when my story ground to a halt, the man said, "Thank you, Mrs. Lamb. We will pass this information along and, if necessary, we will contact you at your college."

"I don't suppose you'd let me talk to one of your detectives?"

"We'll make sure one of them sees this. And thank you again for coming in."

I found myself back on the street, but without wheels. It wasn't far from here to St. Ormond's, but after walking less than one block, my ankle protested. I flagged down another taxi.

MY TAXI COULDN'T take me all the way to St. Ormond's main gate because a limousine was blocking the narrow street in front. I could see a chauffeur behind its wheel, calmly reading a newspaper. My driver sounded his horn but must have had an attack of timidity halfway through the action, because his honk came out as a short peep.

"I can walk from here." I paid him and started down Cobbler's Lane toward the side gate, then decided I'd rather go through the front gate, so I could get a better look at the limousine and possibly discover what notable personage was paying us a visit. The chauffeur glanced at me as I walked by and returned to his *Daily Mirror*.

Inside the gate, the porter's station appeared to be on red alert. Normally there would be one attendant visible through the window and he, as likely as not, would glance up as I passed, nod at me, and go back to whatever he was doing. Now I saw two porters practically standing at attention behind the window. I could see no one in the quad beyond.

I stuck my face up to the little round hole in the window and asked, "What's happening?"

"Lady Attwood is visiting the Wetmores."

"Is this a problem?"

"No. Certainly not."

The finality with which he answered told me not to ask any more questions. In the East Quad, three gardeners with weed baskets and rakes knelt around the perimeter, working like elves before Christmas. It was the first time since I'd been here that I'd seen more than one gardener at work. Climbing the stairs to my room,

I heard Mignon Beaulieu call my name. Her door was open. I found her sitting on her bed, barefoot and with a notepad on her lap.

"I got the autopsy report," she announced.

"And?"

"They called me a few minutes ago. They said they'd already called his family." She heaved a sigh. "It was hypoglycemia, as we suspected."

"They're sure?"

"Sure. They said his blood glucose level was thirty-two."

"That would do it," I said. "Did they say anything else?"

"He had some bruises, but they assume he got them from banging around in his room. He probably got delusional before he passed out, and banged around trying to get out of the room or find a snack or something."

"That makes sense," I said, but I was thinking, *the banging noises I heard were at two a.m., long after he should have been out cold from hypoglycemia.* "What happens next? Will his family come here?"

"Bram will be cremated. It's in his will. His lawyer in Glastonbury keeps a copy of the will in his office, so I called him. Bram wanted his ashes scattered over Glastonbury Tor." Mignon laid her notepad aside on the bed cover and stood. "I also called his mother a little while ago. She didn't know about the will or about his wish to be cremated, but she didn't seem to have any objection to it. To the cremation. But she said she wants the ashes. She's his next of kin, so I don't know how they're going to work it out."

"If his will is legal and it says 'scatter,' they'll have to scatter."

"We have a big group of friends in Glastonbury who will want to perform our ancient ritual. It will enable him to pass through the Star Gate. That's what Bram wanted."

I didn't know what to say.

"Are you hungry?" she asked. "I haven't had lunch yet."

"I've had lunch, sorry. I'd go with you and keep you company but there's an afternoon session I can't miss. Let's go to dinner together."

Back in my room, I let out a scream of frustration. Cremation would wipe out any trace of murder, and I had no way to stop it.

NINE

THE GARDENERS HAD dropped an obstacle course of hoses, sprinklers, and tools in the walkway around the quad. I saw no way to avoid violating the "Don't walk on the grass" sign.

"Stop! Stop it I say!"

I froze in my tracks. Turning slowly, because the command had not come as a shout but as an angry hiss, I wondered what I was in for. I found Daphne Wetmore right behind me, but she wasn't hissing at me. She ran to one of the gardeners, snatched the hose from his hands, and narrowly avoided spraying herself with water.

"This is no time to be watering!"

"But you told us…"

"I told you to pull the weeds. You should have done it last week. This is Sunday, for Christ's sake."

"But you called…"

"I know I called. But Lady Attwood will be coming through here any minute. Pick up your gear and get out of here!"

"Go home? But we…"

I supposed I was seeing the sharp side of Daphne Wetmore. I'd never have thought she could speak that way to anyone. What was so horrible about gardeners watering flowers? This was a Sunday. Was that it? Was Daphne's sister, Lady Attwood, super-religious? Would she be scandalized at the sight of men working on the

Lord's Day? That didn't fit with what Lettie had told me about her assorted scandals involving horses, taxes, and rumors of murder on tropical islands.

I crossed Middle Quad and followed my fellow conferees to the building where we'd had our general sessions, but now they were all heading for a different door.

The afternoon event I couldn't afford to miss was a small breakout session, scheduled to run concurrently with several others and titled, "Treasures from the Bodleian." The session leader was Robin Morris, and they were going to show us actual documents from the Elizabethan period. Would they bring us something in Shakespeare's own hand? That would be exciting, but the most important reason I wanted to be here was to fill a gaping hole in my own knowledge of history. I teach ancient and medieval history and, since I went back to teaching some eight years ago, have had to concentrate on the time from about 3000 b.c. to 1500 a.d. The course I teach ends with the War of the Roses. From the Tudors onward, it's the Modern Age. Shakespeare's plays, to the amazement of most high school students, are considered modern English.

When my dissertation topic veered from "Macbeth, King of Scotland" to "What did Shakespeare know about Macbeth and when did he know it," I found myself trapped in unfamiliar territory. This was all Larry Roberts's doing. He told me, probably correctly, that my topic was too broad. I tried to narrow it down in several different ways but he pushed me into my present box. Shakespeare was partly influenced by the writings of Holinshed and Boece, but most importantly, by James I, who was also James VI of Scotland and keen to reinforce his own legitimacy on the Scottish throne which, since he was of the house of Stewart, meant painting Macbeth as a usurper.

I was out of my field when it came to the Tudors and the Stewarts, but I was doing my best.

I found both Robin Morris and Claudia Moss waiting for us, cotton-gloved to protect their treasures from contact with bare hands, and standing behind an array of documents and items that were not under lock and key, not behind glass, but simply *there.* They assumed we knew how to behave around priceless artifacts. About ten other people, one of whom was Larry Roberts, also drifted in and took seats.

Robin explained that most of these items would eventually be on permanent display in a new part of the Bodleian Library, currently under construction, but now kept in a place that was closed to the public. We all murmured our gratitude for this rare privilege.

Robin said, "Since this conference deals with the Elizabethan era and also with Arthuriana, I've brought items that relate to both. It seems that good old Henry VIII, while doing his best to impoverish the kingdom, nevertheless did us academics a bit of a favor. By sending Thomas Cromwell forth to dissolve the monasteries, and to hang, draw, and quarter the inhabitants, he also confiscated the considerable wealth hidden behind the monastery walls. No one knows what happened to most of the booty. It must have been a huge treasure trove, but thankfully, some of it has come down to us."

"Just like the Elgin Marbles, right, Claudia?" This rude interruption came from Larry Roberts, who apparently thought his comment was funny.

I cringed. Larry was referring to the marble reliefs taken from the Acropolis in Athens by Lord Elgin, and now in the British Museum where Claudia worked. Greece wanted them back.

Claudia's gloved hands turned into fists for a second before she regained her composure and, with the stiff upper lip of her heritage, said, "Dr. Roberts, you should visit the Acropolis today and see the state of the marbles Lord Elgin *didn't* take. We did them a favor."

This unpleasant exchange may or may not have continued. I don't know because my ears still rang with the words "Thomas Cromwell."

Stupid! Stupid! It wasn't Oliver Cromwell, it was Thomas Cromwell! I didn't have Bram Fitzwaring's note with me, but I was certain I'd seen, on one line, the words Sharpham and Cromwell. I should have known it wasn't Oliver Cromwell, Lord Protector of the Commonwealth. He was more than a century later than the time we were interested in.

Now I needed to find out who or what Sharpham was.

I THOUGHT I could use my iPad to discover everything I needed to know, but I soon found the World Wide Web had its limits. I spent the rest of my time until dinner, surfing. I learned that Sharpham was the name of a vineyard on the River Dart, a college, and a town in western England. A map of Devon and Cornwall revealed that the town of Sharpham was only a mile or so from Glastonbury, so I decided Bram's note probably referred to the town.

But I could find no link between the town of Sharpham and King Arthur, or Glastonbury Tor, or the Elizabethan period, or anything else that might have explained why Bram had written the word on the note I found in his room.

Thomas Cromwell yielded more websites than I could possibly read, but I did my best. Cromwell served Cardinal Thomas Wolsey until that worthy fell from Henry's grace, at which time Cromwell danced a little sidestep and distanced himself from Wolsey. Soon, he took Woolsey's place, campaigning to discredit the papacy and clear the way for Henry to divorce Catherine of Aragon so he could marry Anne Boleyn. That marriage didn't work out either, but it did produce Elizabeth, whose long reign spanned the era concerning us at this conference. Cromwell also arranged the marriage of Henry and Anne of Cleves, in whose personal appearance the fat king was so disappointed he sent her packing back to Cleves, marriage still unconsummated.

Thomas Cromwell dissolved the monasteries all over England with shocking brutality, confiscating, as Robin Morris had told us, their gold, silver, and art for the King's coffers. After executing practically all the abbots in the realm, Cromwell himself fell out of favor and was beheaded on the same day Henry married Catherine Howard.

Glastonbury Abbey was one of the wealthiest in England, and in the reign of Henry VIII it was led by the able and highly respected abbot, Richard Whiting. Cromwell had assured Whiting on several occasions that Glastonbury was in no danger of dissolution. But seeing all the other monasteries around him disappear, did Whiting believe that? At any rate, he shouldn't have because, by early 1539, Glastonbury was the only one left. In September of that year, Glastonbury Abbey was destroyed, its wealth confiscated, and in November, Whiting himself was hanged, beheaded, drawn, and quartered.

I found I had lost my appetite and it was time for dinner.

I STOPPED BY Mignon's room on my way down to dinner only to learn she wasn't going with me after all. The owner/operator of The Green Man had invited her and others to his house for dinner. "It's a jolly group, the Oxford gang, but we'll be making plans for the gathering on Glastonbury Tor, so tonight will be a bit more somber than usual."

"Let me guess. You normally drink mead and sing madrigals."

"Oh, we'll have our mead. We won't be *that* somber."

"When will this gathering be?"

"We don't have a date yet, but I've talked to friends back home in Glastonbury, and they're checking around to find a time when we can have the Tor to ourselves, without a bunch of tourists gawking at us."

"I can see how that might spoil the mood."

"You don't believe in any of this, do you?"

"Any of what?" I knew what she meant, but I felt more comfortable with the ball in her court.

"In the unity of the spiritual and physical worlds. We stand at a spiritual threshold, you know, and Glastonbury is its physical center. The only spot in the universe where Mary and Joseph of Arimathea walked, where Arthur came to be healed of his battle wounds, where Excalibur was forged, where Arthur and Guinevere were buried, and where to this day, the power of the ancient stones concentrate their energy like no place else on earth."

Mignon delivered this whole speech in a dreamlike voice while staring out her room's only window and clasping to her ample breast a small sachet tied with black ribbon. The silence that followed demanded some sort of response from me. "I've never been to Glastonbury, but it sounds like an interesting place." I'm afraid I made my answer sound insultingly mundane on purpose; to squelch any idea she may have had about recruiting me.

"Interesting." She cut her eyes toward me, then back to the scene outside her window.

"I've been wondering. What was Bram's speech yesterday going to be about? The program said, 'The Dissolution of the Monasteries,' but it hardly seemed to me like a subject he would have chosen."

"I don't know," she answered in a monotone. She placed the little sachet carefully on her desk.

"I find that hard to believe. I had to listen to Larry Roberts's speech a hundred times. I practically had it memorized. Didn't Bram discuss it with you at all?"

She picked up the notepad she'd left on her bed and slapped it against the edge of her nightstand. "You may find it hard to believe, but it's the truth!" Her head tipped back, she looked down her nose at me. Then, more softly, "Bram probably didn't know, himself, what he was going to say."

That was a lie, but I knew further probing would do no good.

HAROLD WETMORE SHAMBLED across the quad at five to seven, in the same old linen jacket, but tonight he wore a green bow tie. His mustard-colored trousers were too short, exposing the fact that his socks didn't match. We walked to the dining hall together. The hostas along the wall stood wet, weedless, and proud. They reminded me of Daphne's near-meltdown with the gardeners earlier in the afternoon.

"You had visitors today," I said. "I saw the limo out front."

"That was Daphne's sister, Anthea." Harold took my

arm and steered me around a hand rake lying in my path. "Anthea Attwood. Her husband is Lord Attwood."

"And she normally travels by limousine?"

"Or something equally impressive." He turned to me and smiled. "I'm afraid my poor Daphne has always lived in the shadow of her glorious sister. I wish you had met Lady Attwood."

"Your poor Daphne? Why do you call her your poor Daphne?"

"That wasn't a good choice of words. But Daphne is, um, not brilliant, not particularly talented at anything, nor is she beautiful. Not in the usual sense." He touched my shoulder and quickly added, "Oh, she's beautiful to me, of course. Anthea is tall, brilliant—the sort of woman whom everyone who's ever met her remembers. Daphne grew up, I'm afraid, feeling like the ugly duckling. Anthea's only a year older so they were almost like twins in terms of their ages.

"Their parents didn't help. They've always treated Anthea like a princess and Daphne like…well. Anthea got married quite young to a wealthy, titled, ass and since then they've been cannon fodder for the tabloids."

"And Daphne is envious? Why?"

"Oh, I don't know." Harold had paused several times as we approached the dining hall to nod at or shake hands with people headed in the same direction as we. "For fifteen years, though, Daphne lived at home with spinsterhood looming ahead, while Anthea and her jet-set friends made news. It affected her outlook."

"And then you…"

"Came along on my white charger and whisked her off to this old crumbling castle where she gets to serve tea to the boring wives of crusty old academics such as myself."

"My, my. You do have a way with words."

I SAT WITH Larry Roberts at dinner. I felt I could hardly let his atrocious comments to Claudia Moss this afternoon go unremarked, and I was struggling inside my head to find the right words. True, as my major professor, he could make or break me in my bid for a doctorate. On the other hand I felt he was on the brink of making a laughingstock of himself, and I liked him too much to stand idly by and let him.

Daphne Wetmore sat beside her husband at the High Table, looking none the worse for her stressful afternoon. I wondered if she might be hiring new gardeners next week. Tonight's speaker, a man who looked at least ninety, sat on Harold's other side, but he had already nodded off and the first course was yet to be served.

I thought about what Harold told me about Daphne. His insulting comments about her lack of redeeming virtues had distressed me. Did Daphne know he talked about her like that behind her back? I studied her face. She wasn't bad looking. I suspected Harold, like most of the academics I know, preferred a woman who kept his life in order to a woman who presented a challenge in the romance department. Harold was no sexpot either.

"May I sit with you?"

I hope I didn't look as startled as I was. The question came from Claudia Moss. She was pulling out the chair next to me and across the table from Larry. She looked lovely in a burgundy wrap dress and silver earrings. Her nails were done in a flesh-tone polish. *So much nicer than overdoing the red*, I thought.

"Dr. Roberts?" she said, sliding both her hands under the table. "I brought something for you to look at." She handed a half-dozen four by six glossies across to Larry. "I took these on my last trip to Athens. Do you see what

I was talking about? The air pollution in the city has eaten away at the marble until some of the sculptures are unrecognizable."

"What about the ones Lord Elgin dropped overboard bringing them here? How are they doing?" Larry set the photos beside his salad plate, but barely looked at them. "And what about London's air pollution? Huh?"

This was intolerable. I felt like doing a Rodney King: *Can't we all get along?* But it would have sounded too cliché, I thought. Instead, I interrupted them with, "The autopsy report on Bram Fitzwaring is out. He died of hypoglycemia."

"Who?" Claudia asked.

"The nutcase from Glastonbury," Larry said. "He was supposed to have delivered a paper at the general session right after you." He tapped the photos into a neat stack and handed them back to Claudia.

"Really, Larry! You didn't even know him," I said, keeping my voice low. "You can't call him a nutcase if you didn't even know him."

"I can, if he says that King Arthur and his knights of the round table are indisputable fact. You can't talk sense to people who live in a fantasy world."

"You never *tried* to talk sense to him," I said.

"I looked him up online."

"You never told me that."

"You should have done it yourself. If you had, maybe you wouldn't have invited him here."

"I didn't invite him!" That came out too loud. Heads turned.

Now it was Claudia's turn to cool things down. "What about his companion? Mignon? Isn't that her name? Is she still here? I haven't seen her."

"Mignon went to a friend's house for dinner," I said.

"You getting pretty buddy-buddy with her?" Larry looked up as the waiter placed the entrée in front of him, and asked for a bottle of Merlot.

"We stay on the same staircase, Larry. I go past her room every time I go up or down the stairs."

"What does Mignon say about Fitzwaring's death?" Claudia asked. "Was she surprised? Had anything like this happened to him before?"

"Apparently not. She told me he was very particular about his medications, and he checked his blood sugar more often than he really needed to." I paused, then added, "I heard loud noises coming from his room in the wee hours. They woke me up. Oddly, though, I had seen him after dinner and he was acting spacey."

"That sounds like hypoglycemia," Larry said.

"Yes. But not that early. If he was already spacey at nine o'clock, he wouldn't have been banging around at two. He'd have been long dead."

Larry took a big gulp of his wine. His gaze darted from me to Claudia and back again. "What? Don't look at me! I was at the Randolph Hotel all night and I can prove it."

Softly, Claudia said, "No one is suggesting you weren't, Dr Roberts."

DINNER OVER, I CAUGHT a glimpse of Robin Morris leaving the hall, made my apologies to Larry and Claudia, and hurried out to catch up with him. "Excuse me," I said, coming up behind him. I realized I didn't know what to call him. Was it Dr. Morris or Mr. Morris?

"Dotsy Lamb," I said.

"Of course. From America, aren't you?"

"Right. I really enjoyed your presentation this afternoon."

"Thank you."

I saw he was carrying a bottle of wine. In the dim light of the archway where we stood, I couldn't tell if it was an open bottle or not. "I want to talk to you about getting admission to the Bodleian. I desperately need to do some research."

"I see." He looked toward the broad expanse of the Middle Quad. "Are you going to the Senior Common Room?"

"Is that where you're heading? May I walk with you?"

Apparently other diners were doing the same thing, because I found we were going with the flow across the quad. Several people were swinging wine bottles by the neck as they approached the west side of the lawn. I explained that I needed to research the history of Glastonbury Abbey but I made it sound as if it was related to my dissertation topic, which it wasn't.

"Glastonbury Abbey?" Robin Morris paused. We'd come to a pair of doors, and our fellow walkers were stepping around us to enter. "I can help you with that, but actually..." he waved his wine bottle, which I now saw was half-empty, toward the door. "Let's go in. We may be in time to snag a comfortable chair or two."

TEN

THE SENIOR COMMON Room looked as if it had been decorated by my great-aunt Clara—several patterns too many. The carved wood of the fireplace surround, the bookshelves, and the waist-high wainscoting were magnificent. The dozen or so oil paintings in the style of Turner and the tulipy Dutch tiles around the hearth would have been all the extras the room needed, but the walls above the wainscot were papered with a busy print, the floor carpeted in beige with blue dots, the furniture slip-covered in a blue and white vertical stripe damask. A couple of crystal chandeliers Great-aunt Clara would have loved hung from the exposed beams of the Tudor ceiling.

About twenty of our fellow conferees had beaten us here and stood or sat around in conversational groups. On one wall a sideboard held a variety of wine bottles, glasses, and napkins.

"This is the first time I've been here, but someone did tell me about the after-dinner gatherings in the Senior Common Room."

Robin Morris took my elbow and steered me toward the sideboard. "We bring in the wine we didn't finish at dinner and put it here. The waiters also go around the dining hall and gather all the bottles that aren't dead soldiers and bring them in. No need to waste good wine."

As he said this, a door swung open and a waiter backed in, holding his tray full of bottles clear of the doors. He set the tray on the sideboard and turned each of the bottles so the label faced outward.

"These are fair game," Robin said. "Whoever bought it has left it on the table, so if you find one that interests you, pour yourself a glass."

I chose a Chablis with a colorful label. We found two unoccupied chairs on one side of the fireplace and sat. I found a silver coaster on the small table between our chairs and set my glass on it. Robin crossed his legs in a way that American men consider effeminate, and rested the arm holding his wine glass on his knee. "About your research on Glastonbury Abbey. I suggest you come over tomorrow morning. Go in the door just behind the statue of the Earl of Pembroke. I'll take you around Duke Humfrey's Library. You'll love it. Then I'll walk you through the formalities, but I'm going to suggest you not do your work there."

"Why not?"

"Because the material you want will most likely be right here."

"Here?" I felt a thud of disappointment. I wanted to do research at the Bodleian! I wanted to brag about it back on campus at UVa.

"The Fellows Library here is also part of the Bodleian. We have branches all over town, but the one right here, coincidentally, is the best for historical documents and books dealing with England from earliest times up to the Commonwealth."

I felt a bit better knowing I could still brag that I'd done research at the Bodleian. I looked around the room. By now I had met and could have named perhaps half of the occupants. The doors swung open again and this time it was Larry Roberts, holding the door open for Claudia

Moss. I lost track of what Robin was talking about as my gaze followed the pair to the sideboard where Larry poured two glasses of wine, and they walked together to a small settee in the far corner of the room.

"…bring nothing with you but a pencil."

"I'm sorry? I didn't catch that." Larry and Claudia seemed to have buried the hatchet. I'd need to keep an eye on this because Claudia was a pretty woman and Larry, although a decade or more older than Claudia, was a handsome man. But he was married, and his wife was a friend of mine. I wondered if Claudia knew that.

I STOPPED IN at Mignon's room on my way up the stairs. She opened her door for me, a plastic cup in her free hand. I caught a whiff of flint, like a struck lighter, as I walked by her. "Is that mead?" I asked.

"Oh right. I should… Do you want to taste it?" She held out the cup. A lavender unicorn wrapped around its side.

I declined the offer. "How was your party?"

"It wasn't a party. It was a gathering of friends. We broke bread together and remembered Bram."

"Of course. Sorry." I hate dealing with this sort of person. The sort who make you feel like you're a complete lunk. "Did you ever find all Bram's things? His luggage and all?"

"It was in the Porter's Lodge. I asked them for it and they were about to give it to me, but Mrs. Wetmore came in and said she'd promised to have it delivered to The Green Man."

"To the store? Why?"

"Simon—that's the man who runs the store—knows Mrs. Wetmore. He called her as soon as he heard about

Bram and asked her to send his belongings to the store. Said he'd see that they got delivered to Bram's family."

"Didn't you think that was strange?"

"Rather. Then I realized Simon didn't know I was here. If he'd known I was here at the college, he wouldn't have worried about it."

"Worried about what?"

"His things not just being thrown away."

I supposed that might make sense, but I wondered if there might be something important in Bram's luggage. Something more than clothes and lecture notes. I shook my head when Mignon nodded toward the room's only chair. She plunked herself down on the side of her bed with an audible grunt, the mead in her unicorn cup splashing over.

"So Mrs. Wetmore knows the owner of The Green Man?"

"Small town. Well, not really a small town, but you know how it is. The business owners and the college brass—they all know each other. *Town and gown,* they call it."

BACK IN MY ROOM, I made plans for tomorrow. First thing in the morning, I'd go to the Bodleian and meet up with Robin, get settled in at the library, and work until noon. Would I be able to find anything helpful? I wondered if the place would have an old card catalog or a computer. One of the few advantages of being over the hill was knowing how to use a card catalog.

I wished I could spend the whole day in the library, but my own breakout session, the one I was to lead, was scheduled for one-thirty in room 106 of the building where Robin and Claudia's had been held. My topic was "Shakespeare's Historical Sources and References to Arthurian Legend in his Plays." I pulled out my notes and made sure they were all there. Before I left home I had loaded a few photos onto my iPad, but would they be large enough to show to a group? I wished I had one of those projectors you can hook up to your computer like the one I use in my classroom back home. Wait a minute. Didn't I hear someone else talking about finding the AV man? Surely I wasn't the only one with this problem. *I'll ask around at breakfast.*

I took Bram's little note to bed with me, looked at it again, and was immediately struck by its resemblance to something else I'd just seen. My own presentation notes! Why hadn't I seen it before? This was probably the note Bram planned to have tucked in his hand when he delivered his address. If he intended to make use of projected images, he'd probably step to one side, away from the podium, to give the audience an unobstructed view. He'd want notes with him, nothing elaborate like his lecture notes, just the names and numbers he'd be most apt to forget. Items one through four could refer to four slides he intended to show.

Item 2. *bone 51.9 (x2.6+65) = 2m.* I'd worked that out yesterday and it made no sense in either English or metric units. Maybe I'd done it wrong. Would a man, writing cheat notes to himself, worry about the order of operations that most of us haven't thought about since high school? Wouldn't he more likely have written *bone 51.9* then said, "What if they ask me how I got two meters? I'd better write down the numbers I used."

It's funny how things you've learned in one part of your life come in handy in another. In my research for my ancient history classes, I've become fairly conversant in the field of archaeology. In fact, I've even worked on a dig. Somewhere along the way I'd seen a formula for calculating the height of a person from the length of the long bone, the femur. I punched up the calculator on my iPad, but this time I did the operations in order, ignoring the parenthesis:

$51.9 \times 2.6 + 65 =$?

I got 199.94. Rounded off, 200. Centimeters? If so, that would be two meters. How much would it be in feet? I turned back to my iPad and to Google, metric to English conversions. Found a chart. Two meters equal 6.56 feet or about six feet, six inches. This felt right. I knew it was right!

I looked up at my window, open to the night air, and felt like shouting out to the whole city, "It's the leg bone of a man who was six foot six!" I jumped out of bed and did a dance reminiscent of the Mashed Potato. The "no exit" sign on my little window didn't seem silly now, because in my present mood I was sure I could fly.

I crawled back in bed when my ankle reminded me, sharply, of its delicate condition. Picking up the note again, I looked at item four, 450 ce. This would be a reasonable date for the death of King Arthur. That is, if he ever lived. Which, of course, he didn't.

ROBIN GAVE ME a quick tour of Duke Humfrey's Library, a part of the Bodleian more suitable for gawking than for research. He administered the mandatory oath: "I hereby undertake not to remove from the Library, or to mark, deface, or injure in any way, any volume, document, or other object belonging to it or in its custody; nor to bring into the Library or kindle therein any fire or flame, and not to smoke in the Library; and I promise to obey all rules of the Library."

He called ahead to the Porter's Lodge at St. Ormond's to have someone waiting with the keys to the Fellows Library. He explained, "Most of the time, particularly in summer, no one is using the Fellows Library. Undergraduate students use the modern library in the Smythson building. I've told the porter you should be allowed to work any time and as long as you like. Only one caveat. They will lock the door when they leave you there. You can still open it from the inside, but you won't get back in."

"I'd better use the bathroom before I go in."

"In case of fire, you wouldn't want to be locked in."

"After the pledge I just made, you've pretty much eliminated the possibility of fire."

Robin laughed, and then added, "Remember, no biros, no highlighters, no crayons. Only pencil and paper—and don't mark in the books even with your pencil."

Before sequestering myself in the Fellows Library, I dashed over to the wing of the Smythson building where classrooms filled most of its three floors. I found the room where I was to do my presentation and checked out its size, the number of chairs, and the location of outlets. I climbed the stairs to the top floor where I'd been advised I would find the audiovisual room. It was my lucky day. The AV room was open and the AV man was inside, applying a screwdriver to a computer keyboard.

I introduced myself and asked if I could have a projector from one-thirty until two-thirty. The man, who told me his name was Pete, wrote my name and room number on a schedule sheet in the correct time slot.

"I have another question. Did the speaker scheduled

for Saturday afternoon, Mr. Fitzwaring, have any equipment reserved?"

"The man who died?"

"Yes." I assumed an appropriately solemn tone.

Pete had to look in his trashcan for Saturday's schedule because they were kept on a tear-off pad. Luckily the trash hadn't been emptied recently. He unfolded the sheet and spread it out on his workbench. "Here it is. Yes. He signed up for the projector for four o'clock. Looks like he was going to show some photos he had on his own device because he wanted an Apple VGA adapter as well."

"Oh! I'll need one of those, too. One that will work with an iPad." While he wrote this down, I asked, "Did you, by any chance, see the photos he wanted to show?"

"No. I just set things up. He can show porn for all I care."

THE FELLOWS LIBRARY WAS, like the dining hall, in the wing that separated East Quad from Middle Quad. After the porter locked me in, I pinched myself. It was as if I had walked into Hogwarts School. Ancient oak shelving on both sides of a long aisle were punctuated by a dozen or more cubbyholes also lined, floor to ceiling, with books. All the chairs were wooden and straight-backed, reinforcing the idea that you were not here to get comfortable.

My first shock came when I scanned a few rows of leather-bound volumes and found they were all in Latin. Uh-oh. Given a Latin-English dictionary I could translate about two sentences an hour. Walking up and down the aisle, I eventually found a section dealing with British History and the volumes were in English. I selected a big book entitled *Documents Regarding the Suppression of the Monasteries, 1539,* and took it to a plain wooden desk beneath a modern fluorescent lamp.

The next time I looked at my watch, I found I had almost missed lunch and realized how easily I could have also missed my presentation. I get into a zone sometimes when I'm looking for answers in books. I carefully placed the dozen volumes I'd consulted back in their proper spaces on the shelves and left, closing the door behind me. I checked to make sure it was locked.

I had learned a lot. I had learned that a man named Frederick Bligh Bond in the early twentieth century had allegedly excavated the bones of Richard Whiting, the last abbot of Glastonbury Abbey. Bond, it seems, was an archaeologist but also a psychic, so I automatically put his work inside a mental parenthesis, knowing that I couldn't mention him among my peers without precipitating a chorus of jeers and snide remarks. But bones had been dug up, and I wondered how they could have belonged to Richard Whiting, since that good man had been beheaded and the rest of his body chopped into pieces for exhibition throughout the realm. The execution took place on Glastonbury Tor in 1539, but what would have remained for burial at the Abbey?

Richard Whiting was given no notice he was about to be arrested and the Abbey destroyed, yet he must have had a suspicion. If he had a suspicion, wouldn't he have hidden the Abbey's treasures? I found a reference to the possibility that he had, and that his hiding place was in nearby Sharpham. Bingo! Sharpham was a name on Bram's note. If so, what else would he have hidden? What did the Abbey have that would've been more precious than silver or gold?

The bones of King Arthur.

Or at least bones they *thought* were those of Arthur and Guinevere. I learned that the Abbey burned down in 1184, and during its reconstruction in 1191, monks discovered bones deep down and inside an oak log. Several feet above the bones they found a stone slab and under it, not visible to anyone standing at ground level, they found a leaden cross inscribed, *Here lies the famous King Arthur and his second wife, Guinevere, buried in the Isle of Avalon.*

The exact wording varied according to the source, and its authenticity had been roundly challenged through the ages. The cross itself hasn't been seen since the early eighteenth century.

As for Arthur's and Guinevere's bones, when the Abbey was finally rebuilt about a hundred years later, King Edward I had them placed in a black marble coffin under the high altar of the new church. Every aspect of these events had been challenged, ridiculed, accepted, and disproven by scholars and clerics from that time until now.

Legend has it that Arthur was a giant. People in fifth century Britain were short, not due to genetics, but to diet, to frequent illnesses, and to the challenges of just staying alive. So a man could have grown to six feet six if he came from genetically tall stock, if he led a charmed life, and if he had a good diet from birth to adulthood. But in western Britain in those days, a man six and a half feet tall would have looked like a giant.

Heading for the dining hall, I seriously considered skipping the afternoon session and holing up in the Fellows Library. If I hadn't been in charge of it, I would have.

LUNCH WAS COLD meats and cheeses. We were to make our own sandwich at the buffet table and sit anywhere we wanted. I saw some people walking out with sandwiches wrapped in paper napkins, heading for the lawn. I found Larry, Claudia, and Harold sitting at the end of a long row of tables and joined them. They were finished with their sandwiches, but lingering over their plates.

"Eat up, Dotsy." Larry tapped his watch. "It's ten after one. Your presentation starts in twenty minutes."

"I've been working in the Fellows Library all morning. Lost track of time."

"How did you get in?" Harold Wetmore looked at me over the rims of his glasses.

"Robin Morris. He swore me in and everything."

Larry glanced at Harold, then quickly back to me. "Why are you working in the Fellows Library?"

"I'm trying to find out exactly what Shakespeare's sources would have said about King Arthur."

"You already know, Dotsy. You've been reading nothing else for the past year!" Larry's face was redder than it should have been upon discovering his student was reading more than necessary.

I saw Claudia's arm move as if she had laid a hand on Larry's knee, but I couldn't see under the table. Harold Wetmore frowned and rubbed the stubble on his chin with the back of his hand.

"But I've only been reading about Shakespeare's sources that related to Macbeth. This afternoon thing is about Shakespeare and the Arthur legends." I took a big bite of my sandwich.

"Like, what did Willie know and when did he know it?" Claudia said.

"Exactly," I mumbled through the food in my mouth and swallowed sooner than I should have. "What? Don't look at me like that, Larry! My God, you'd think I was researching fairies and crop circles."

Larry wasn't expecting that. I'd never talked to him like this before. His jaws clenched. "You could just ask your friends from Glastonbury. They can tell you all about such crap."

"Friends? Make that 'friend,' Larry. Only one left."

Larry couldn't or wouldn't answer. He pulled at his ear with his left hand and I noticed his wedding ring was missing.

"Speaking of Glastonbury," I said, "I may go there myself for a day or so when the conference is over. It's not far."

"Why the hell would you go there?" Larry's face darkened. "There's nothing in Glastonbury but fruitcakes and magic shops."

"I'd like to see the place, okay? I'll have a free day before we go home."

Harold mumbled, as if to remind us to lower our voices, "Our library has a lot of old books, but remember, they weren't subjected to peer review. In today's market, none of them would pass."

"And some were complete fiction," Larry added.

ELEVEN

I WAS HAPPY to see fifteen people show up, filling almost all of the chairs in the little room they'd assigned me. Claudia and Robin's presentation yesterday had not drawn so many. I had already started my spiel when Larry Roberts walked in. My stomach lurched.

I emphasized the pageantry, citing examples of courtly love and gallantry in Shakespeare's stories. These were uncontroversial topics, even for Larry, and I felt I was in safe territory as long as I stuck to them. I'd totally forgotten that, in Oxford, I might come face to face with a die-hard Oxfordian—one who believes that Edward de Vere, Earl of Oxford, was the author of the plays and poems attributed to William Shakespeare.

A prune-faced man interrupted me defiantly. "And you believe the son of a glove maker from Stratford donned the soul of a nobleman and wrote all this as easily as he could have donned one of his old man's gloves?"

While considering my response, I gave him one of the looks I used on my boys when they were growing up and acting like asses. "I'm continually amazed that *anyone*, from *any* social background, could write so many beautiful works, but someone obviously did."

I got smiles and a few winks from most of my other listeners. Having spent half my allotted time in safe territory, I had to venture out. After all, my topic was "Shakespeare's Historical Sources and References to Arthurian

Legend in his Plays." So far, I hadn't mentioned Arthur. I killed a few seconds by pouring myself a glass of luke-warm water from the pitcher someone had brought me.

"Shakespeare relied heavily on the work of Holinshed, as most of you know," I said, hoping no one would dispute that well-known fact. "But remember, Holinshed was also influenced by earlier writers. He didn't write centuries of history from memory." That got a laugh. I felt emboldened. "Holinshed read Malory, William of Malmesbury, Geoffrey of Monmouth, and even Gildas. Gildas was a near-contemporary of the events attributed to Arthur." I paused for breath. "So the story of King Arthur, be it history or myth, was firmly fixed in the brain of Raphael Holinshed."

Larry Roberts stopped me there. "You're suggesting the possibility Arthur is a myth and the possibility he's history are equally likely?"

"That isn't what I said."

"'Be it history or myth,' isn't that what you said? Or is there a strange echo in here?"

"You're twisting my meaning!"

"I'm listening, but what I'm hearing sounds like it came straight from the grey-haired hippies of Glaston-bury."

By this time, everyone in the room was glaring at Larry. He looked around quickly, then stood and headed for the door.

Someone said, "Of all the nerve!" loudly enough so that Larry, now hurrying across the threshold, must have heard it too.

He turned and looked at me, his face nearly purple, and said, "And you can forget about that PhD."

At least I thought that was what he said.

I WENT STRAIGHT back to my room and paced, talking to myself. I'm sure my blood pressure was sky-high. I checked my iPad and found an email from my son Brian, informing me that business (he has a John Deere farm equipment franchise) was booming, his wife and children were well, but his father, my ex-husband, Chet, was drinking himself into oblivion almost every night now. Too bad, I thought. All in all, his message cheered me up a bit. I decided I couldn't stay in my room and brood. I needed to go for a walk.

I plodded down the High Street, trying not to think about Larry. The shops along both sides were a hodge-podge of the ancient and the new. An open door, its wood frame painted so many times old nicks and dings were nearly obliterated, spilled hip-hop music onto the sidewalk. I love the mixture you can only find in a college town.

My feet turned in at the Covered Market, a collection of some fifty stores spanning the middle of the block between Market Street and the High. This was the first time I'd been inside. The smell of a leather shop gave way to the sweet aroma of pastries, then fruits, cheeses, meats, and fish. The fish markets were wisely placed near the wide open north exit.

I stopped in front of the fish market and studied the display of mussels, clams, and shrimp on a long bed of ice. That reminded me of the canapés I blamed for the stomachache I and others had suffered. Was it because of the seafood? I only remembered eating one bacon-wrapped mussel, but I may have had more. I still couldn't get the picture of Bram's trashcan out of my mind. Placed at one corner of the mattress he'd put on the floor, it was so eerily like the one I'd pulled over to the head of my bed.

I thought about saxitoxin and the oysters in the pan at St. Giles's lab. He'd told me the oysters were sucking up the poisonous soup, concentrating the toxin in their tissues. I'd read about how animals high on the food chain could get toxic doses of chemicals that don't harm the animals they eat, because predators don't eat just one, and over time the toxin builds up. Like the bald eagles and DDT. They got such a big dose, their eggshells wouldn't harden and the chicks died before they hatched.

In this case it would be people rather than eagles at the top of the food chain. The algae in the water would produce the toxin in tiny amounts. Shellfish, all filter-feeders, get their food by pumping huge amounts of water in one siphon and out the other, removing the algae in the process. The toxins, useless as food, remain behind and build up until the tissues of the oyster, mussel, or whatever has a much higher concentration than the algae had. Then a human comes along and eats a couple dozen of these. That can be a fatal overdose.

Had the mussels they served at the party been contaminated with saxitoxin? Were the algae that produce saxitoxin found in the waters around the British Isles? Might someone have deliberately tainted the shellfish? Again, I found that hard to believe. No one at the party, except possibly Bram, got all that sick. If the object was to inconvenience us, they had succeeded on a small scale, but if it was murder, who was the target? If the target was Bram Fitzwaring, how would the killer know Bram alone would die?

Bram was about six feet four, I guessed, and weighed

about 250 pounds. It would have taken a lot of bad mussels to kill him.

What if someone knew Bram was inordinately fond of mussels and prone to eat huge numbers of them when available? That someone would've had to have access to the canapé trays before they were brought out. Someone in the kitchen, a cook, a server, or—Daphne Wetmore, who had supervised every detail of the event. Motive? None that I knew of. The only person likely to have known Bram's favorite foods was Mignon. She could possibly have intercepted the food trays somewhere along their route from the kitchen to the Master's Lodge, but again, where's the motive? Perhaps it was simply that the mussels were tainted, collected, and sold without anyone in the supply chain knowing they weren't safe. I had no idea whether shellfish were subjected to any sort of inspection in the British Isles, or indeed, if saxitoxin could be detected in a batch headed for market. St. Giles Bell mentioned collecting from the cold waters of the North Sea. But was he collecting oysters, saxitoxin, or the algae that produced saxitoxin? I'd read about people dying from shellfish poisoning, but I thought it only happened in the Gulf of Mexico and US coastal waters.

Might that be because I live in the United States and I'm hearing mainly US news?

I'd been staring at the mussels nestled in their bed of ice, so, naturally, the fishmonger asked if he could help me. "Mussels are beautiful, no? Only two quid per kilo!" He had an Indian or Pakistani accent.

"Beautiful," I agreed. "Where do these come from?"

"From the distributor," he said, then grinned when he realized that wasn't what I meant. "One minute." He stepped back from the display and called to a man who was filleting a flatfish. Turning back to me he said, "Sussex."

"Have you had any complaints about people getting sick from eating these?"

"Sick? No!" He looked confused and a bit insulted.

"Sorry, I didn't mean to suggest... I mean, the other night at St. Ormond's we had mussels at our cocktail party and several people got sick."

"They did not come from us, did they?"

"I don't know where they were bought, or who bought them."

The blood-spattered man from the worktable, still wielding a filet knife, stepped forward. "You'd best find out where they came from before you start accusing us of selling bad mussels!"

I made hasty apologies and dashed out into Market Street. This wasn't my day. I felt as if I could do with a Kevlar vest. Turning left onto busy Cornmarket Street, the town's retail hub, I kept walking until Cornmarket turned into St. Aldate's and ahead I saw the great Tom Tower of Christ Church, the bell tower named for Thomas à Becket and stubbornly set to ring nine o'clock at five after nine, because Oxford is, in fact, five minutes west of Greenwich, which is officially zero degrees longitude. Only in Oxford.

I kept walking south toward the river Thames—locals called it the Isis—trying to fill my mind with the sights around me and forget my horrible afternoon, but my mind stubbornly returned to Larry. What didn't make sense was *how angry he got!* I'd never seen him so upset. I'd rarely seen *anyone* that upset over anything. Okay, so he didn't go for the idea that King Arthur may have been a real man. Okay, so there isn't any actual proof he ever existed. I understand that historians get upset when non-historians start making things up and proposing them as though they really happened.

But Larry's anger was out of proportion. Off the charts. Why? I remembered Claudia Moss telling me about the curious exchange she'd heard between Larry and Harold. Something like, "Got your loins girded?" and "Frankly, I'd rather be elsewhere." This was just prior to Claudia's presentation and an hour or two before Bram was scheduled to take the stage. It was also about the same time Mignon walked into Bram's room and found his body. Bram was already dead and had been so for hours.

I knew, from talking to John Fish the ghost tour guide, that Harold Wetmore was an active opponent of all things paranormal. He'd tried to force city council to do away with the ghost tours. The Arthur legend was mixed up with the paranormal—Celtic gods, crop circles, veils between worlds, all that sort of thing—and I could safely assume Harold would have taken a dim view of whatever Bram Fitzwaring had planned to tell us in his afternoon lecture. But active opposition does not call for murder. I've seen historians argue for hours as if they might come to blows, then slap each other on the back and order another drink.

All in all, Larry's reaction to my harmless statement at my breakout session, and to my reading up on the Arthur links in the Fellows Library, made no sense.

And if Bram had indeed been murdered, I had to know by whom and I had to know why. But was he? No one but me seemed to have any doubt that his death was natural. No one including the medical examiner, who knew a lot more about such things than I. It was time for me to re-think the whole thing. I had not one scrap of evidence.

Turning back, I walked uphill and passed Alice's Shop, a store that found its way into Lewis Carroll's *Through the Looking-Glass* as the Old Sheep Shop. Now it specialized, not in Alice's barley sugar, but in children's clothing and Alice memorabilia. A little way past Alice's Shop, I spotted John Fish stepping out of a bookstore and already dressed in top hat and black coat for his evening ghost tour. I called to him.

John waited on the sidewalk for me to catch up. "How are things at St. Ormond's? Grey Lady still afoot?" His yellow-toothed grin tightened at the corners and quickly faded, perhaps because he was self-conscious about the condition of his teeth.

"I saw her again the other night, and I chased her, but she got clean away."

He shot me a look of alarm. "Again? But that's not possible!"

"Why not?"

His head lowered, he didn't answer me.

"Oh, I get it. You *did* know about it. You were be-hind it!"

He still didn't answer but I caught a glimpse of his face beneath the brim of his black hat and saw a mixture of indecision and chagrin. I had almost given up waiting for a response, when he said, "It was supposed to be a joke. Daphne Wetmore and I thought it up. We thought it would be a good conversation-starter on the first night of your conference."

"You certainly succeeded. The talk at dinner was of nothing else."

"Aye, that's what you told me. I haven't seen Daphne

though, to find out what she thought of it. The Grey Lady, as your group called her, was played by Bumps McAlister. She's the wife of the bloke who owns The Green Man on the High."

"I know The Green Man. I was in there the other day." I told him, as briefly as I could, the connections between Mignon and Bram and the proprietors of The Green Man. "My friend Mignon, in fact, had dinner with them last night."

"Aye. Oxford's a small town when you come right down to it."

"But why did the Grey Lady come back again Saturday night?"

"She didn't."

"She *did*. I chased her across the quad and nearly broke my ankle."

"I can't explain that."

"And she disappeared more or less into thin air. I thought I'd catch her at the back gate. It was the only place she could have possibly gone, but when I got there the place was empty and the door was locked." I stole another glance at John's face and realized I was providing him with fodder for a brand-new ghost story. "I gather that you and Harold Wetmore aren't the best of friends, but apparently you and Daphne are. Am I right?"

"She's a good woman," John said. "Does everything she can to help St. Ormond's, too. Harold is nothin' but an arrogant old ass. Gets by on his reputation."

"He certainly has a great reputation as a historian. My major professor, the man I came over here with, practically genuflects every time he sees him."

"Daphne, too. Don't ever let her hear a bad word about her Harold. I made that mistake once and she nearly took my head off. Hero worship, if you ask me. Makes me sick."

We'd reached Carfax corner where I vaguely intended to turn right, but when John kept walking straight ahead, up Cornmarket Street, I followed him. "Did you hear about the man at St. Ormond's who died? It was Bram Fitzwaring, the man I was just telling you about. He was staying on the same staircase as I am."

John said he hadn't heard about it, then asked, "You say he knew Simon McAlister?"

"Is that the shopowner's name? Yes. Mignon and Bram were from Glastonbury but they're all connected, apparently, by this New Age thing. Bram was scheduled to deliver a paper at our conference and they both had rooms on Staircase Thirteen. Mignon is still here."

"What did he die of?"

"Hypoglycemia, they say. He had diabetes, like me." I leaped out of the path of a bicycle that came my way from the right as I stepped off the curb. "But several of us got sick that night, and I've wondered if it might not have been caused by the food they served at the cocktail party that evening. Since Bram was diabetic, if he got sick and threw up, that could bring on the hypoglycemia."

John nodded, somewhat disinterested, I thought. As if his mind had wandered off on another track.

"I suspect the mussels," I said.

"Why?"

"Yesterday I went out to the Radcliffe Hospital to see the daughter of a friend of mine. She took me through their research wing and I met a man who was working with a poison found in shellfish. It just made me wonder."

"That's what happens when you get one thing on your mind. You start wondering about everything."

Technically, that made no sense at all, but oddly enough, I knew what he meant. "He had a pan full of oysters sitting in a poisonous bath. He told me he's using it for his work on nervous disorders." I thought about him again. So charming. Too charming? I don't trust men with too much charm. "Odd name, he had." I searched my mind to remember it. "St. Giles was his first name. St. Giles Bell."

John Fish stopped. He lifted his stove-pipe hat and ran his hand through his greasy hair. "Well, now! That's a name I do recognize. From the papers."

"Oh?"

In his best funereal tones, he said, "His wife died last year. Fell down the stairs and broke her neck." We had reached another intersection. John paused again and his body language told me his destination lay somewhere down Beaumont Street. If I intended to return to St. Ormond's for dinner, I needed to walk in the opposite direction, so I stopped, too.

"And you remember this from the papers? You mean the obituaries?"

"No, it was on the front pages for a while, then the back pages. Nothin' ever came of it." He took my elbow in his hand and looked at me through knitted brows. "But there were those as said it weren't no accident."

"You mean she was *pushed*?"

"Nothin' ever came of it so who knows?" He shrugged, turned, and headed down Beaumont Street leaving me with a bunch of questions still forming in my mind.

TWELVE

I KNOCKED ON Mignon's and Lettie's doors as I passed by
on my way up the stairs. Nobody home. In my room, I
found myself pacing with the same nervous energy as
before. I moved the fresh towel the scout had left me
from the foot of my bed to the radiator beside the basin.
I threw a plastic shopping bag and a couple of receipts in
the trashcan. I checked my blood sugar, found it too low,
and ate the Chocolate Kream cookies the scout had left
on my tea tray. It was too early to dress for dinner so I
kicked off my shoes, sat on the bed with my back against
the wall, opened my iPad, and googled "saxitoxin."

Over the next hour I learned:

1. Saxitoxin is one of several poisons produced by
   a few marine algae and it is the most potent non-
   protein poison known. A mere 0.2 milligrams
   could kill a person. (Doing the math, I found that
   one gram, the weight of a paper clip, could kill
   5,000 people.)
2. It is specifically a sodium channel blocker, and as
   such is proving to be a valuable tool in neurologi-
   cal studies (as St. Giles Bell had already told me).
3. It is unaffected by heat, so cooking tainted fish
   or shellfish does not make it safe to eat.
4. It has been a subject of study by the United States

CIA and is rumored to have been given to spies as suicide pills.

5. Saxitoxin poisonings, worldwide, are not uncommon.

6. After receiving a lethal dose, death usually occurs in two to twelve hours.

7. There is no cure, but if the person suffering from the effects of saxitoxin can be hooked up to a respirator in time, he can survive. Death usually comes from lack of oxygen due to the fact that the breathing muscles are paralyzed.

8. It may be possible to detect saxitoxin in the brain of a victim. (But not if the victim, like Bram, has already been cremated.)

All this dove-tailed nicely with what I'd learned in Bell's lab, but I still wondered how Bram could have received a lethal dose. If it was from the mussels at the party before dinner, wouldn't he have felt the effects by the time he joined me on the bench in the quad? That was at nine o'clock. One of the websites listed numbness of the lips as an early symptom. A feeling of constriction in the throat and incoherent speech might follow. Bram certainly was talking crazily, asking me if I wanted to go out for pizza when we'd all just had a huge dinner. But that wasn't incoherent speech. He wasn't slurring his words. I needed to talk to a real doctor. Lettie's daughter Lindsey was a real doctor.

I already had Lindsey's number in my cell phone. I called it and immediately wished I hadn't because if Lindsey was still at the hospital, the call might interrupt something important. My next thought was that if she was doing anything important, she'd have the turned the phone off or switched it to vibrate.

"Hello?"

Lindsey's voice surprised me and for a minute I stammered around trying to explain why I'd called. Lindsey told me I'd caught her eating a very late lunch in the hospital cafeteria. I explained in as few words as possible, then asked, "How hard would it be for someone to filch a bit of saxitoxin from Dr. Bell's lab?"

"Impossible."

"You mean difficult. Nothing's impossible."

"And it's possible the NBA will draft me next season. No. Impossible. You would not believe the security around St. Giles's tiny stash of saxitoxin. First of all, he doesn't have that much on hand at any one time. He has a system of labeling that would make it impossible for anyone but himself to know what was what. He stores it in several different concentrations, some so weak they'd be harmless to humans. It's all kept in a time-lock safe so anyone sneaking in after hours couldn't get to it if they were holding a gun to St. Giles's head. There's an electric eye on every door and a motion detector that covers the whole lab."

"Okay. One more question," I said. "I know that people can die from eating shellfish tainted with saxitoxin, and that cooking doesn't make it safe. But what about an injection? Could it be injected?"

"Oh, sure. It probably wouldn't take as much if it were injected. It would probably work faster, too."

"How fast?"

Lindsey laughed. I could tell by her voice her mouth was full of food. "You've got me there. Would you like to talk to St. Giles again? Mom told me you're like a blood-hound when you sniff something rotten."

"I miss your mom. I've hardly seen her for a week."

"Sorry about that. Did you say you do want to talk to him again or not?"

"I don't know, Lindsey. I'll talk to you later."

DAPHNE WETMORE WAS leaving the college as I walked across the quad on my way to dinner. She stepped out from a side door of the porter's station swatting at a drooping tendril of wisteria that encircled the door, her face slick with sweat. The breeze I'd felt earlier now departed, the quad was sweltering under a hot, heavy blanket. Daphne was always in a dither it seemed, but this was the first time I'd seen her without makeup and with her baby-fine hair in disarray. She had the kind of hair that had to be washed and fluffed daily, otherwise she would look like a wet cat. Without mascara, her eyes almost disappeared beneath her heavy auburn brows. Her skin was splotchy and flushed.

"Oh, Dr. Lamb! I'm glad I caught you. I've told the porters, but they may forget to tell Harold. I have errands to run and I don't know exactly when I'll be back so I'll probably miss dinner. Will you tell my husband not to worry? I've taken the car, and I'll be back as soon as I can."

"No problem," I said. "Car? I didn't know you had a car. Where do you park it?" I hadn't seen any places nearby where you could park a car without paying by the hour.

"We keep it in a resident's parking lot just off St. Cross Road. Oh! One moment!" Daphne scrambled through her purse, dropping a lipstick, a cell phone, and a spray of loose change onto the grass. "There's something else I have to tell Harold, but…" Her hands shook as she pulled out a notepad with a short ballpoint attached to one side and turned, searching for an appropriate writing surface. "It'll be better if I write it. You'll never remember…" I offered my back as a writing surface but, after scribbling a few words, her pen quit due to its inverted position. "Oh, damn!"

I handed her a pencil over my shoulder.

She finished writing, ripped the note off the pad, folded it twice, and handed it to me. "Give this to Harold." She scrambled through her purse again and pulled out a key ring with the college's magic button attached. "He needs it *before* dinner. Do you mind? Thanks ever so much."

The note she handed me was wet with perspiration, partly hers and partly mine, I suspected. I could feel my shirt sticking to my back. I unfolded the note carefully to avoid tearing. It said, "His name is Malcolm. Tell him you're sorry for his loss. His wife died last week."

I believe I could have remembered that.

I had some extra time before dinner and I considered checking the SCR to see if there was a pre- as well as post-dinner gathering. I suspected there might be, but looking around the East Quad, I thought of something else. Perhaps, in the daylight, I'd have better luck figuring out where the Grey Lady had gone that night. The last I'd seen of her, she was dashing through the north archway while I hopped on my good foot, giving way to my twisted ankle. I walked through and turned left, as I had done that night, into a dead end. The late afternoon sun poured gold across three roofs, their weathered gargoyles leering down at me from the overhangs.

Ahead stood a solid brick wall, some three stories high, and flanked by two ancient stone walls. To the left, the backside of the wing that housed the rooms of Keith Bunsen and several other faculty members. The one on the right incorporated bits of the ancient city wall, much repaired over the last eight hundred years. Behind me, the Master's Garden and a door to the Wetmores' lodgings.

White curtains fluttered out from an open window in the second floor of the building on my left. I imagined a fan in the room beyond, because there was no moving air to produce any cross ventilation. Voices, so low I couldn't make out the words, slipped out as well. This window would be at about the same place as Keith's rooms on the staircase closest to the northwest corner of the building. I listened for another minute, hearing an angry or perhaps excited voice and a deeper, calmer one. I heard a long scrape, as if someone was pulling a chair across the floor. Then, quite clearly, perhaps because the speaker had moved closer to the window, a girl's voice said, "If looks could kill, I'd be dead right now!"

NOT WISHING TO be caught eavesdropping, I turned right and stepped into the archway where I felt the Grey Lady must have gone. At the far side stood the small door cut into the gigantic wooden nail-studded gate. Then I saw it. An iron railing to the left of the door sloped down, disappearing into the cobbled stone floor. Stepping across and peering over the rail, I spotted a door below ground level, at the bottom of a stairwell so dark I could hardly read the sign on the black, water-stained door. "No Admittance." Whatever lay beyond the door must run beneath the wall itself.

If the Grey Lady had slipped down these stairs I would

have missed her, whether she went through the door or not. She could have hidden in the stairwell in her black, hooded cape and I wouldn't have seen her. I checked my watch and decided there wasn't enough time to visit the SCR, so I wandered around the Middle Quad, admiring the borders. The gardeners stuck small brass plaques, with common and scientific names, in the ground beneath some of the more exotic plants. I stopped at a huge black flower with a plaque that read *Aeonium arboreum* and wondered if I could raise one of those in my garden back home. If I saw a gardener before I left I would ask him; that is, if the gardeners hadn't quit following Daphne's verbal harangue.

"I've tried to grow those with a singular lack of success," a voice behind me said. I turned and found Claudia Moss.

"Claudia. I need to talk to you." Still studying the flower border as we both moseyed in the general direction of the dining hall, I said, "Have you talked to Larry Roberts this afternoon, since, say, three o'clock?"

Claudia hesitated as if she might be revealing more than she should by answering, then said, "I had tea with him at the Randolph at four."

"Did he mention my presentation? He came in, but left soon after. He was angry with me. Furious would be a better word."

"He did mention it." She paused again and her next words seemed to have been carefully weighed. "He said you were being taken in by our visitors from Glastonbury. He's adamant, you know, that history must be done scrupulously and objectively."

"I know. He and I have had these discussions before, but what I said in my presentation was not the least bit controversial. I was careful in the way I worded my one and only reference to Arthur in Glastonbury, and none of the others thought anything of it. Once I got the Oxfordian squared away, and after Larry stormed out, we had a nice discussion."

"I knew this sort of thing would come up as soon as I heard the topic they'd selected for the conference."

"Who selected it, by the way?"

"I don't know. Dr. Wetmore, perhaps?"

"I doubt it. Did Larry also tell you he said I could forget that PhD?"

"Give him time to cool down." We had reached the doors to the dining hall. "Would you join us for dinner?"

"I think not. He needs more time to cool down and so do I."

THIRTEEN

A SMALL GROUP of diners waved me over, and I was ever so glad for their invitation because otherwise I would've had to sit by myself or go up to someone I didn't know very well and ask, "May I sit with you?" A perfectly normal thing to do in America, but here? Not always. And you might find yourself with a group speaking another language, although all the conference attendees spoke English well enough to understand the lectures and discussions.

I recognized two of them as participants in my breakout session today. We introduced ourselves all around. "Your presentation today has given me so much to think about. I took three pages of notes," one said.

"I've never fully appreciated the fact that historians in Shakespeare's day were no more writing from personal knowledge than we are today," another added.

"Correction. We may be writing from personal knowledge when we write about recent events," yet another said and looked at me. "As an American, do you remember the assassination of President Kennedy?"

"I was in high school, but yes, I remember."

"You were there. You could write that story from personal knowledge."

"But I wasn't in Dallas. All I know is what I saw on TV."

"Exactly! Just my point!"

We paused while the server straightened out our first courses, two of our group having ordered vegetarian and unwilling to accept the salads with prosciutto.

"That man who stormed out! It was Dr. Roberts, wasn't it?"

I explained as quickly and calmly as I could.

"What's his problem? If I were you I'd find another mentor to work with."

"And the man who brought up the Earl of Oxford! There's always one in every crowd."

Having established ourselves as moderate historians, we had a lively discussion through the rest of the meal. We were starting on dessert, which the English call "pudding" whether it's pudding or not, when I looked up and saw Lettie standing in the door, looking around the room.

I stood to get her attention and pulled out a chair for her.

"I'm not eating," Lettie said, grabbing my coffee spoon and helping herself to my cake.

Introductions complete, Lettie said, "Lindsey is staying home tonight—for a change. I felt like I should introduce her to her own children." To the others, she added, "I've been babysitting my two grandchildren while my daughter works at the hospital. Don't get me wrong. I love to spend all the time I can with my grandchildren. They are the sweetest things. But enough's enough, you know? Children need their mothers, as well, don't they?" She paused for breath and looked at me. "Sorry. I'm running off at the mouth, aren't I?"

"I understand," said the man sitting across from me. "You haven't talked to an adult all day, and the freedom makes you feel quite giddy."

Lettie purchased a bottle of Merlot from our server

and we took it with us to the SCR. She wasn't sure she was allowed, but I assured her this wasn't part of the history conference and she had as much right to relax in the faculty room as the rest of us.

The air had turned chilly while we were at dinner, from hot and still to a cool breeze and that eerie change in pressure that you can't exactly feel, but register, somewhere deep down. The city's lights reflected off low-hanging clouds and archway lanterns began creaking on their chains.

Someone had raised all the windows in the SCR. As if responding to the change in weather, most of us took chairs and bunched them around the unlit fireplace. The last time I was in this room, with Robin Morris, the occupants had wandered about the room or gathered in little conversation pods.

"Poor Harold. Did anyone else notice how shaky he was tonight?"

"Daphne wasn't there. That's why. He needs her to tell him when to stand up and what to say."

"Where was she? She's always there."

"I can answer that," I said. "I ran into her about a half-hour before dinner and she was leaving to run some errands. She gave me a note to give to Harold and I did give it to him, but all it said was that his guest tonight was named Malcolm and Malcolm's wife died last week."

"Harold called him Martin when he introduced him."

I threw up my hands. "Hey, I did my best! I gave him the note."

The man who had challenged me on the authorship of Shakespeare's works spoke up. "I hope I didn't offend you today, Mrs. Lamb. The debate over the authorship of the plays and poems is a long-standing one. It's ground we've all been over a hundred times, but to an American perhaps it seems like a minefield."

"No offense taken," I said. His apology sounded sincere but with a touch of arrogance.

"Too bad we had no Baconians," said the woman who had invited me to sit with them at dinner. "We could have had a right jolly row."

"I'm glad we didn't. I wouldn't have had time for my prepared remarks."

Lettie, sitting on the settee beside me, had a bewildered look on her face so I said to the group, "This is my lifelong friend, Lettie Osgood. She's a librarian, but her own interests are not especially along the lines of British history. I doubt she knows what a Baconian is."

"A Baconian, Mrs. Osgood, is one who believes Sir Francis Bacon wrote the plays attributed to Shakespeare."

"And then there are the Oxfordians, who believe Edward de Vere, Seventeenth Earl of Oxford, wrote the plays."

"All perfectly silly of course," said a thin woman with a deep voice and black hair cut in what they used to call a Dutch boy style. "Because it's all based on the idea that a working-class man couldn't possibly have written so intelligently."

"And the idea that a common man couldn't possibly have known so much about the places where he set his stories," another added.

All eyes seemed to be on Lettie, the lone pupil in a room full of tutors. Lettie shifted uncomfortably in her chair, clasped her little hands tightly in her lap, and straightened her back. "Does it matter? After all, *somebody* wrote those wonderful plays, and whoever did *deserves* the name Shakespeare."

I threw my arm around her shoulders and laughed, letting the others know they could too, but not too much. Lettie didn't get it. I looked beyond her bewildered face and saw Larry Roberts as he stepped through the door, surveyed the scene, turned, and left.

We heard voices, then rhythmic, hollow, thumps wafting through the open windows on either side of the fireplace. No one spoke for a minute while we listened. Drums? Then a high-pitched voice singing something that sounded like classical church music broke through, alternating with the drumbeats. I, sitting closest to the right-hand window, jumped up and looked out while the Oxfordian man dashed to the other window.

They were marching in, two by two, the New Agers. Dressed in long robes and carrying flashlights held aloft as if they were torches. I counted ten marchers, their robes of uncertain color in the dim light of the East Quad.

"Oh, Lord! It's an invasion!" said the Oxfordian.

The overhead lantern under the college's main entrance cast the invaders in silhouette as they turned toward Staircase Thirteen. The last pair carried the drums. Striking in unison they sounded like one. The marchers in back stopped to allow the front ones to go up the stairs in single file. Stepping up and onto the stone threshold, they entered, lowering their flashlights and giving me a quick glimpse of their faces, but I really didn't need to see their faces to know they were Mignon Beaulieu and her friends.

As the doorway swallowed the last one, a tremendous bolt of lightning lit up the courtyard. A deafening thunderclap followed less than a second later. I jumped, and I heard several startled cries from the room behind me. Then the rain began, and it came in undulating sheets.

The front of my shirt and slacks caught the first of it so I quickly lowered the window, the sheer drapes sticking to my raised arms. I turned and saw others rushing to close windows along both exterior walls.

Another flash and another clap, and the lights in the room went dark. I stood there stupidly, wondering whom we'd find lying on the floor, murdered, when the power came back on.

"Oh, my Lord! My brolly is in my room! Who has one here?"

"Those damned hippies! How did they manage to start a storm?"

"I don't know about you, but I still have a half bottle of Merlot. I'm staying right here until it blows over."

"Are the lights out all over college?"

"Dotsy! Where are you?" This came from Lettie.

A man said, "May I suggest we all either leave the room or find a seat? We're going to start banging into each other if we don't."

Another flash of lightning showed me where I was in relation to the settee, so I groped my way over, found Lettie's spiky hair with my hand, and guided both of us to the same seats we'd left earlier.

"Any good ghost stories?" someone said.

I heard the door open and close several times as people left to brave the elements. Lettie and I waited until the rain slackened. Meanwhile we joined the other stragglers in making silly comments about dark and stormy nights. Fifteen minutes later the pounding tapered off. I returned to the window and pulled back the curtain. A small figure leaning into an umbrella turned the corner at the Porter's Lodge and hurried toward the Master's

Lodge. I recognized Daphne by her size and her determined gait.

Lettie and I grabbed sections of yesterday's *Oxford Daily Mail* for our heads and made a run for it.

CLIMBING THE STAIRS, I wasn't the least surprised to see yellow light slipping under the door of Bram Fitzwaring's former room. The electricity was still off, so it had to be candlelight, I thought. I stopped and grabbed Lettie's arm, shushing her.

Now they were doing a really strange chant. One at a time, in voices high and low, they uttered sounds that might have been words, but I don't think they were in English. We kept climbing. Lettie fumbled for her keys and asked me in. I groped my way around the wall until I felt the back of her desk chair. We talked for a few minutes, mostly about Lindsey. Lettie said she thought Lindsey and her new boyfriend, St. Giles Bell, had broken up because Lindsey came home to her apartment that day with red, swollen eyes and told Lettie to leave. Whatever the problem was, Lindsey wouldn't talk about it.

I left and felt my way up the next flight to my room. My footsteps sounded like gunfire on the wood floor outside my door. Opening the door with one arm while pressing my body against the wall, I saw a pale stream of light slanting through my little garret window and onto my bedspread. I managed to dress for bed and brush my teeth in the dark. I had to use my travel flashlight to read the number on my blood glucose meter. As the light brushed my face, I looked in the mirror over my sink. My hair was dripping wet and beginning to kink up around the ears. The hair dryer was plugged in and draped over the unheated radiator. I flipped the

switch. No electricity, of course. I'd need to wash and
style my hair tomorrow morning.

I SKIPPED OVER the machinations necessary to restore my
rain-soaked and sleep-flattened hair the next morning.
The power was restored sometime during the night, and I
heard Lettie's hair-dryer through her closed door as I descended the stairs on my way to the bathroom. I knocked.

Lettie used the same gel/mousse hair product Rod
Stewart was reported to employ for his famous spiky
look, but Lettie's hair was red rather than blond. After
she opened the door for me, she flicked the dryer off and
slathered both palms with hair product. "I may actually
have a day off. I just tried to call Lindsey to see if she is
working today, but she didn't answer. This is supposed
to be her free day."

The door to Bram's room stood open, the aroma of
sandalwood drifting out into the narrow hall. I found Mignon still there, staring out the open window. It looked
as if all traces of Bram's short stay had been erased.

"Are you okay?" I asked.

"Of course. I'm just taking one last look before I
return the key to the porter." She jangled the key and
sighed. "His spirit is no longer here."

"When will you go back to Glastonbury?"

"Bram's mother and I have divided his ashes. She's
gone home already and I'll take my half back to Glastonbury where we'll scatter them on the Tor."

I paused a minute before I dropped my big question.
"What was Bram intending to reveal in his speech?"

Mignon's face flushed and her hefty frame wavered. I
thought she might actually pass out. She bent over Bram's
bed, turned, and sat with a grunt, both feet leaving the

floor. She inhaled through tight lips and said, "What are you talking about?"

"I know he was planning to show slides of the Tor, and he had something to tell us about bones, and about Richard Whiting. He planned to mention the little village of Sharpham, which is very near Glastonbury, isn't it?"

"And you know this, how?"

"I found a note on the floor when you and I came in together, remember? It was on the floor. There." I pointed to the floor of the closet, its door hanging open. "Apparently the scout missed it when she cleaned."

"What did it say?" Mignon required a complete description. Her head jerked nervously, setting her neck fat in motion as I told her what the note said. "Where is the note now?"

"I still have it."

"I need it." In case I had any doubt, I knew now that Bram's speech before the whole group on Saturday was to have been a blockbuster. Hadn't he told me he was going to blow the doors off this place? Mignon seemed to be in a state of inner turmoil, as if she was weighing the wisdom of taking me into her confidence versus diverting me with lies.

I tried everything I could think of, but to no avail. She knew what Bram's speech contained and she wasn't about to tell me. More than ever, I was convinced it was to have been something important. Was Mignon now planning to confer with the group back in Glastonbury and reach a mutual decision, or was she planning to strike her own bargain with the press and reveal it herself?

I went for the gut. "I know his speech had something to do with the bones of a large man, perhaps six and a half feet tall. I know that King Arthur was reputed to have been a giant and, in his day, six foot six would have been a giant. I know that bones thought to be those of Arthur and Guinevere were found in Glastonbury after the old abbey and church burned down in eleven eighty-four. I know that King Edward the First and Queen Eleanor attended the reburial of the bones in a black marble tomb in front of the high altar of the new church when it was completed, about a hundred years later. I know that Henry the Eighth destroyed the abbey and church in fifteen thirty-nine. That was the title of Bram's speech, wasn't it? The Dissolution of the Monasteries in fifteen thirty-nine?"

Mignon's head bobbed rhythmically as I talked, but she said nothing. Her sausage-like fingers grasped the bedcover, their knuckles white.

"It doesn't take a huge leap of imagination," I said, "to suppose Abbot Richard Whiting saw trouble ahead before the king's men arrived. There were reports that Whiting took the abbey's most valuable possessions to nearby Sharpham. Gold and silver and probably some relics of saints. But what was, far and away, the abbey's most valuable possession? Arthur's bones, of course.

"And, since Bram's lecture notes mention both Whiting and Sharpham, I figure Bram *had King Arthur's bones!*" I stopped, demanding a response.

Mignon laughed. "Ridiculous! I've never heard anything so ridiculous in my life."

"But true, isn't it?"

"Of course not. If Bram had King Arthur's bones, do you think he'd announce it in an insignificant little conference like this? A conference full of dusty old snobs moldering in their crumbling ivory tower?" The sneer she didn't try to hide bared her front teeth on one side.

"This is precisely where I *would* expect him to an-nounce it. He, in fact your entire Glastonbury group, has been ridiculed by these dusty old snobs for years. This would be a perfect way to throw concrete proof of King Arthur and Camelot right in their faces." I tilted my head to one side and lowered my voice. "Tell me. Have you had the bones dated with carbon fourteen?"

Mignon continued to deny my whole theory. She could have cleared it all up by simply telling me what Bram's speech was to have been about, but she refused to go there. I felt certain my idea was right. Or mostly right.

FOURTEEN

TUESDAY, JULY TENTH. A day Lettie Osgood will never forget.

Lettie and I ventured outside the college to breakfast at The Mitre on the High, navigating leaf-strewn streets, still wet from last night's storm. The building that houses the restaurant, a part of Lincoln College, dates back to about 1630, but an inn of some sort has stood on this site since perhaps 1300. With Henry VIII and the dissolution of the monasteries fresh on my mind, I told Lettie the story about the tunnel that ran under the High and joined The Mitre to The Angel, another inn across the street. "Henry's soldiers chased a group of monks into the tunnel and walled it shut on both ends with the living men inside. They say you can still hear their screams sometimes."

Lettie stopped and threw her pudgy hand to her mouth. "And you expect me to eat breakfast here?"

"It's only a legend. I'm sure it never happened."

"How do you know it never happened?"

"Why would a bunch of monks just stand there while they're being walled up? Wouldn't they fight to the death before they let that happen?"

"What if Henry's men knocked them out, and when they came to, they were trapped?"

THE MAITRE D' TOOK us to a back room with exposed beams and lots of little alcoves. Lettie switched her cell phone's ringer to vibrate. Mine was already turned off to save the battery. We placed our orders and considered what we'd do with our day. Tomorrow would be the last day of the conference but today's schedule held nothing I couldn't miss. Larry Roberts was in charge of a break-out session I wanted to attend, mainly to harass him as he had done to me. If my PhD was already in the toilet, I figured, I might as well enjoy myself. Lettie and I decided we'd shop first and then take a tour of the castle.

Lettie was buttering her scone when her phone vibrated. "I'll take this outside," she said, "I hate when people talk on the phone in restaurants." She walked through a short passage to the front of the restaurant and out the main door, but I could still see her from where I sat. The front was all windows. Her caller was probably Lindsey, I figured, asking Lettie to babysit again today. I did wish Lindsey could be more considerate of her mother. Lettie needed time off, too, and much of her babysitting had been when Lindsey wasn't even working but was out somewhere with St. Giles Bell.

Through the front window, I saw Lettie turn, cell phone to one ear, and press her forehead against the glass. Then slowly, slowly, she sank until all I could see was the points of her spiky hair above the windowsill.

I stumbled through the front door behind a couple of waiters who also saw Lettie faint and beat me to the sidewalk. One knelt beside her, felt her pulse, and called out, "Get a doctor!"

Lettie's eyes fluttered open.

"I'm her friend," I said. "Give us a minute. If we need a doctor, I'll let you know." They stood back and I knelt beside Lettie, her legs sprawled out on the wet concrete, one shoulder against the wall. I took the cell phone from her hand and checked to see if the call was still open.

"Hello?"

I waited for an answer, then looked at the screen. It said, "Thames Valley Police."

"Hello? This is Mrs. Osgood's friend," I said. "Mrs. Osgood has passed out. Can you tell me what this is about?"

"Where are you? We'll send officers to help, straight away."

I told them, then repeated my question.

"Dr. Scoggin, Mrs. Osgood's daughter, has been shot. She's in hospital."

Lettie raised her hand to me. "Let me have it."

I handed her the phone and sat beside her, the wet sidewalk soaking the rear of my slacks. Waiters and a few patrons poked heads out and asked if they could help. I asked one of the waiters to bring me our check, as we wouldn't be finishing our meal. He waved my request away with a sweep of his hand. "No charge."

Lettie's face was still an unhealthy grey, but her eyes shed no tears. Not yet. "She's at the Radcliffe Hospital," she said. "Emergency room. We need a taxi."

I dashed into the street and flagged the first one I saw. Lettie struggled to her feet and lurched toward the rear door of the cab. Before the driver could manage to hop out and open it, Lettie opened it herself and fell in. I fell in beside her.

"Radcliffe Hospital," I said.

"And hurry!" Lettie added.

We had both left our purses with all our money at our seats in The Mitre. I explained this to the driver, who wasn't pleased, but handed me his card and explained how I could pay him later. It was in his own best interest not to say what I'm sure he wanted to say. As the cab weaved through the outskirts of town past rows of homes and shops, Lettie sat like a stone, her gaze straight ahead and her hands clamped on the edge of the seat. I talked to her throughout the whole trip but she didn't appear to hear me. The driver dropped us off at the emergency entrance.

Lindsey was in one of the emergency rooms, but a nurse told us they needed to take her to surgery right away. They'd been waiting for us since the police had called and told them we were on our way. Lettie apologized for having no identification and had to establish that she was indeed Lindsey's mother by answering a couple of questions they pulled from their staff contact files. They let us go in briefly while they prepared to move Lindsey to surgery.

Lettie may be a scatterbrain, but when circumstances call for bravery and calm, she rises to the occasion. Lindsey lay on a gurney, her mouth and nose covered by an oxygen mask. Naked to the waist, she had a blood-spattered sheet on the lower half of her body. Lettie slipped between two nurses and placed a hand on Lindsey's head.

"You're going to be all right, Punkin. They're taking you upstairs to remove the bullet and I'll see you as soon as you come out. Okay? Dotsy is going to take care of Claire and Caleb. Don't worry about a thing."

Her composure in the face of this great uncertainty brought tears to my eyes, and mine weren't the only wet ones in the little room. An attending physician had told us on the way into the room that she had been shot below her rib cage and above her navel so they didn't know exactly what sort of internal damage they'd find.

Lettie's simple "remove the bullet" sugarcoated what might be a life-threatening injury. Lettie squeezed her daughter's hand and kissed her on the forehead as they wheeled her away.

Then Lettie broke down.

I had to lead her to a chair in the hall and hold her until she started sobbing out loud. Until I heard sounds, I was afraid she was choking on her own tears. When, after some minutes, I looked up, I saw two plainclothes detectives flashing badges at us.

"She was shot coming out of her flat at eight thirty-three this morning. We don't know who or why. We're talking to all the neighbors, but so far we've found only one who thinks he saw someone running away, down a path behind the building, but we're hoping we'll get better information when we locate others. Most of the residents are at work now."

"Do you have a description?"

"No. Dark colored anorak, he thought. But nothing definite." One of the detectives had a notepad in hand. The other one said, "Wait here a moment, please. I'll find us a room where we can talk."

The room the hospital staff found for us was a fair distance away and Lettie worried we wouldn't know when they brought Lindsey back from the operating room. I had to ask the detectives their names again, since I hadn't listened when they told us before. The man was Chief Inspector Child, an efficient-looking man of about fifty. His assistant was a shiny-faced young woman named Detective Sergeant Gunn. In less dire circumstances I'd have made a comment about the appropriateness of her name.

We were in an office with a large desk, upholstered

chairs, and bookshelves. Chief Inspector Child rolled a utilitarian office chair across its protective PVC mat for himself, and waved Lettie to an armchair. He turned to me. "I suppose we should conduct these interviews one at a time, but under the circumstances I think it will be all right if you stay, Mrs... ."

"Mrs. Lamb."

"Officer," Lettie said, pulling a tissue from the box on the desk, "my friend needs to go to my daughter's apartment and take care of my grandchildren. They're seven and five. They're too young to be left alone."

"Dr. Scoggin's children are in good hands. We have a woman officer at the flat now looking after them."

"But still! They need someone they know."

I hoped Lindsey's children would remember me. I'd seen them only once since I arrived and, before that, not since Christmas. These poor kids were already dealing with the breakup of their parents' marriage and the insecurity of spending their summer in a foreign country. Now this. I knew Lindsey had tried to keep the custody squabble away from little ears, but children are so perceptive you can hardly ever keep them from sensing trouble.

"Perhaps you're right, Mrs. Osgood. Mrs. Lamb is not directly involved in this anyway." He turned to me. "A couple of questions before you go. What is your relationship to Dr. Scoggin?"

I told him. He asked me to tell him about the last time I'd seen Lindsey and if I could think of anyone who might want to kill her. Having nothing of value to tell him, I was allowed to leave. "One problem," I said. "I'll have to take a taxi to the apartment and I have no money. Lettie and I have both left our purses back at The Mitre."

Chief Inspector Child asked DS Gunn if there was a squad car here at the hospital. Gunn made a call on her radio and turned to me. "There's an officer outside waiting to take you. He'll also drive back into town and pick up your purses from The Mitre." She returned to her radio and dictated the address of Lindsey's apartment to the officer in the parking lot.

Before I left, I looked carefully into Lettie's eyes. I saw fear. I wished I could stay with her, but I knew she'd feel better knowing I was with her grandchildren.

THE APARTMENT BUILDING was what the British call a "terraced property," a single row of two-story apartments, each with a small, walled-in front yard and a somewhat larger space in the back. Lindsey's place was conspicuous with the yellow crime scene tape strung across the front. A small front stoop stood between a large plate-glass window on one side and wood siding with an inserted air-conditioning unit on the other. Above, brown shingle siding with smaller, probably bedroom, windows and two more air-conditioning units.

My police escort saw me to the front door and rang the bell. I tried to ignore the big pool of drying blood on the walkway, only a couple of yards outside the front door, but I turned and looked at it again while we were waiting for the door to open. "That's where it happened," I said.

"Aye. We think she was just popping out to pick up the morning paper."

"Did the children…?"

The door opened and a policewoman showed me in. My driver tipped his checkerboard hat to us and turned to leave, but the policewoman stopped him. "I need to ride back with you," she told him. "Just a moment. Won't be a tick."

My heart thudded. In the living room ahead, I saw Lindsey's two children, sitting side by side on the sofa as if they were in church, minding their manners and enduring a sermon they didn't understand. Claire, the seven-year-old, was in pink shorts, blue T-shirt and flip-flops. Five-year-old Caleb looked as if he'd dressed himself. He wore a plaid shirt with only one button done, and Disney character pajama bottoms. White socks, but no shoes.

"Hi, kids, remember me? Aunt Dotsy?"

Both nodded their heads.

"I'm going to stay with you a little while, but your Grandma Lettie will be here just as soon as she can."

"Are they taking the bullet out of Mommy?" Claire asked.

"Oh, so you know." I turned to the policewoman who was standing at the front door, one hand on the knob.

"Hard to keep anything from those two. They seem to deal with fact better than fantasy. They know everything. I've given them their tea, so I don't think they'll want lunch before noon."

"Thanks. We'll be all right now." When the front door closed behind the policewoman, I told the children, "They're taking the bullet out right now, and Grandma Lettie will be there to see her when she comes out of the operating room."

"Wheoh did the bullet hit huh?" Caleb asked.

Oh golly! These kids go straight to the point. "It went in under her ribs, about here." I stuck my forefinger into my own stomach at the approximate spot.

"It hit her in the pancreas?" Claire said.

"I don't know. Is this where your pancreas is?" I knew it was, but I couldn't believe a second grader could be so well-versed in human anatomy.

"Why did that puhson shoot my mommy?" Caleb asked.

"I thought they had strict gun laws in the United Kingdom," Claire said.

I found an armchair on the other side of the coffee table and sat. "As a matter of fact, Claire, I was thinking the same thing myself on the way out. I don't think individuals are supposed to have handguns here."

"Maybe it was a rifle."

"Or a shotgun."

"Well! I think the very best thing for us to do is whatever you normally do this time of day. What would that be?"

"Sometimes Grandma takes us to the store with her."

"How do you get there?"

"We walk. But that's when we need some groceries," Claire said, "and we don't need any right now."

The children, it turned out, wanted to talk about it. I don't think they'd felt they could talk freely to the policewoman, but they did talk to me. They'd both been asleep when it happened. Claire thought she heard a pop. Caleb heard nothing. Claire had hopped out of bed and run to her window when she heard a neighbor from across the street shout.

"I ran down the stairs but I couldn't get past the front door because Mrs. Champion from next door was already there and she wouldn't let me go out. But I saw Mommy lying on the sidewalk and she was bleeding. I think she was still awake but I can't be sure because Mrs. Champion was hiding my eyes and the man from across the street was kneeling over Mommy."

"Did you hear anyone say anything about seeing the shooter?"

Both children shook their heads.

"Is Mommy going to be all right?" Caleb asked.

Claire slapped him on the back of the head. "Of course she'll be all right, stupid!" Her voice quivered a tiny bit, and she raised her small chin, as if swallowing had suddenly become difficult.

A half-hour later a squad car pulled up in front. An officer got out and handed me my purse. "Any word from the hospital?" I asked.

He hadn't heard anything, but now I had my cell phone and I had money. My phone had Lettie's number on speed dial. "I hate to use you kind people as a taxi service, but if you're going back into town, could the children and I go with you? We want to visit the Pitt Rivers Museum." I stepped back inside, set Claire to the task of finding the keys to the apartment, and sent Caleb upstairs for shoes and outdoor pants. These children were so amazingly mature for their ages, I found myself treating them as if they were teenagers.

THE PITT RIVERS MUSEUM, with its stuffed dodo bird and other extinct animals, enthralled both children. I asked a docent where they kept the shrunken heads I'd heard about and tried to steer the children away from that aisle, thinking it too gory to be age appropriate. But Claire found them anyway, and backed off, saying, "Uhhgg!" and "You don't need to see this, Caleb. Are they real, Aunt Dotsy?"

"Yes."

"But how do they do it? Does the skull shrink, too?"

"I don't know. Let's go outside. I want to call your grandma."

FIFTEEN

We found a bench on the lawn outside the museum and I called Lettie. The mercury was climbing toward ninety and Caleb was starting to act cranky. I reminded myself that, prodigy though he might be, he was still only five years old. It was nearly one o'clock and he was probably hungry.

Lettie answered on the second ring and told me Lindsey was still in surgery. "I'm scared. They should have finished by now."

"They may be holding her in the recovery room," I said.

Claire grabbed my arm with both hands, and looked up at me, expectantly.

"They said they'd let me know as soon as she was out of surgery. I'm waiting in the room they're supposed to bring her to when she's out. If she were in the recovery room, they'd have told me," Lettie said. "The police are lurking."

"Lurking?"

"Like they're ready to pounce on her with a million questions."

"It's their job, Lettie. Besides, we want to know who did this, don't we?"

"Absolutely! But I wonder if Lindsey will remember anything."

I held the phone to my ear for several seconds after

Lettie had hung up, hoping to think of the right words to report to the children. Claire still held my arm, waiting. Caleb, his head down, looked at me sideways, as if he was afraid to ask. As if he knew the news wasn't good. I had to tell them something, and I knew these kids were too perceptive not to intuit a lie. When I could delay no longer, I hit the end call button on my phone.

"Your mom is still in the operating room, but Grandma says to tell you she'll call the minute she's out."

"It's been more than two hours," Claire said.

"Yes."

"It doesn't take two hours to remove a bullet."

"A bullet in the chest has to be treated carefully. I'm sure they want to check everything and make certain—"

"There's no internal bleeding." Claire finished my sentence for me.

"Will they sew up her pancreas?" Caleb said.

"I'm sure they will, if it needs to be sewn up."

I felt as if I was walking on eggshells. These poor children's lives were threatened and they—at least Claire—knew it. What would happen if Lindsey didn't make it? I pushed the thought from my head and tried to smile. "Let's get some lunch."

With Caleb on one side of me and Claire on the other, I ushered them down Museum Road to the Eagle and Child Pub, known to locals as the Bird and Baby. "We're going to the same pub where C.S. Lewis and J.R.R. Tolkien hung out and drank beer when they were in school here."

"Who?" Caleb asked.

"Have either of you read *The Lion, the Witch and the Wardrobe*? How about *The Hobbit*?"

"I have. I've read three of the *Narnia* books," Claire said. "But can we go to a pub? Will they let children in?"

"In England, pubs are open to everybody, kids included."

"Can we get beer?" Caleb danced sideways, looking up at me.

THE EAGLE AND Child had a children's menu. Once fed, we took to the street and I called Lettie again. She was still waiting for the first word from the operating room. I told her, "I'm taking the kids back to St. Ormond's for a while. If she wakes up and wants to see them, I'll bring them out to the hospital. Otherwise we'll head back to Lindsey's apartment."

By the time we entered St. Ormond's gate, Caleb was whining about his legs hurting. I took them up to my room. Caleb flopped down on my bed and immediately went to sleep. I had to wake him up to explain things to him. "If Claire and I go outside for a while will you be all right?"

"Yes."

"Are you going to wake up and wonder why you're in this strange place?"

"No. I won't be scared."

"Good boy. We'll be back soon. You'll probably still be asleep when we get back. If you do wake up and we're not here, you can stay here, or you can go down the stairs to the Porter's Lodge. Do you remember? It's where you waved to the man in a round hat a few minutes ago. He can help you find us." Fortunately with my own grandchildren in various stages of childhood, I never really get out of practice talking to young children. You have to keep it simple and tell it in little steps. Having raised five children, I'm good at it.

Claire and I walked the perimeter of the East Quad, surveying the flowerbeds. Claire, I thought, was feigning more interest in the flowers than she really felt, and I knew her mind was on her mother. When we'd made a complete loop, we ran into Harold Wetmore heading for his own lodgings along the north wall of the quad. He bent and shook hands politely with Claire when I introduced them.

"Just popping back for a few minutes before the last afternoon session," he said. "I believe Daphne is having a few people in for tea. Would the two of you join us?" To Claire, he said, "We have some lovely raspberry jam and scones. Would you like that?"

His tone was entirely too infantile, but Harold had no way of knowing how mature Claire was, and Claire was too well-mannered to roll her eyes. We accepted the invitation and found a half-dozen of my fellow conferees already there, milling about in the Wetmores' library with their teacups rattling on little saucers. One of those present was Larry Roberts. I supposed it was time to smooth our troubled waters.

Pretty Georgina Wetmore, Harold's niece, led Claire to the sideboard full of goodies and I wondered if the poor kid would be able to force anything else down, given the hamburger and fries she'd put away at the Eagle and Child less than an hour ago. Unlike the other guests, Georgina was wearing grunge casual today. Distressed jeans, thin yellow T-shirt, and flip-flops. Her blond hair was pulled back in a red rubber band.

Larry Roberts stood in a corner, alone with his teacup, so I had him trapped. Approaching him, smiling, I said, "Can we call a truce, Larry? We seem to have for-gotten we really like each other."

That got to him. He was expecting me to challenge him, to apologize, or to grovel. He wasn't prepared for an appeal to his humanity. His teacup jittered on its sau-cer and for a minute I thought he was going to cry. That would be horrible. Before he embarrassed us both, I knew I'd better steer the conversation onto a more intellectual track so I said, "Isn't scholarly discourse, disagreements included, what conferences like this are all about?"

His face brightened. "You're right. As usual."

"Can I have that in writing?"

He laughed as if a weight had been lifted. "Where were you this morning? I hoped you'd come to my break-out session, but when you didn't show, I said to myself, 'I think I'm getting the cold shoulder but I guess I de-serve it.'"

"Oh! You haven't heard." It hadn't occurred to me that no one here knew Lindsey had been shot. No one here even knew who she was and wouldn't have recognized the name Dr. Lindsey Scoggin if they *had* heard about a shooting in another part of town. For the first time, it dawned on me that the shooting would have already been all over the TV. In a town like this a shooting, espe-cially when it involved a doctor, would be huge news. But the conference members were, by and large, staying in rooms without TVs. Those who, like Larry, were staying in hotel rooms wouldn't make a connection between the victim and our group even if they heard Lindsey's name.

I started to explain, but Claudia Moss walked in at that moment and Larry looked toward the door, saw her, and waved her over. I felt a tug at my elbow.

"Aunt Dotsy? Come over here. Georgina and I want

to show you something." Georgina stood by a glass display case nestled beneath the tall, mullioned, east window. I got a chill when Georgina greeted me. The last time I'd heard that voice it was coming from the second floor of the faculty wing and it was saying, "If looks could kill, I'd be dead!" I hadn't recognized her voice when I was standing beneath the back windows of the faculty rooms, possibly because I'd never really talked to her long enough to register its tone.

"Look at these guns, Aunt Dotsy. Aren't they great? Georgina says this one was used to kill Catesby in the Gunpowder Plot." I wondered if Claire knew anything about the Gunpowder Plot or if she was merely repeating what Georgina had told her. The glass top of the display case wasn't far below Claire's eye level.

I looked at the one Claire indicated, a long pistol in burnished wood and engraved steel. It lay on a green felt mat with perhaps ten other firearms. All of them looked very old. I wondered how Claire could so casually look at guns while her own mother lay in the hospital suffering from the result of one's use.

"Uncle Harold loves old guns," Georgina said. "He inherited some of these from a former master of the college, and he bought some of them himself. Each one is probably worth thousands."

"Since Harold's field is Anglo-Saxon England, I'd have thought he would collect swords and spears," I said.

Claire spoke up. "I asked Georgina how her Uncle Harold could have these if the United Kingdom doesn't allow people to keep guns and she said gun collections like this are allowed."

"I don't imagine your average criminal would know

how to fire one of these even if he managed to get in here and smash the glass," I said.

"I can shoot," Georgina said, then added, "clay pigeons." She closed one eye and aimed a pretend shot at the ceiling with her forefinger.

Claire's face screwed up.

"Not real pigeons," I told the child. "Clay pigeons are just small discs people use to practice shooting."

"Oh."

When Claire and I left the party, Georgina went with us. I sent Claire up the stairs to check on Caleb and asked Georgina to sit with me on the bench in the middle of the quad. This was the same bench Bram Fitzwaring and I had shared on his last night alive, and the same one Daphne Wetmore and I had shared while we waited for the EMTs to emerge from Bram's room.

The Elizabethan "serving wench" of our first night's party in the Master's Lodgings was gone, replaced by a typical—albeit prettier than average—college student. Georgina wore no makeup. Straight brows above China blue eyes and a tiny space between her two front teeth lent a touch of character to a strictly symmetrical face. Her gaze lingered on the entrance to the staircase into which my young charge had disappeared. "I like Claire, don't you? She's clever for her age."

"Very," I said. "Did she tell you about her mother getting shot this morning?"

"Bloody hell!" Georgina recoiled as if she herself had been hit.

"Her mother was shot this morning, coming out of their flat out near the Radcliffe Hospital." I told her the story and ended with the fact that Lindsey Scoggin was still, as far as I knew, in surgery.

Georgina was clearly shocked at the crime, an anomaly in a town where crime usually meant bicycle theft. "Lindsey Scoggin, you say? That's Claire's mother?"

"Dr. Lindsey Scoggin. Why? Do you know her?" It would be too coincidental, I thought, to have mentioned the shooting to someone who actually knows the victim. Lindsey was new in town and hadn't had time to make more than a few acquaintances.

"The name sounds familiar, but I don't know where I've heard it. Oh, wait! At my friend's house this morning. On the telly! It was all over the news." She slapped her hand against her forehead. "That was Claire's mum?"

Our conversation wandered onto Georgina herself and what she was doing in Oxford. She was a student, she told me, of Keble College and would soon begin her third and final year. Keble was widely regarded as the ugliest of Oxford's forty colleges, she said. Reading chemical engineering, she hoped to work in pharmaceuticals (which she pronounced "pharma-CUTE-icals") upon graduation.

"Speaking of pharmaceuticals," I said, giving the word the American pronunciation, "I take it you know Dr. Bunsen."

Her expression froze for a second. "Why? I mean, I know he's a fellow here, and he's staying for the summer. I see him around."

"You were in his rooms last evening. I heard you because his window was open. I wasn't snooping. I was looking for the back gate and Dr. Bunsen's rooms are directly over that walk. I heard you say, 'If looks could kill, I'd be dead right now.'"

Georgina flashed me an incredulous sneer of the sort you get when someone is desperately buying time. "Last evening? What time last evening?"

"About dusk. About six-thirty."

She stared at her feet for a second before answering. "Right. I was there. I went up to see him because I'm writing a paper on liver enzymes and I need some reliable sources. What I meant…what I was talking about when I said that…was this girl I caught trying to nick my iPhone."

I decided to let that pass as if I believed her. "I gather, from the fact that your last name is Wetmore, it's Harold rather than Daphne to whom you are actually related."

"What's keeping Claire? Do you think we should go up?" Georgina looked toward Staircase Thirteen, then returned to my question. "Right. Uncle Harold and my father are brothers. My parents live out Cowley Road. I'm staying with them until Michaelmas," she said. Michaelmas was Oxford's word for the fall school term.

"Perhaps we'd better check on the kids," I said.

We met Claire clattering down the stairs. "Caleb's crying. Can you come up?"

"What about?"

"He's afraid Mommy's dead."

I lunged ahead of Georgina and clambered up the last two flights. "You have the key, Claire. Open the door."

We found little Caleb lying face up on my bed, tears streaking across his cheeks and into his ears. After a minute of cuddling, he consented to stop crying long enough to talk to Grandma Lettie on the phone.

I called her. Before I handed the phone to Caleb, Lettie gave me the latest news. "She's out of surgery but they've got her in intensive care. They've put a breathing tube down her throat and a drainage tube in her side. They're worried about fluid collecting in her chest. Oh, Dotsy! They let me peek in for one second and I just about passed out! She looks awful."

Hiding my gut reaction, I said, "Caleb is so worried about his mom. He's right here beside me. Could you talk to him and tell him she's going to be fine?"

Caleb took the phone and swung his feet off the side of the bed. He listened, mumbling an occasional, "Yeh," between hiccups and sniffles. Then, he said, "Are you sure? Are you really sure?" Apparently Lettie told him she was sure because Caleb said, "Okay, bye," and handed me the phone.

Lettie said, "That was tough. Does he look all right now?"

I assured her he did.

"Can we come to the hospital now, Grandma?" Claire said, loudly enough for the phone to pick up her words.

"Stall them for an hour, Dotsy. Then bring them out."

"You sure?"

"Give me an hour. I'll figure out how to handle it. Claire is too smart to believe us if we lie to her."

"You got that right!"

While Claire took her little brother downstairs to the toilet, I seized the moment to talk to Georgina. "Lettie needs an hour. After that, I can take the kids to the hospital."

"I can go with you. I can look after the children while you and Mrs. Osgood go in to see their mother."

"Thanks, but we'll be all right. What I do need you to do is figure out how to keep them entertained until it's time to go."

Georgina sat on the side of my bed and stared at the floor for a minute, then said, "Bubbles." She jumped up and stepped across to the door. "I'll meet you in the quad in five minutes."

With no further explanation, she dashed out and down

the stairs. When the children returned, I helped Caleb wash his hands at my sink and gave him a comb for his hair. By the time we emerged into the quad, Georgina was there with a ten-gallon bucket and a long tube attached by rings to a mesh belt. She waved the contraption in a sweeping motion and produced a bubble about the size of a MINI Cooper. It started as a long, caterpillar-like, undulating form, then, picking up rainbows in the afternoon sun, morphed into a sphere. The children were captivated. I was, too.

Georgina showed them how to make their own bubbles by dipping their hands in the soap and glycerin mixture, their fingers curled into okay signs. Conferees walking across the quad to the afternoon session stopped to watch. I asked, "How did you just happen to have this all close to hand?"

"Pure luck," she said. "Last week Uncle Harold, Aunt Daphne and I went to a fete they had at Attwood House. Aunt Daphne's sister is Lady Attwood, and they have more money than God. You should see their house.

"Anyway, it was outdoors on the lawn and they had games for children and adults. That's where I saw this bubble thing and the lady who was in charge had several of these tube contraptions. I bought one from her."

"Is that where you learned to shoot clay pigeons?" I asked.

"Right! But not last week. The Attwoods have a bunch of people out in the autumn for a pheasant hunt, but they have a trap shoot set up for people like me who don't want to kill birds." Georgina made a face, then turned to applaud the bubble Claire had produced. "You should go. Aunt Daphne can get you an invitation. Oh, I guess you won't be here in October."

SIXTEEN

Georgina went with us to the hospital, but left us almost immediately for the research wing. By this time I knew without asking that she and Keith Bunsen were lovers. I knew it by how often she mentioned him, by her tone of voice when she did, and by how often she looked toward his window while we were playing with the children in the quad. I'd never heard either of them mention or even speak to the other when Daphne or Harold Wetmore was present, so I further speculated that this was not a match approved by the family. She told me she was living with her parents for the summer but would share quarters with two girlfriends when school started. "My mum and dad were against it. Thought we'd be bonking every bloke in town. But I'm so knackered most nights after ten hours in the lab, I can't think of taking the bus out Cowley Road. I'm ready to pack it in."

We found Lettie in Lindsey's room, or rather, the room they'd bring Lindsey to when she left the intensive care unit. Lettie grabbed her grandchildren and kissed them. Both kids teared up, but Lettie, stoic as a gladiator, sat them down to talk. She explained about how they would only, because of germs, be allowed to peek in at their mother from a distance. Nothing was wrong. The tubes and equipment they would see were standard for chest wounds. Their mother would be well soon.

"Does she have a breathing tube down her throat?" Claire asked.

Lettie rolled her eyes at me as if to say, *I forgot how smart this kid is.* "Yes, but it doesn't hurt her. They're keeping her asleep until they see there's no fluid left in her chest."

"Medically induced coma," Claire said.

"Is that what Aunt Dotsy told you?" Lettie's tone had a sharp edge.

"That's what doctors call it. I've heard Mom call it that."

With a sigh, Lettie rose and led the children out. Having nothing to read, I studied the view out Lindsey's third-floor window. Long shadows stretched across the grassy fields lined with green hedgerows. I heard a peck on the open door behind me.

It was Chief Inspector Child again. This time he was alone. He asked where Lettie had gone and I told him. "She has Dr. Scoggin's children with her?" He seemed concerned.

"The children really need to see that their mother is still alive. Lettie can handle it."

"Several of Mrs. Scoggin's neighbors have called to say they will stay at the flat and care for the children. You don't have to do all the work yourself."

"I don't mind at all. I'll work it out with Lettie when I have a chance." I sat on the bed and motioned CI Child toward the room's only chair. "Will the bullet they removed tell you what kind of gun it was?"

He paused as if considering how much he should tell me. "The bullet is an unusual caliber. Our lab has it now, but the firearms man says it may be from the sort of gun used by German infantrymen in the Second World War."

"Wow! That would narrow it down, wouldn't it?"

"Not really. Guns have to be registered, you know, and a big percentage of the ones in private hands are old. Collector's items, and a lot of them are German and date from the nineteen forties."

"But you do have records."

"Even if forensics tells us the type of gun and it turns out to be German and from the Second World War, that won't tell us much. It seems like every home in nineteen fifty had at least one weapon swiped from a German soldier, and a lot of them are still around."

Chief Inspector Child hitched up his trouser leg at the knee and cleared his throat. "Mrs. Osgood has told us Lindsey Scoggin was seeing Dr. St. Giles Bell. Do you know him?"

"I met him once. Lindsey took me around the hospital here a couple of days ago, and we went to Bell's lab in the research wing. We talked for a few minutes."

"It's critical that we find out who had a motive for trying to kill Lindsey. So far we have nothing. Dr. Bell, as her frequent social companion, is the most likely suspect, but he was apparently in London at the time of the shooting. Do you know of anyone else? Even if it seems far-fetched, we need to know. Anyone who had argued with her? Anyone who might consider her a rival?"

"A rival for the affections of St. Giles Bell?"

"Any sort of rival. Or anyone who might want to keep her quiet. About anything at all." CI Child was casting his net as widely as possible.

"I'm sorry, no. But there is something. On Sunday I went to the police station myself and made a report."

He sat up. His hand went to his jacket pocket and drew out a small notepad.

"This was on Sunday just after Lindsey and I had toured the hospital together. The day before, one of my fellow conferees, a man named Bram Fitzwaring, was found dead in his room shortly before he was to have addressed the entire conference. His room was on the same staircase as mine but below it. His death was ruled natural and due to hypoglycemia. He was diabetic, and so am I. That's why I think his death *wasn't* natural. He managed to wreck his room before he died. With hypoglycemia he'd have died quietly in his sleep. And several of us who ate the mussels at the party earlier that night had gotten sick. Dr. Bell's research involves a potent shellfish toxin called saxitoxin. In fact, in his lab I actually saw a pan of oysters in water laced with saxitoxin."

Inspector Child marked through a line he'd just written in his notepad, held his scratchings at arm's length, and shook his head. "You are suggesting that Dr. Bell killed Mr. Fitzwaring? With a toxin he keeps in his lab here at the hospital?"

"No. I'm suggesting that someone did. Someone who had access to his lab."

"Such as Lindsey Scoggin?"

"No!" This was not going right. "Of course not. What motive would she have had?"

"What motive would *anyone* have had?" Child made a hand gesture that I took to mean *Go on. You started this.*

"I'm not accusing anyone, but some of the people at the conference didn't think Fitzwaring should be there, and they certainly didn't think he should be delivering a paper on the first day."

"Why not?"

This brought up the whole thing about King Arthur as legend vs. King Arthur as real man. It would have

taken me hours to do the subject justice and to relate all the various comments I'd heard from other conferees. Bram's top two opponents, and, by extension, the most likely suspects, would be Harold Wetmore and Larry Roberts. I made up my mind that I would not, under any circumstances, mention either man's name. Chief Inspector Child could do this dirty work himself.

"Can you be more specific about who didn't want him there?"

"Not really. I heard some comments from people I don't even know."

"Might anyone have had a more personal reason? I have a hard time believing someone could commit murder for purely academic reasons."

"You don't know these people."

"I've lived in Oxford all my life. I believe I do."

"Of course. As for a more personal reason, he and a friend, Mignon Beaulieu, both came here from Glastonbury. They were friends with the owner of The Green Man on the High."

"I know the place."

"I think there's a larger group of friends that might be called New Agers. They're into magic and ancient rites and Celtic stuff."

"Did this companion, Mignon, say anything that led you to think she or anyone else might have wanted to do away with Mr. Fitzwaring?"

"Not at all. No. But there is something going on that I don't understand." I immediately wished I could take that back. If he didn't already have me mentally measured for a straightjacket, he would if I mentioned King Arthur's bones.

"Like what? Explain."

"I can't explain because I don't know. But you could talk to Mignon yourself. She's still in town."

"And you say you reported this on Sunday?"

"At Thames Valley Police Station on St. Aldate's. You can check."

It seemed to me that Child had weighed in his mind the benefits of referring me for counseling versus the possible benefits of treating me like a well-informed consultant, and the latter won. "Is this"—he looked at his notes—"saxitoxin, a chemical that would show up in autopsy?"

"If a fluid sample from the body was chemically analyzed, it might, but Fitzwaring's body has already been cremated."

"The body was autopsied *before* it was cremated, I'm sure."

"Yes, but the medical examiner put down hypoglycemia as cause of death."

"You don't understand. Fluid samples are sent to a lab. The lab would have no reason to test for a strange poison like saxitoxin. They'd only test for common things like oxycodone. But they don't throw these samples away immediately. They hold on to them for a time."

"You're right! I hadn't thought of that. His blood could be tested *again*."

LETTIE AND THE children returned, somber and subdued. She said, "I'm going to take Claire and Caleb home and see that they're taken care of for the night. They tell me they'll be all right if a neighbor stays with them, as long as they can call me anytime they want."

I told her I'd be glad to stay with them, and their new friend, Georgina, had also volunteered. Georgina must have been waiting out in the hall, because at that moment she stepped through the door and confirmed my words.

While Georgina talked to the children, Lettie pulled me aside. "Before I took the children to the ICU, I worked with the staff down there to rearrange the equipment around Lindsey and hide some of it under the bed. All the kids saw was the breathing apparatus." She put the back of her hand up to the side of her mouth and added, "I also brushed her hair and added some blusher to her cheeks."

"They let you do that?"

"I explained how important it was."

SEVENTEEN

ON THE TAXI ride back to town, I reviewed the events of the last few hours in my mind. When Lettie said the children would be well cared for by Lindsey's neighbors, I felt relieved because I needed the evening to follow up on questions that the day's events had brought up. Why was Mignon still here? If the Grey Lady was actually Bumps McAlister, wife of the owner of The Green Man, did that mean Mignon and Bram were also in on the stunt? What about my second sighting of the Grey Lady? Was it Bumps again? This was probably not important, so I reminded myself to stick to the important matters, the death of Bram Fitzwaring and the shooting of Lindsey Scoggin.

Were the two related? I couldn't see how, but I knew they were. The connections were tenuous at best. Shellfish, poison, Staircase Thirteen. Shellfish in Dr. Bell's lab and shellfish served at the cocktail party. Lindsey's mother and Fitzwaring both staying on Staircase Thirteen. Fitzwaring, a participant in a study conducted by a man who lives only yards from Staircase Thirteen and has a lab only feet from Dr. Bell's lab where saxitoxin, potent shellfish poison, is stored in quantity. None of this connected up but somehow, taken all together, there were too many threads not to indicate some sort of cloth.

I knew Lettie had my cell phone number, but I drew my phone from my purse and called her to make certain.

The children were settled in for the night, and a neighbor they trusted was with them. Lettie was just climbing into Lindsey's rental car to return to the hospital when she answered my call. Remembering Lettie's poor driving record in countries where they drive on the left side of the road, I cautioned her. We'd had a wreck at a round-about in Scotland that resulted in Lettie driving a pencil through the roof of her mouth.

I browsed through the contacts on my phone, then tapped on the photos. I hadn't taken any recently, and the first ones I saw were those I took that day in Bram's room after they'd taken his body away. They gave me a little shiver. I shielded the phone display from the fading afternoon light and saw a picture of Bram's open closet door, another of his bare bed frame strewn with clothes and shoes, and a third of the tea tray on his table. Beside the tray stood a plastic water bottle. I recalled he had been using it as a sharps container. How many used syringes did it hold? I couldn't see clearly because of the label on the bottle.

I expanded the photo on the display and zeroed in on the bottle. Three. I thought I could make out the barrels of three syringes resting, needle-end down and at varying angles, in the bottle. That would be about right, I thought. He arrived at St. Ormond's that day and may have taken an injection of insulin about that time. Another before dinner or, more likely, before the cocktail party. Then the third—when? Before bed? No. He was showing signs of hypoglycemia then because he had eaten nothing at the dinner, and must have realized the situation because there were cookie wrappers, tea bags, and empty sugar packets in his trash, I recalled. He wouldn't have taken another dose of insulin under those circumstances.

Unless he was confused.

I know too well the confusion brought on by low blood sugar. But he would have had to go back down the stairs to the fridge beside the bathroom on the first floor, retrieve a syringe, and return to his room. He had followed me up the stairs and left me at the level on which his room was located, so he would have had to go *back* down to get his insulin and, given the state he was in at the time, he couldn't have made it.

I thought. I couldn't be sure.

I had to find that plastic bottle. Where was it now? Our scout would have taken it away when she cleaned the room. Then what? As soon as the cab let me out in front of the college gate, I flew in and asked the porter, "What do you do with sharps?" This made no sense to him, of course, so I explained.

He nodded and told me, "We have a container where the scouts put sharp objects like needles. Once every week or so, the city picks it up and leaves us an empty one."

"When was the last time it was picked up?"

"I don't know. To tell the truth, they don't really pick it up that often. More like once a month, I'd say."

What luck! "Where is the container?"

"They keep it in the broom cupboard…" He pointed to a wall of the Porter's Lodge where I could see no door, then realized he was indicating a broom closet you had to enter from the quad. "Who is your scout?" he asked.

"Patricia," I said. "But I can't wait until she comes in tomorrow. This is urgent. Don't you have a key? Please?"

He mumbled and fumbled around with the papers on the small ledge on his side of the window. "We're not to mess around with the sharps container. Regulations."

"I just want to see it." Not true. I wanted to open it, but one thing at a time. The porter grabbed a key and led me into the quad where he stopped at the first door on the left and opened it. Inside, scores of brooms, buckets, rags, and the distinctive smell of dirty mops. A bright red sharps bin sat on the floor near the back wall.

"There it is, but it's against the law to open it."

"May I pick it up and shake it?"

I took his silence as permission. The bin looked large enough to hold several weeks', if not months', worth of sharp instruments discarded in a place like this. I picked it up and shook it, listening.

"It's empty."

Two possibilities. The city had picked up hazardous waste in the last three days or our scout hadn't put the syringes in the bin at all. I'd have to wait now and talk to her tomorrow morning. I prayed she'd remember what she did with them—and that she'd tell me. Given the black market for used syringes among addicts, I couldn't count on it.

Climbing the stairs as far as Mignon's room I knocked, expecting no answer, but she surprised me by opening the door. "Would you like to go to dinner with me?" I asked.

This was the night before the end of the conference, and I figured the dinner would be a good one. I hoped they'd have pheasant again. Mignon seemed glad of the invitation. "I was thinking of going out to eat, but this is already paid for, isn't it?"

"Certainly. Why waste food we've already bought?"

After a quick change and freshen-up, Mignon and I walked to the dining hall together. I was wearing my last clean blouse and Mignon sported the long, blue, crushed-velvet dress she'd worn the first night.

Before we walked in, Mignon stopped me with a hand on my arm. "I need to tell you something."

We shifted sideways, away from the dining room doors, so diners wouldn't have to swerve around us. I didn't want to miss a word of whatever Mignon had to tell me. She looked into my eyes so directly and intently it was a bit uncomfortable.

"You were right about the bones," she said in a hoarse whisper. "About us having Arthur's and Guinevere's bones. That TVRA you saw on Bram's notes? It stands for Thames Valley Radiocarbon Accelerator. They do carbon dating. They've tested the bones Bram found in Sharpham and they date to four hundred fifty a.d., give or take, so we know they are Arthur's and Guinevere's. The size of that leg bone, they figure, would have made the man nearly seven feet tall! Who else could it be? The problem now is that I don't have money to pay for the lab work, and they won't give me the bones until I pay them. They ran five tests and I owe them a thousand pounds."

"How did Bram plan to pay for it?"

"He had the money in cash, but I don't know where he put it after he got here. He must have hidden it, but I've searched his room with a fine-tooth comb."

"What about Bram's mother? Did you ask her?"

"She would've laughed at me." Mignon made an ugly face. "I've put the problem to my friends and they're with me. We're trying to raise the money, but until we do, I can't leave Oxford. I can't leave the bones of our immortal king with people who don't know or care about their sacred power!"

I passed over the oxymoron, *bones of our immortal*

king, and asked, "Where in Sharpham did Bram find these bones? How did he know where to look?"

"Well now, that's for later. It'll all come clear in good time."

She was refusing to tell me! Saving it for a press conference, I didn't doubt. Or a book deal.

"But I know you're on our side. You're the one who got Bram on the speaker's list to begin with! It's only a thousand pounds. I'm sure you paid more than that for your flight over here. Could you? I hate to ask but I don't know who else to turn to."

She was refusing to tell me where they found the bones and asking me to get them out of hock for her, in the same breath! "Excuse me," I said. "I need to go to my room." I backed away from her. "And I wasn't the one who put Bram on the program. I knew nothing about it until I read it that morning."

I left by the north gate of the college and tramped down to the Pret a Manger on Cornmarket Street for something to eat. I resented Mignon's forcing me to miss the last dinner at St. Ormond's and realized that hadn't been her plan, but the nerve of her! Refusing to tell me where they'd found the bones while asking me for money to pay for their tests. From a purely practical standpoint, I'd have been smarter to swallow my fury and try to get more out of her during dinner, but I hadn't, so that was that.

I ATE IN my room, phoned Lettie, and found there was no news about Lindsey, then gathered my things for a trip to the shower. Once there, I draped my robe over the dormant radiator and went into the toilet niche in an L off the shower space. The window was wide open, letting in a cool breeze, and I heard distant voices, probably diners going to or from the SCR. Again, I cursed Mignon Beaulieu for making me miss not only dinner but the last night our group would gather in the SCR. I imagined there'd be a lively discussion tonight, now that all the papers and workshops were over. A masculine guffaw drifted across the lawn and through the window. I could still go to the SCR. There'd be plenty of wine and it might be the last time I'd see some of these people.

A huge shadow, a human head and torso, undulated along the uneven stones on the opposite side of the quad. Its shadow legs stretched across the lawn to a spot not far from my window. I stood on my tiptoes and looked down, past the wisteria vine clinging to the wall below, and saw Keith Bunsen ambling past no more than five feet away from me. Actually I saw his head, his lower body obscured by tendrils and leaves. I started to call to him, realized I was in the toilet, and decided a shoutout would be potentially embarrassing. I stepped out and down a few steps to the staircase entrance.

By this time Keith was in the arched entrance at the main gate. The shadows, I saw, were made by a floodlight attached to the side of the building at a height that played shadows of passersby across the lawn and onto the north wing of the quad. Returning to the shower room, I got a flash of déjà vu. I'd seen the same shadow phenomenon a few nights ago, but I'd spotted no one I knew.

I intended to go over the day's events before I fell asleep. So many new pieces had to be fit into a picture that seemed just beyond my reach. It seemed as if the whole thing would come clear if I were only a little bit smarter. As if one or two more observations, correctly interpreted, would bring this whole mess into focus, and make me slap my head. *Why didn't I see it sooner?* I climbed into bed, clicked off the bedside lamp, and reviewed two facts I thought were relevant. That Bram Fitzwaring was in Keith Bunsen's diabetes study, and that he was in the control group, not the experimental group. Keith was worried about losing more subjects in that latter group, because the math—I recalled his mentioning the *old chi-square monster*—would go wonky, even if most of the remaining subjects were doing well. But what about losing one more person in the control group? My own math skills didn't include chi-squares, but I'd heard other graduate students back home refer to the test. Students whose work involved statistics—mine didn't—had to use a certain formula to find out if the results of their work meant anything.

I sat up, switched my light back on, and pulled my iPad from under my bed. Typing "Chi-square" into Google, I found a site with a truly scary algebraic equation—the chi-square formula—but scrolling down a bit farther I came to a simple little chart where you could plug in numbers and it would do the math for you. It required two numbers each for two different groups (control and experimental.) I played with it until I discovered that smaller numbers in the experimental column could drive the results into insignificance, but smaller numbers in the control column as well could drive it back to significance.

In other words, it was possible that a researcher could see years' worth of hard work go down the drain by the loss of a single person from his test group, but it was also possible to fix the problem by eliminating one person from the control group.

That suggested an ugly new possibility.

MY FIRST THOUGHT upon waking Wednesday morning was that my plane home was leaving in a day and a half. Lettie, of course, wouldn't leave until Lindsey was either recovered from her gunshot wound or…well. That didn't bear thinking about. King Arthur's bones, if they were Arthur's bones, would be left in the hands of people who would do God knows what with them. Charge admission to see them? Throw them back to "The Lady in the Lake"? I couldn't imagine, but I knew Mignon Beaulieu wouldn't hand them over to history scholars and archaeologists for proper study.

The morning was one of those bright but misty ones that brought Matthew Arnold's "dreaming spires" to mind. From my tiny third-floor window, I looked out across domes and steeples that had changed little in hundreds of years. I decided to take a walk before breakfast. This time I went south off the High, down Magpie Lane past Oriel College, and, as on my last early morning foray, met John Fish, the ghost tour guide, trudging up past Merton College. I wondered if he ever slept or if he wandered the streets all night. I turned and joined him.

He'd already heard about the shooting of a visiting doctor at the Radcliffe Hospital. He knew the victim was going out with St. Giles Bell. He didn't know she was the daughter of my best friend.

"Oh." He stopped and looked at me. "I'm sorry to hear that. Have they arrested the bastard?"

"Bell? He has an alibi. He was in London."

"They'd better look close at that alibi. He's a slick one. He'll get people to lie for him."

"Maybe I'll learn more today."

He told me more about the circumstances surrounding the death of Bell's wife earlier that year, while I struggled to separate rumor from fact, and fact from newspaper speculations. As John talked, I found myself looking in vain for anything that would exclude an injection of saxitoxin as a reason why the poor woman fell down the stairs. One of the poison's first effects, I knew from my recent reading, is the loss of muscular coordination.

"Are you sure," I asked, "that your friend only did her Grey Lady act one time?"

"Bumps McAlister? Sure. Why would she have done it twice? It was hard enough to talk her into doing it once. She weren't keen on the idea." He stopped and poked at something on the sidewalk with his skull-headed cane. "Thought somebody might chase her down and hurt her."

"Bumps is the wife of the owner of The Green Man?"

"Right."

"But Daphne Wetmore was in on it? Did Harold Wetmore know about it?"

"I doubt it. He'd probably have put paid to the whole thing if he knew. At first Mrs. Wetmore didn't like the idea, either. Thought it would be *unscholarly*. Then she thought better of it and decided it might be just the thing to get Harold's conference off to a great start."

"So it was your idea. For publicity, was it?"

"For fun. Just to see what those stuffed shirts would do if they saw a ghost."

We were almost back to the High. As I looked ahead through the narrow gap that was Magpie Lane, I saw the Grey Lady again. "Whoa!" I ran as fast as I could up the lane and turned left to catch her. "Excuse me?"

She stopped and turned. It was Georgina Wetmore and she was wearing a plain old black anorak with the hood up. In the misty morning light and in the narrow space at the entrance to the lane, I realized, she had appeared fuzzy and rather ghost-like. She said, "Good morning! Going to St. Ormond's? Me, too."

John Fish remained behind, none the wiser for my silly mistake. He called out to me, "I'll see you later."

AT BREAKFAST I sat with Claudia Moss. Some members of our group were already rolling luggage out the gates. Claudia and I talked, mostly about Larry Roberts. I didn't feel comfortable with this because I knew Larry's wife personally and, to my knowledge, neither of them was considering a separation or divorce, so this thing between him and Claudia was simply an extramarital fling. Funny thing was, Claudia was perfectly okay with that. She knew Larry was married and, as she calmly drizzled honey on her toast, mentioned that she didn't plan to ever see Larry again. "I'm taking the train back to London and I may not see him before I leave. If I do miss him, give him my best, all right?"

Just like that? As if she'd no more than had dinner with him! Am I that out of touch with the times?

"My PhD is still in limbo," I said. "Larry's last words on the subject were, 'You can forget that PhD,' but since yesterday at the Wetmores' tea we've sort of made up."

"Don't worry about it. He was in a terrible state earlier. Once you're home, it'll all come round right."

"I still don't get why he was *in* such a terrible state. He's normally laid back. At this whole conference it's been as if he was out of control. Totally beyond reasoning."

"It's Harold Wetmore."

"What?"

"It's Harold. If Harold hadn't been here, Larry would have been a different person."

"Sorry. I don't get it."

"You know how people are. We all have someone whose approval we require above all others. Someone we have to impress." Claudia paused for a sip of her tea. "Don't you have someone who lurks in your brain? I call it my inner audience. I don't often admit this, but mine is a roommate I had at Cambridge." She paused again, and I had enough sense not to interrupt. "She was always better at everything, her parents were classier, her beaus were handsomer, her clothes were trendier, her hair was…!" Claudia waved the memory away with one hand and lowered her voice. Others were turning to look. "Anyway. However many times I tell myself it's quite silly, I can't change the fact that she's always there in my head and I'm playing to her. My audience."

I thought about it. Was she right? Who was my inner audience? Chet Lamb? Much as I deplored the thought, I feared he was. Always there, watching, while I show him I'm doing great without him. "So you're saying Harold Wetmore is Larry Roberts's audience?"

"Larry studied under Harold when he was a student here. He worked like hell to support his ideas in debates with Harold, but Harold bested him every time. He knew so much more. Of course! Harold had been at it longer. Now Larry is more like Harold's equal in that they both have good posts at good universities, but he's still trying to prove himself to Harold and he always will be."

"And Harold hates the romantics who perpetuate the myths of English history."

"Exactly. And Larry tries to out-hate Harold. If Harold is outraged that some of the Glastonbury crowd wormed their way into our conference, Larry is doubly outraged."

"I wish we had time to know each other better. If you're ever in America, look me up."

"I won't look you up unless you promise you won't tell Larry."

ON MY WAY back to my room, I met Daphne, scurrying across the lawn like a little mouse. "Will you be needing help moving your luggage out, Dr. Lamb?"

I told her I wasn't leaving yet and, at any rate, could manage my own luggage.

"This poor woman who was shot yesterday. Harold tells me she's Mrs. Osgood's daughter? How is she?"

At first I was taken aback, then realized all Oxford was probably talking about it. Would it be in this morning's *Daily Mail*? "I haven't talked to them this morning but I'll call in a few minutes."

"Give them my best, will you? And tell Mrs. Osgood the room here is hers for as long as she needs it."

"Thank you. I'll tell her." It hadn't occurred to me that the rooms here might be unavailable past the time for which we'd rented them. "Oh! If you see Georgina would you ask her if she wants to go out to see Dr. Scoggin's children again? She was so nice to help me with them yesterday."

Daphne looked puzzled. "I'll give her the message."

Of course, Georgina would have talked to the Wetmores about the shooting if she'd seen them. I knew Daphne wouldn't have seen her niece this morning because the young woman didn't go to the Master's Lodgings after we came in. She went to Keith Bunsen's apartment.

MY PHONE BUZZED in my pocket as I was opening the door to my room. It was Lettie. "My God, Dotsy! You're not going to believe this! But first, Lindsey is awake and it looks like everything's okay. No fluid in her chest and her lungs are in good shape."

"Oh, I'm so glad!"

"But after she got her bearings, and yesterday started coming back to her, she wanted to talk to the police. She knows who shot her. It was Georgina!"

EIGHTEEN

THE NEXT FEW minutes were like standing in a wind tunnel. Lettie was talking in one of my ears while my brain struggled to process what I thought I knew about Georgina. How wrong could I possibly be? Fact was, I didn't know anything about her for certain. That she and Keith Bunsen were on intimate terms was an assumption based on the voice I heard through his open window. I'd had an *aha* moment an hour ago when I mistook her for the Grey Lady. I'd also figured she was the phantom I chased across the quad and that, rather than hiding in the little stairwell by the back gate, she had slipped into Staircase Ten and up to Keith's rooms.

Lettie was still talking. I made her repeat everything.

"Lindsey says she found out Georgina—she didn't know her last name—was also having an affair with St. Giles Bell and that's why she ran out of the hospital and came home crying. Lindsey, that is. I told you she came home in bad shape. Well, it seems that Lindsey went down to St. Giles's office—the one he keeps in the research wing—and found an eleven by fourteen photo in St. Giles's top desk drawer. It was signed, 'All my love forever, Georgina.' She says she's seen Georgina hanging around there a couple of times but never even wondered what she was doing there."

"Wait, Lettie. This is the same area where Keith Bunsen has his lab."

"Who?" I started to explain, but Lettie's next statement sent me off in another direction. "The police are trying to find Georgina right now. They found out her last name is Wetmore—isn't that a coincidence?—and they're on their way to her house."

"Her house?"

"Her parents' house. She still lives at home."

I ended the call and tried to figure out what to do next. Georgina was probably still at Keith's apartment across the quad, unless I had this whole thing figured wrong. If she was, I needed to warn her. If she wasn't, was she still here at the college? Where else might she have gone after we walked in together? What if it was true? Could it be?

I should trust the police to do their job.

That, bottom line, was the simplest and easiest way to proceed. Trust the police. Could it be true? Could Georgina possibly have been the shooter? I didn't know her that well. She told me she could shoot. There's a case full of guns in her uncle's library. Lindsey's neighbor told the police they saw someone, possibly a woman in a dark anorak, leaving the scene. As I made more and more connections, I began to suspect Georgina's motive for being so damned friendly with the children.

And there I sat, on the side of my bed, agonizing over a hundred unanswerable questions, my phone still clasped in my hand, while the police barged into St. Ormond's and arrested Georgina Wetmore.

I emerged into the quad to the sight of Georgina Wetmore, two policemen and a policewoman leaving through the front gate. As soon as the door within the gate closed behind them, a dozen porters, scouts, and college guests emerged from their various holes in the surrounding stone, questions on their faces. Poor Daphne Wetmore stumbled out of the passage that led from the Master's Garden and leaned against a wall, her shoulders heaving with her sobs. I ran over to her, but others reached her first.

"They think she killed that doctor," I heard her say. Then, in bits and pieces, "in for questioning," and "don't know," and "I tell you *I don't know*! They wouldn't tell me anything!"

I flew back to my room for my purse, then out the front gate to hail a cab.

I BOUGHT A vase of flowers on the ground floor of the hospital and took an elevator up to Lindsey's room. Lettie, with Caleb on her lap, tried to rise and offer me her chair, but I waved the offer aside. Lindsey thanked me for the flowers and pointed to the windowsill. She looked pretty good considering what she'd been through. Claire stood at her mother's head, one hand under the pillow, caressing the sheet, as if it were an extension of Lindsey herself.

"They may let her go home today," Lettie said.

Caleb pumped his little fists.

"Did Mom tell you the latest?" Lindsey said.

I nodded, but glanced at both children. Did they know? How awful for them to discover yesterday's playmate was today's suspect.

Lindsey answered that question by telling the children to run downstairs and get her a newspaper. Claire took a five-pound note from her mother's purse and joined Caleb in the hall. "They don't know," Lindsey said.

"I'm glad. Did Lettie tell you Georgina came out here

with us yesterday? She and the children had a great time blowing bubbles in the quad."

"How very sweet." Lindsey's voice oozed sarcasm. "I wonder if the police have found her yet."

"They have. She was at St. Ormond's when they came in and told her they wanted her to go with them and help them with their inquiries."

"That's what they say when they really mean they're arresting you," Lettie said.

Lindsey took a deep breath, winced, and used her elbows to adjust herself against the pillow. "I take it that Georgina and the Wetmores of St. Ormond's are actually related. I was wondering about that. I only just learned her last name an hour ago."

I had to think. Lettie hadn't, as far as I knew, ever met Georgina before yesterday and I didn't think I had mentioned her last name. She sat forward in her chair, banging one fist on its arm. "The nerve of that hussy! She befriended the children to get closer to Lindsey and find out what was going on. Probably couldn't stand it that the shot didn't kill her. I wouldn't put it past her to sneak a gun in here and finish the job."

"Lettie! We don't know anything yet, so don't jump to conclusions. In fact, I've been thinking Georgina was in love with someone else entirely." I glanced at Lindsey, then back to Lettie. "And nobody says 'hussy' anymore."

Lettie scowled and picked at the arm of her chair.

"By the way, has St. Giles been in to see you?" I asked the young woman in the bed.

"I should hope not! I don't ever want to see him again. I was told he called the nurse's station on this floor to check on me." Lindsey gasped. She tried to cough but couldn't, and the effort contorted her face. "Lucky for him, he was in London at the time. If he'd been here, he'd have been a suspect. The police wanted to know all about how long we'd been together, and the only neighbor who thinks he saw the shooter said he *thinks* it was a woman, but he isn't sure."

I shifted my vase of flowers to one side and rested my butt on the windowsill. "Lindsey, how much do you know about St. Giles's late wife?"

"She died. Fell down the stairs at their home."

"The police apparently had their doubts about it being an accident."

Lettie's eyes widened. "Where did you hear this?"

"From a perhaps not totally unimpeachable source, but it would be easy enough to get back issues of the newspaper and read about it."

BACK AT ST. ORMOND'S, I realized I'd missed the morning session titled, "Elizabethan Poetry: Faeries, Fiends, and Star-Crossed Lovers," but by now I was resigned to purchasing the CDs of the meetings I'd missed. I hoped to at least make it to the general session this afternoon.

I tracked down our scout, Patricia, and found her in East Quad broom closet sharing a cigarette with a man from the kitchen. I asked her about the plastic bottle with used syringes left in room four after its occupant died. She acted as if she remembered, but I doubted she was telling the truth.

"We always put sharps in the sharps bin," she told me.

"That one?" I pointed to the red container behind her left foot.

She mumbled something, bent over, and picked it up. Shaking it, she said, "They musta made the pickup already."

"Are you sure you put it in there?"

"Not the whole bottle. Just the syringes."

"And you would have put the bottle, where?"

"In the reg'lar trash."

"When is that picked up?"

"Thursdays."

"Tomorrow."

At this, the man in the kitchen apron stepped forward and pointed the still-burning butt end of their shared cigarette at me. "Hey, if you got a problem with trash, you take it up with the porter. We's on our break in here."

"Awfully sorry," I said. "But this would have happened on Saturday. It should be still here."

"Talk to the porter."

Having been summarily dismissed from the broom closet, I did talk to the porter, who told me the trash bins were kept inside the north gate. This took me back to the arched gateway where I'd found the sunken stairs I suspected the Grey Lady of hiding in. I now saw that it contained an array of trash bins in a variety of colors: blue, brown, and green, and the smell in this tight space below the cobblestone floor was foul. Did I really want to do this?

I started with the brown bins and found they held garden cuttings. These seemed to have been recently filled and didn't smell bad. The blue ones held bags of general trash and smelled awful. I simply didn't have the stomach to open any of those. Green, I found, was for the recyclables: glass, plastics, paper, and, with a few exceptions, these were fairly clean. I grabbed a sturdy limb from one of the brown bins and stirred. Of the two recycle bins, one contained nothing but empty wine bottles, their liquid dregs now aging from alcohol to vinegar. In the other recycle bin, I found the plastics but after several minutes of determined stirring found no plastic water bottles. I gave up.

Trudging back across the quad toward my room, I decided I'd try a call to the local hazardous waste folks, then I had one more idea. I'd been awakened one night— I couldn't remember which night—by loud noises from Sycamore Lane beneath my window. Clinks and clanks that could have been someone dumping trash into the large bin I'd seen in a cubbyhole on street level. But the scouts didn't work after five o'clock. Still, what if a scout had discovered something left undone? Something that needed to be disposed of without going back into the college? Something perhaps squirreled away for possible resale or reuse, then reconsidered? It was a million to one shot, but my OCD tendencies compel me to finish what I start. Wipe that last bit of marker from the whiteboard. Eat that last Cheerio. This was, I believe, the first time in my life it's paid off.

I walked out the front gate, turned right into Sycamore Lane, and found the large bin. It stood in a space that might have once been an entrance to the East Quad. In this bin, the contents weren't neatly separated as they were at the north gate. I swung the lid open and stepped back, bowled over by the smell. I simply couldn't rummage through this mess.

Instead I backed out, closed my eyes long enough to let them adapt to the gloom inside the bin, and took a deep breath. I held the bin lid open and looked as long as I could hold my breath, then returned to the lane for another breath. It only took three trips before I saw a plastic water bottle nestled into the right front corner, as if someone had carefully tucked it there.

Inside the bottle, its plastic cap still intact, stood three small syringes.

NINETEEN

I SHOWERED AND changed clothes before I headed for the police station. The smell of the dumpster clung to me like greasy fog. I zipped the water bottle into a plastic bag and tucked it inside my purse. At the station on St. Aldate's, I spoke through the bulletproof glass partition to a duty officer I'd never seen before. I didn't know if this was good or bad because, although the reason for my visit made little sense when presented, cold, to an uninitiated ear, it also enabled me to momentarily escape the nutcase label I'd have gotten from anyone who'd seen me before. I asked to speak to Chief Inspector Child or to Detective Sergeant Gunn.

"They're both in interview at the moment. Can you speak to someone else? Is it about a charge you wish to file?" This woman looked about sixty. Her wide leather belt cut deeply into the fat around her waist and looked positively painful.

"It's actually about a crime I've already reported. I have some evidence to give them."

"Evidence?" She paused a minute, as if this was a different matter. "Let me get someone to help you."

She disappeared into a large room I could see only partially through the glass partition. A minute later, another uniformed officer popped through a side door and waved me through. He led me to a cluttered cubicle with a chest-high partition, no different from a dozen others I saw lining the walls on three sides of the room.

"I talked to Chief Inspector Child yesterday at the hospital. The gunshot victim, Lindsey Scoggin, is the daughter of a friend of mine." This established a certain level of credibility. I knew someone who knew someone who was a bona fide victim. "But Mr. Child and I also talked about the death of a man at the conference I'm attending. That's why I asked to see him today. I'm afraid this will all sound a bit strange to you, but Chief Inspector Child knows the background."

"I'm listening."

I described the death of Bram Fitzwaring as succinctly as I could, but it was becoming a long story. I felt I had to mention at least a couple of motives and a couple of circumstances that led me, a person of sound mind, to suspect his death wasn't natural. When I got to my suspicion that the causative agent may have been saxitoxin, I let the name of St. Giles Bell slip.

The officer stiffened as if he'd heard a fire alarm. "St. Giles Bell? Dr. St. Giles Bell from the Radcliffe Hospital?"

"Yes."

"So how does this… I mean, where's the connection to the shooting of Lindsey Scoggin?"

"That's the million dollar question, isn't it?"

Now I got the look reserved for nutcases.

"I know it all sounds crazy. That's why I really wanted to talk to Chief Inspector Child. But, look. How about you just don't worry about it? How about taking the bottle full of syringes I have in my purse, mark it however you're supposed to do, and take my name and number."

"Bottle full of syringes?"

As I searched for a better way to explain, Chief Inspector Child himself walked past. "Oh, speak of the devil!" I said. Not, perhaps, the best way to greet a policeman.

He stopped, shook my hand, and asked what I was doing there.

While explaining, I drew the plastic one-gallon bag containing the plastic bottle from my purse. "From the dumpster just outside St. Ormond's. I've touched the outside of the bottle but I haven't removed the cap."

"Have you touched the cap?"

I had to think. Had I? If I had, my fingerprints would be on the cap, and he wouldn't know if I'd messed with the contents or not. "No. I haven't."

He handed the bag to the officer I'd been talking to. "Bag and tag this. Leave it in the bag it's in and put the whole thing in an evidence bag."

I breathed a sigh of relief. I would have given anything to ask him if they were still questioning Georgina, but he wouldn't have told me anyway.

"Phone call, sir," the woman from the front desk stepped around her partition and announced. She directed this announcement to Child.

"I'll call them back," he said.

"I think you should take it now, sir. It's Lord Attwood." She spoke the name as if it should be preceded by trumpets. "He wants to report a missing gun."

CHIEF INSPECTOR CHILD took the call at the front desk, and I stood no chance of hearing any part of the conversation. But Lord Attwood was the brother-in-law of the Wetmores, and he was reporting a missing gun. I'm not one of those people who say *I don't believe in coincidence*. I do. Coincidences happen every day, but the coincidence here was not that Lindsey was shot yesterday and Lord Attwood reports a missing gun today. The coincidence was that I was here when the call came in. I had no doubt that the former two events were connected. But how?

I dawdled, asking to use the bathroom before they ushered me out, but I only caught one more glimpse of Chief Inspector Child as he dashed through a door on the opposite end of the big room.

I raced back to St. Ormond's, making calls as I went and letting oncoming pedestrians worry about the dodging. First I called Lettie and got the main number for the Radcliffe Hospital. I played touch-tone roulette with the recording until I connected with Keith Bunsen's lab in the research wing. An assistant told me he wasn't in. I talked her into giving me his cell phone number. No luck again. I left a voice message.

SCREWING UP MY courage at the front gate, I turned right at the Porter's Lodge, continued around to the garden entrance of the Master's Lodgings, and banged the hefty brass knocker. Daphne Wetmore herself answered, barefoot and wearing leotards and T-shirt. "Come in, Dr. Lamb. Lovely to see you. You've caught me at my yoga."

"Sorry. I can come back later."

"Of course not. Do have a seat." She padded over to one wall of the sitting room, where she punched a button on a small device, and the soothing white noise I hadn't noticed until then stopped. "My sister introduced me to yoga. We took classes together. I find it helps manage stress."

"Your sister, Lady Attwood?" I tried to guess where Daphne would sit so we would be at a comfortable talking distance apart, and decided on a well-worn slip-covered chair. "I'm worried about Georgina."

"You're worried! Why do you think I'm doing yoga in the middle of the day? I promised Harold I wouldn't go to the police station. I talked to Georgina's mother on the phone, but they don't know any more than I do. Harold is busy with the closing ceremonies for the conference, and says he can only do one thing at a time. Says he'll worry about Georgina when the ceremony is over." Daphne curled up into a scattering of throw pillows on one end of a sofa, her bare feet beneath her.

"I came out this morning when they were taking her away," I said. "I heard you say, 'They think she killed that doctor.'"

"They think she *shot* her," Daphne clarified. "The woman isn't dead, and I heard they're letting her go home soon."

"That's why I was taking care of her children yesterday. We came to your tea."

"You did? I'm sorry. I was so busy, I didn't notice everyone who was here. Did I talk to you at all?"

"I don't think so, but Georgina was here, too. She helped me take care of the children, and she even went out to the hospital with us."

"Wait! One thing at a time! Are you telling me Georgina actually visited the woman who was shot? In her hospital room?"

"No. Lindsey was still unconscious at that time in the ICU."

Daphne paused a minute. "Okay. Here's what happened this morning. Harold and I had just finished breakfast when Georgina came in. I gave her a cup of coffee, and then Harold had to leave. We talked for a few minutes, about nothing in particular. Then she got a phone call from the police and they said they needed to talk to her. Asked her where she was. Georgina told me she had no idea what it was about, but almost immediately the police were at the door. They asked her if she knew Dr.... Sorry. What is her name?"

"Lindsey Scoggin."

"Georgina said yes, that's the woman who got shot. She said, 'I don't know her but I've met her children.' They said they needed to talk to her and it would be better to do it at the station. I said I'd leave them alone if they wanted to talk here, and they asked her where she was Monday night. She said she was at home. That's when they told her she'd have to go to the police station with them."

"And you haven't heard anything since?"

"No."

"Georgina told the police she was at home Monday night?"

"Yes." Daphne's eyebrows knitted. "Wait. When I talked to her mother, she said the police asked her where Georgina was Monday night and she told them she had spent the night with girlfriends."

"Uh-oh."

"Uh-oh, is right!" Daphne's hand flew to her mouth. "Why didn't I notice that? If the police had already talked to her parents, they *knew* someone was lying. As you Americans say, 'Houston, we have a problem.'"

"Daphne, I may be stepping out of line here, but I suspect Georgina is involved with Keith Bunsen."

"Not possible! Keith is a dear, but he's close to fifty and a nerd as well."

"I've seen how they look at each other."

"You mean how Keith looks at her? *Every* man looks at her as if he'd like to eat her up."

"I could be wrong."

"Her parents would go ballistic. He's more than twice her age!"

"What would they say to a charge of attempted murder?"

Daphne paused, and I figured she was letting my words sink in. This was rather a lot to take in all at once. "Do you think she might have been with Keith Monday night, and she's lying to protect him?"

"It's worth considering."

"But Dr. Scoggin told the police…"

"I don't think Lindsey actually saw the shooter. I think she's reacting to a photo she found in Dr. Bell's desk."

"Dr. Bell?"

"St. Giles Bell. He also does research at the Radcliffe."

"At the hospital?"

"Yes."

"And right after that she was shot? Where? In the parking lot? Surely not inside the hospital."

"No. She wasn't shot at the hospital. She was shot the next morning, coming out of her flat. Apparently, the shooter was waiting for her. Lindsey lives in one of those new developments north of the hospital."

"Regency Flats?"

"Belle Glen, it's called."

"Same difference. Depressing little things, with their cheap little fake Art Deco doors and their postage-stamp yards. I wish city council would…" Daphne turned, as if she'd heard someone at the door, and surprised me with, "Do you mind if I call you Dorothy? Dr. Lamb seems so formal now."

"Everyone calls me Dotsy—Daphne." I'd given up explaining that I wasn't a doctor. Her mind seemed to be wandering and, for the first time, I considered the possibility that Daphne Wetmore wasn't all that bright. From the size of yards in the new housing to what we should call each other, her mind appeared to be not wandering but bouncing randomly around inside her cranium. I reminded her of Job One. "We really need to find Keith Bunsen. We don't have to tell him what I just told you. We can tell him the police are questioning Georgina as to her whereabouts on Monday night. If I'm right, he'll know what he has to do."

Daphne talked me into a cup of tea. Determined to make sure I'd made my point, I followed her into the kitchen while she put on the kettle.

"Oh, I almost forgot!" I said. "You and Lady Attwood are sisters, aren't you?"

"Yes," Daphne sang the word in the same note as the boiling kettle, then turned with a jerk. "Why?"

"Because I… I had to take something to the police station this morning and while I was there, they got a call. I heard the desk sergeant say it was Lord Attwood and he was reporting a stolen gun."

"A stolen gun?"

"Right. And the policeman told me, yesterday, that the bullet they took out of Lindsey Scoggin was of an unusual caliber."

Daphne let the cup she was pulling down from a cabinet crash on the floor. She ran straight to the library and to the glass case where Harold kept his antique firearms. "They're all here, I think. And the case is locked."

"Do you suspect the gun came from here?"

"No! Of course not. But when you said 'unusual caliber,' my first thought was of these. I suspect they're all of an unusual caliber."

"Does Lord Attwood also keep old guns?"

"He has a whole room full. I don't know how he'd notice if one was missing."

"Are you sure none of these is missing?"

"Well, look. They're all arranged just so. If one was missing there'd be a space."

"Unless the thief moved them to cover the space."

"Still, there's no reason to think my brother-in-law's missing gun has anything to do with the shooting of Dr. Scoggin."

"Coincidence? Is there any connection you can think of between Dr. Scoggin—or St. Giles Bell—and the Attwoods?"

Daphne paused a long moment, running her hands along the wood frame of the gun case. "I can't think of any, but they have so many friends. Dr. Bell could be one of them."

My cell phone rang. "Keith Bunsen," I mouthed to Daphne. He was responding to the message I'd left. "Dr. Bunsen, you're going to think me an awful busybody but I think you should know the police are presently questioning Georgina about the shooting of Lindsey Scoggin on Tuesday morning. There seems to be some doubt as to her whereabouts on Monday night into Tuesday morning. She told them she was at home but her parents say she was spending the night with girlfriends."

"Where are they now?" Keith's tone was grave.

"At the station on St. Aldate's, unless they've…"

"Talk to you later. Thanks."

I CARRIED MY empty cup back to the kitchen and was preparing to leave when Daphne asked me, "Is the woman from Glastonbury still in room three? Miss Beaulieu?"

"She was there last night. I haven't seen her today."

"Do me a favor, please. Let me know when she does leave. I don't want to talk to her. I only want to know when she's gone."

In case I thought Daphne and Mignon were bosom buddies, I now knew better. I ventured a noncommittal, "Harold didn't like having them here, did he?"

"No. He and the Glastonbury crowd don't get along."

"Still, it's too bad, Fitzwaring dying so suddenly."

"Indeed. And such a young man, too. But diabetes can take its victims without warning." Still barefoot, she followed me to the door. "Such a horrible thing, and so common these days."

"Do you know what he was planning to say in his address that day? He was going to announce that he had the actual bones of King Arthur."

Daphne spluttered—a derisive hiss and guffaw combined. "Where did you hear that?"

"From Mignon herself."

"And where are these bones?"

"At the lab where they do carbon-fourteen dating. Mignon is trying to raise the money to get them out of hock."

"I can't wait to tell Harold! He'll love it!" The way she laughed told me she wasn't giving the idea any serious thought at all.

"Apparently they're from the right time period."

"So are a lot of things." She opened the door for me. "Thanks for dropping by."

TWENTY

THE MIDDLE QUAD was almost deserted when I crossed it heading for the closing ceremonies in Smythson Hall. A quarter of the group had already left and the rest were inside the hall. I was a bit late. I slipped into a seat near the back. On the dais, Harold Wetmore sat in the lone chair while a man I recognized as Pete, the audiovisual man, explained how we could purchase CDs of the various sessions. I scribbled the web address he gave us on a cash register receipt from my purse. Next, one of the porters gave us instructions for checking out of our rooms.

A minor commotion on the right caused heads in my vicinity to turn. Mignon Beaulieu was bundling her bulk along a row of listeners, forcing those she passed to shift their knees to one side. Finding two vacant seats together, she plopped herself into one and an olive-drab duffel bag into the other.

Harold Wetmore stepped up to the podium and tapped the microphone with one finger. The magnified thunk resounded throughout the room. "It is with regret that I bring this most productive gathering to…" Yada, yada. My mind wandered and I looked around the audience. Larry Roberts sat in the front row, nodding frequently, as I could tell from the back of his head. I couldn't find Claudia Moss. Daphne wasn't there either but, given her anxiety level, I figured she'd have returned to her yoga as soon as I left. I located Robin Morris and reminded myself to thank him for helping me with my library work.

Harold said, "It is now certain that one can hardly overstate the importance of sexual attraction and lure of palace intrigue to the Elizabethan psyche. We've been reminded of the tremendous influence the French had upon the mores of the English court. We've seen how the literature of France…"

I heard more rustling from my right and turned to look. Mignon was scrambling through the contents of her duffel, a drawstring pouch clinched in her teeth. People sitting near her looked irritated.

"But the greatest good that invariably comes from a conference such as this," Harold droned on, "indeed one may argue that it, alone, is sufficient justification to hold such a conference, is the contacts one makes. We may read one another's published work, we may confer by email or phone, but there is nothing like the bond one forms when sitting down and talking face to face. I'm certain that, when we go back to our respective offices and homes, we will continue to talk. By phone, by email, or…"

"But not one of you will ever call me!"

The shout came from my right. I turned, as did everyone in the hall, and saw Mignon, now standing, sweeping her jiggly arm around to include the entire assembled group. It felt as if she pointed directly at me, but I suspected we all felt the same. Her eyes danced with anger.

"You're blind! All of you! King Arthur was real. *Is real.* The greatest king England will ever know, and not one of you will allow his name to be spoken in this bloody ivory tower, unless the word 'myth' goes with it. Well, you almost got corrected! Almost, but not quite, because Bram Fitzwaring died before he could set you straight."

Harold Wetmore thumped on his microphone, for attention I supposed, but it didn't work. He looked chagrined, peering toward the back and side doors, as if he'd give his kingdom for a horse—or a policeman—or anyone who knew what to do in a situation like this.

Mignon went on. "Bram had a thousand pounds with him and he intended to use it to obtain the proof you all need to open your stupid eyes, but he didn't get the chance. I'll give you a hint. The proof is right here in Oxford!"

Stirrings around the room.

"But I don't know where Bram's money is. Undoubtedly someone here stole it from his room. All I need is a thousand pounds, and I'll show you proof positive that King Arthur and Queen Guinevere were as real as you or I!"

Harold's voice boomed through the microphone. "You insult us, then ask us to give you a thousand pounds? That's not likely to happen, Miss Beaulieu."

Nervous laughter.

Mignon lurched forward as if she were about to trample over the people in front of her, then staggered left and into the center aisle. But before she could reach the front of the room, Harold had scurried for the steps at the side of the dais and a number of men from the audience had risen to block Mignon's progress. They surrounded her. I didn't wait to see the rest. I slipped out the back.

I felt my phone vibrate in the purse I held clinched under my arm. Pulling the phone out and checking the screen, I hoped it was Lettie calling, but it was the airline with its automatic "time to check in" prompt. I wasn't ready for this! Home tomorrow? No way. Could I wrap this mess up before tomorrow? Could I leave not knowing what the lab would find on or in those syringes? Not knowing who shot Lindsey? Not knowing why Bram upended his furniture in the middle of the night, and then died?

Could I leave without ever seeing Arthur's bones? I had to admit it. I was more than curious. Bram must have taken *something* to the radiocarbon dating lab. What was it? Would Mignon raise the thousand pounds, call a press conference, sign a major book deal, and stun the world as I watched from my TV back home?

When I reached the center of the East Quad, the windows all around began to sway. Low blood sugar. I'd eaten no lunch and it was four o'clock. I didn't think I could make it up all those stairs to my room so I stumbled to the bench and sat. I could feel my brain pulsating behind my eyeballs.

"What did I tell you?" For a second I thought it was my mother chiding me because I'd done it again. I turned toward the sound of the voice and saw Larry Roberts, waving like a stalk of corn in the wind. "What did I tell you? Complete wackos. Both of them."

"I need something with sugar. Go up to my room, and get the cookies on my tray."

Larry knew about my condition. "Where's your room key?"

"In my purse."

He grabbed it off the bench, dumped the contents on the ground, and picked up the key with the magic button attached. "What's your room number? Never mind, it says six right here." He must have flown the whole way because I was still conscious when he returned.

"Cookies," he said, handing me two cellophane-wrapped packages. "And I found your orange juice." He punched the attached straw through the foil opening on top and handed it to me.

I waited for the sugar rush, hoping I wouldn't throw up first. When it came, like a blessed chorus of angels, I smiled. Larry was still standing there. I heard him ask some passersby to wait in case we needed more help. "I'm better, now."

Larry insisted I wait a minute and volunteered to find me a proper meal, but I didn't need one now. "You were in the meeting just now?" he asked. "You saw Mignon's performance?" I let him gloat for a minute, but he was getting on my nerves. When I get low blood sugar everything gets on my nerves.

"Where did they take her?" I asked.

"Harold told them to bring her to the Master's Lodgings."

"They aren't hurting her, are they?"

"Of course not. What kind of people do you think they are?"

"I don't suppose Harold's writing her a check for a thousand pounds."

Larry laughed. For a second it was like old times, as if we were back in Charlottesville, discussing Shakespeare and *Macbeth*.

OUTSIDE THE COLLEGE GATE, I hailed a cab and headed for the hospital. I rode the elevator to the third floor and walked to Lindsey's room. It was empty. Fresh sheets on the bed, and the flowers I'd brought her were gone. My heart leaped. The room felt cold and sterile, and I felt faint. *Did I get off the elevator on the wrong floor?*

I hoped. Somewhat shakily, I walked to the nurses' station where they told me Lindsey had been released a couple of hours earlier.

My main reason for coming here was not to see Lindsey, but to gain entrance to the research wing. I wanted to see St. Giles Bell's lab again and I wanted to talk to Keith Bunsen. I knew Keith wasn't in his rooms at St. Ormond's, but he might still be talking to the police or he might be here. If he was here, he'd probably be in his lab. This presented a couple of problems. I couldn't walk into the research wing without clearance. The only other time I'd been there, Lindsey had called ahead, given her name, and someone had buzzed us through.

I started to tell a nurse at the station that I had a message from Lindsey for Dr. Bell and I needed to deliver it personally. That wouldn't work now because I'd just expressed surprise that she wasn't here, so when would she have given me this message? And if talk around this hospital was like most hospitals, every nurse in the building knew all about Lindsey, about St. Giles, and about Lindsey tagging Georgina as her shooter. They'd know Lindsey had given strict instructions that St. Giles was not to be allowed anywhere near her hospital room. So what excuse could I use?

I retreated to a nearby visitors' waiting area and pretended to make a call, then sauntered over to the station again, and called one nurse over. Whispering, I said, "I suppose you know that Dr. Bell and Dr. Scoggin were seeing each other?" I waited for an affirmative nod, but my confidant wasn't willing to make that commitment. "Well, they were. And that set him up as the police's prime suspect."

"But Dr. Bell was…"

"In London. I know.

"But here's the thing. Dr. Scoggin and Dr. Bell have had a misunderstanding. So sad, but she was so angry with him yesterday she never wanted to see him again."

"Wasn't there another woman?" The nurse stiffened as if she'd revealed more than she'd intended—which she had.

"Dr. Scoggin thought so, but that's been cleared up. Anyway, I just called her. She's at home now and she gave me a message to give Dr. Bell. It's confidential, I'm afraid, but I promised I'd try to find him and give him the message personally."

"Why doesn't she call him herself?"

"I said the misunderstanding has been cleared up. I didn't say she was ready to talk to him yet. She's at home now with her mother and her children. She's on pain meds and she's simply had all the trauma she can deal with for the moment."

"I quite understand. One moment. I'll see if Dr. Bell is in the building." She pushed another nurse away from the phone, made a couple of calls, and at length I heard her say, "A Mrs. Lamb is here. She's a friend of Dr. Scoggin and she has a message for you. May I send her down?" Hanging up, she told me, "He's in his laboratory on ground floor. Take the elevator down and ask at the front desk. They'll see you get there straight away."

A COUPLE OF white-coated assistants were working in Keith Bunsen's lab across the hall from Bell's lab. I saw them through the bulletproof glass wall, but I didn't see Keith. On the opposite side of the hall, Bell's door was closed. I peeked through the glass wall beside it wondering if I should knock or what. I knocked. A minute

later St. Giles opened the door and ushered me in with
more amiable hospitality than I deserved. I'd forgotten
how attractive he was.

"You have a message for me? From Lindsey?"

"I'm afraid I misled the nurse upstairs. Actually, I
want to talk to you *about* Lindsey." The room smelled
like a tidal mud flat, with oysters bathing in pans of
toxic soup.

"Come in, come in." He looked around, ran his hand
through his hair, and frowned. "There's no comfortable
place to sit here. Let's go to my office across the hall."
He led me across to a door that was only a foot or so
from the door to Bunsen's lab, plied the knob with a key,
and waved me in.

I'd been here before. This was the same room in which
I'd talked to Keith about Bram's participation in the diabetes study. On that occasion, Keith and I had walked
in from the opposite side of the room. I recognized the
partition that separated this office space from Keith's
laboratory.

"Dr. Bunsen and I share this. His work is on diabetes."

"I know. When I was here before, I talked to him and
he brought me in here." The two desks on opposite walls,
each with its own computer, chair, and filing cabinets,
made sense now. I grabbed the chair at Keith's desk and
turned it around. "By the way, I was talking to someone
the other day about shellfish poisoning, and I recalled
the work you told me about. What was the name of the
chemical you are using?"

St. Giles blushed, then stammered, "Are you talking
about saxitoxin?"

"I think that's it. A friend of mine died recently after
showing symptoms oddly similar to shellfish poisoning,

and after both he and I ate some mussels and got sick. I'm sure he didn't eat enough to kill him, but with my visit here fresh on my mind, I wondered. Is it possible someone could have stolen this—what did you call it— saxitoxin and injected him with a strong dose?"

"From my lab? No. I keep careful records." He smiled bravely in spite of the fact that my question carried with it an accusation of sloppy record-keeping.

"Of course. I didn't mean that. But suppose someone broke in and stole some of your supply. Unless they left traces of the break-in, you wouldn't know about it until you compared your supply with your records."

Was it my imagination, or did I see beads of sweat in his hairline?

"Look. Here's where I keep my supply." Without standing, he swirled his wheeled desk chair around to a safe mounted under the counter near his own work- space. He blocked my view of the dial with his body and opened the thick metal door. I peered around him and saw several glass vials inside. "See? This is it. After I purify the saxitoxin in my oysters, I record it and put it in here. It's a time-lock safe. After hours, even I can't open this safe. Even on orders from the queen. And how many people know the combination?" He held up one finger. "Me. No one else."

"What about Dr. Bunsen?"

"He has his own safe. It's around the corner."

"But anyone who has ever watched you open it could have…"

"I'm careful, Mrs. Lamb." His tone told me I'd taken this far enough. "I thought you wanted to talk to me about Lindsey."

"I suppose you've heard Lindsey told the police she thinks it was Georgina Wetmore who shot her."

He nodded.

"Do you know Georgina?"

"No. The police have already interviewed me today. I told them I haven't the vaguest idea who Georgina Wetmore is."

"Lindsey's mother told me Lindsey found Georgina's picture in your desk."

"What?"

"You didn't know that?"

"The police asked me about her, but they didn't mention a photograph."

"Didn't they ask to see inside your desk?"

"I was at home at the time."

I looked at the desks on both sides of this small room. "Which desk is yours?"

St. Giles rolled himself back to the desk opposite the one at which I was sitting. "This one, but I also have a desk in my office upstairs and in my home office as well." As he talked, he slid open the drawer above the kneehole space. "Bloody hell!"

He pulled out a full color, eleven by fourteen photo of the lovely young woman who'd blown bubbles with Lindsey's children. He turned it toward me and I couldn't help noticing she was completely nude. I read the inscription: *All my love forever, Georgina.*

"I swear to God, I've never seen this in my life!"

"And this is Keith Bunsen's desk?" I pulled out the drawer nearest my chair. Inside it lay a scattering of pens, rubber tubes, and USB cables. "It's obvious what happened. Whoever put the photo in your desk—probably Georgina—got the desks mixed up."

St. Giles nodded, studied the photo, and tapped the face. "I've seen her, but I can't think where."

"Right here, probably," I said.

Before I had a chance to explain, the phone on St. Giles's desk rang. I picked up my purse and, as I slipped out, heard, "How long? Yes, Chief Inspector Child, I'll be here. I'll tell the front desk you're on your way."

TWENTY-ONE

LINDSEY WAS DOZING, Lettie told me. At her flat, I found Claire and Caleb both in manic states, hugely relieved that their mother was home again, but also suffering from cabin fever. I promised I'd walk to the store with them after I talked to their grandmother.

Lettie thought my news was important enough to wake Lindsey. She led me up the stairs and into a darkened bedroom. Lindsey was sleeping on her back, snoring softly. I imagined her throat was still raw from the breathing tube. When Lettie pulled the blinds open, her daughter moaned and squinted, smacking her dry lips as she raised her arm to shield her eyes.

"Dotsy's here," Lettie said. "And she's made a very interesting discovery."

Lindsey tried to pull herself up while Lettie shoved a couple of pillows behind her back. After I spilled the whole story, Lindsey nodded, went silent for a long moment, then started to cry. "Oh, my God. It wasn't Georgina at all. He doesn't even know her. Oh, the poor man. I have to call him!"

"Wait a minute," Lettie said. "The photo may belong to Keith Bunsen, but that doesn't mean you should go running back to St. Giles. There are still a few problems you need to consider before you do anything drastic."

"Calling him isn't drastic! I owe it to him."

"It's to Georgina Wetmore you owe an explanation,"

I said. "She's spent a most unpleasant day at the police station, defending herself against a murder charge."

Looking her daughter straight in the eye, Lettie said, "Did you actually *see* the shooter?" Lettie sat on the side of the bed and took Lindsey's hand. I noticed she kicked a cell phone under the bed with the side of her foot as she sat. "Or did you *assume* it was Georgina because of that picture you found?"

"I'm fuzzy on that."

"Understandably so," I said. "But all is not well, Lindsey. You still have a bullet hole in your chest and the person who put it there has not been caught."

"I'll leave that up to the police."

I COULD TELL Lindsey's had nothing on her mind but making up with St. Giles, and I said so to Lettie after we'd left Lindsey's bedroom. "I don't know if John Fish would qualify as a reliable source, but I think Lindsey should learn all she can about the death of St. Giles's wife."

"What has he said?"

"He told me St. Giles's wife died last year after a fall down the stairs at her home. There were suspicious circumstances. I don't know what they were, but John Fish refers to St. Giles as 'the bastard.' And I don't think he means it in a nice way."

"What can I do?"

"Find out when the wife died and learn all you can online. Then go to the newspaper office and get back copies from that time period."

"I'm on it!" Lettie tripped down the last few stairs and ran to the small alcove where Lindsey's laptop sat on a dining table.

"All right if I take Claire and Caleb for a walk?" I asked.

Lettie was most appreciative since she could see for herself the children had sunk to entertaining themselves by picking their noses and showing each other what they found.

THE CHILDREN LED me past the neighborhood's small playground and I stopped to let them burn a few calories on the equipment. While they played, I studied the layout of this relatively new subdivision. By climbing to the top of the slide, I got a better view. There seemed to be three or four parallel rows of two-story dwellings that in America might be called townhouses. Here, they were called terraced flats. The long streets running past the front yards led to a small cluster of businesses on one end: a grocery, probably a dry cleaner, a pizza place, the sort of places you'd find near any suburban housing. I spotted a sign for a movie rental store.

In the opposite direction, I could see pastureland sprinkled with sheep. A parking area, barely visible behind a grove of trees, served, I figured, as guest parking. Each of the apartments had room for only one vehicle to park in front. *Where would Lindsey's assassin have stood in order to get a clear shot?* Suddenly I couldn't wait to take the children home so I could figure this out for myself. A neighbor had told the police they saw a person in a dark jacket, possibly an anorak, walking along a nearby path. From my perch on the next-to-top rung of the slide, I couldn't see anything that looked like a path.

The children and I walked as far as the grocery store where I bought each of them an ice cream on a stick. Walking home again, Claire said she was making a book of thoughts for her mother. "Not really poems or stories. Just things I've been thinking about while she was in the hospital." Caleb, obviously jealous he hadn't thought of it first, said he was making her a book, too. A book of pictures. A chunk of the chocolate shell on Caleb's ice cream cracked and fell on the street. He seemed about to cry but considered it again and simply shrugged.

Each flat we passed had a small front yard surrounded by a brick wall some four feet high. An opening in the exact middle of each wall led to a brick walk, which led straight to the front door. A small overhang above the doors displayed house numbers in brass. I noticed most of the yards were virtual works of art, more evidence of the English love of gardens, but a few needed tending. Lindsey Scoggin's yard was neat but simple, with river rock and a few small shrubs. Nothing to mow.

"The woman who stayed with you last night," I said to the children. "Where does she live?"

"There." Claire pointed to the house directly across from Lindsey's.

I walked past Lindsey's yard, still thinking about where the shooter would have stood, when Claire brought me back to reality with a tug on my hand. "Whoops!" I said, backtracking. "Ready to go in?" I watched the children until Lettie opened the door for them, then trekked on to the north end of the street where it dead-ended in a bush-covered hill. I picked my way through the bushes to the top of the hill and found the parking area I'd spotted from atop the slide at the playground. Only a few cars were parked in it now.

Beyond the parking area was pastureland set off by hedgerows. A road from somewhere beyond entered the parking area on the west side, and I surmised it probably connected to the A-road I had recently travelled by taxi. With nothing else of interest nearby, the parking lot had to be for visitors to the terraced flats. Did Lindsey's shooter park here? If so, where did he or she stand to do the deed? Turning, I had a bird's-eye view of the street with its continuous row of dwellings on both sides, but I was seeing it from an odd angle. The walls obscured my view of most of the yards. Turning all the way around, I spotted a dirt path. It skirted a stand of trees along the top of the slope.

Picking my way carefully through the deep hardwood mulch around the shrubbery, I reached the path and followed it down and around a bend. *Maybe this is why they call it Belle Glen*, I thought. Beautiful glen. Waist-high woodland flowers lined both sides of the path. This had to be where the person in the anorak was walking when spotted by a neighbor down below.

Certainly the crack of gunfire from here would have made anyone outside or standing near a window or door that morning turn this way—unless it produced an echo. The nearest homes backed onto the slope. I was looking at back yards with clotheslines and barbecue grills. Beyond, the next row of houses, of which Lindsey's was one, faced the street. By the time a neighbor hearing the shot located the path up here, the shooter would have been leaving.

Looking down the slope again I wondered which unit was Lindsey's. How to tell? At once I knew because I was looking through a front gate, up a perfectly straight, paved walk to a front door, which, by its frosted-glass tracery, I recognized was Lindsey's.

This was the spot where the shooter stood. This would've been perfect. Fairly well concealed in a dark jacket by the dark trees behind, the assassin could have stood here until Lindsey came out, as she would have had to do if she was parked in front and if she was working that day. The shooter could have stood right here and waited, gun at the ready. From this distance, I figured I could hit a human target myself. Maybe. And a skilled marksman? No problem.

Had the police figured this out? Had they come up here already and reached the same conclusion I had? If they hadn't, might there be a shell casing still lying around? I looked carefully, found nothing, but wasn't surprised. Any reasonably competent hit man would know to pick up shell casings, and if the Thames Valley Police were any good, they'd have already looked.

Somewhere on my way back down the hill, it hit me. *Who the shooter had to be.* Unfortunately I didn't *know* I knew until much later that night.

IN THE TAXI motoring back to St. Ormond's, my mind returned to Mignon and the closing ceremony. I felt sorry for her. Right or wrong, she felt she knew the truth and no one believed her. For the first time, I considered a whole new possibility. Had Bram been murdered by a thief? He had £1,000 tucked away somewhere in his room, and it wasn't there now unless he'd found a really clever hiding spot. This idea was much simpler and much more likely than anything I'd considered so far.

But how mundane! How ordinary. A thief? How disappointing.

THE DAY'S LAST rosy rays warmed the limestone walls on the High as my taxi passed The Green Man, a few blocks from my destination. Its green front door stood open to the street and its lights were still on.

"Excuse me! I need to get out here."

"You sure?"

My driver swung the cab into the bike lane while I paid him and hopped out. I heard voices now. It sounded as if The Green Man was having a party. I took a deep breath and walked in, expecting something like the bar scene from *Star Wars* but seeing mostly normal-looking folk. Of the fifteen or so people in the store, the only one I knew was Mignon, and she seemed to stiffen a little as I approached her.

"I'm leaving tomorrow, Mignon, but I just wanted to tell you I've enjoyed getting to know you and I wish you luck with your pursuits."

"Pursuits. That's an interesting choice of words."

"You know what I mean." I probably reddened, but carried on. "And, again, I'm so sorry about Bram. I wish I could have known him longer." My words echoed in my head like the drivel you hear in a reception line.

"Did you go to the closing ceremonies this afternoon?" she asked me. "The thousand pounds I need, not surprisingly, was not forthcoming from the academics, so I've turned to my real friends. We've put a collection jar on the counter and Simon has called his best customers to drop in for a drink and donate whatever they can. Help yourself to a glass of mead. It's in the back room."

I turned and located the curtain I already knew separated the back room from the front. Standing beside it was a spectacularly beautiful woman. Tall and willowy, she had hair as black and shiny as obsidian, cut in a wedge with bangs that drew attention to her large hazel eyes. She wore a crisp white blouse over a moss-green pencil skirt.

"That's Bumps McAlister. Do you know her?"

I must have been staring. "No," I said. *This was the Grey Lady!* "I'd like to meet her."

Mignon introduced me to Bumps and to her husband, Simon, owner of the shop. Simon was short, withered, and going bald. I learned that Bumps was an actress, busy at the moment with a local production of *Twelfth Night*. While she talked, I saw John Fish walking toward us. I reached out and drew him into our little circle.

"So now you know the Grey Lady," he said.

"Pardon?" Bumps tilted her head to one side. I wondered how she got her nickname, but decided it was best not to ask.

"You really did a number on us at St. Ormond's the other night," I said. "John told me you were the apparition that drifted by the doors at the party. You should have heard the speculation later, at dinner!"

Bumps laughed. "That was one of my easier roles. All I had to do was walk by and slip into the priest's hole under the stairs."

John Fish left us and stepped behind the curtain to pour glasses of mead for himself and me. Simon moved along the counter and I spotted the donations jar, about a quarter filled with folding money. An impulse grabbed me. I pulled out my wallet and extracted what was left of my spending cash, about £120. I already had my return bus ticket to the airport, and the only thing I could think of that I'd need money for was dinner tonight and a tip for the scout tomorrow. I put thirty pounds back in my wallet and stuck the rest in the donations jar.

Mignon gasped. "Dotsy! Thank you! Are you sure?"

"Sure. You need to get those bones out of hock."

"But I thought you were one of *them*," she said, her head bobbing in the approximate direction of St. Ormond's.

"I *am* one of them."

"Then why?"

"Why what?"

"Why are you helping me? I'm going to prove that King Arthur was not a myth. It's going to shake their beliefs to the very roots. Their ivory tower will come crashing down like a house of cards!" She trembled at her own words.

"Then so be it."

Simon McAlister spoke up for the first time. "What do you believe, Mrs. Lamb?"

"I believe it's always good to find the truth. Whatever it is."

I quickly grabbed the glass of mead John Fish was holding for me and took a sip. Everyone was looking at me and a mouthful of liquid helped me resist the urge to light into a speech of Shakespearean proportions.

IT WAS DARK by the time I left The Green Man. I stopped at the King's Arms Tavern for fish and chips, spending a good bit less than the twenty pounds I'd allotted for my last dinner in Oxford. Back out on the street, I stood under a streetlight and called Keith Bunsen's cell phone.

"Mrs. Lamb," he said, "I thank you for telling me about Georgina. I was able to get her released, and I'm sure you'll be happy to know she's home, safe and sound, with her parents right now."

So we're playing that game, are we? Rather than tell me the police released her after Keith told them she'd been with him all night, he's skipping that part and going straight to "home, safe and sound." Poor little Georgina. If Georgina was indeed home right now, I imagined she was in the middle of a tense family conference. Who would win? Georgina with her *but I love him and you can't stop me,* or her parents? They'd be countering with, "He's twice your age and you're too young to know what you're doing." I've been through this before with my own daughter and, trust me, it's no fun. Georgina was above the age of consent and she'd win in the end.

Under these circumstances, it was not my problem and none of my business so I decided to let Keith continue the ruse. "I'm so glad," I said, "but I need to talk to you anyway. Are you free right now?"

"I'm at St. Ormond's. You know how to find my room. Come on up."

KEITH BUNSEN WAS in shirt and tie, bedroom slippers, and an old holey cardigan. He reminded me somehow of Mr. Rogers and the way he used to start every show by changing his shoes and jacket but leaving his tie in place. Keith led me to his small office at one side of his sitting room.

"I know why the police think Georgina shot Dr. Scoggin," I said, taking the guest chair.

"*Thought,*" he said. "Past tense. They know now that she couldn't have."

"Right. I know why they thought it."

"Something about a picture found in Dr. Bell's desk, I believe. It made no sense. Georgina told me she hardly knows Dr. Bell."

"Georgina meant to put it in *your* desk in the research

wing. Your desk is three feet away from his." I paused, and then added, "I visited Dr. Bell there this afternoon."

I saw the blood rise from his collar to his face. The tops of his ears turned bright red. "I—I—I thought they said it was in the desk at Bell's home."

"Confusion due to Lindsey Scoggin's state of mind when she came out of the medically induced coma."

"I see."

I let him mull that over.

"So I guess there's no use pretending."

"That you and Georgina are in love? No."

Now it was relief that flooded his face.

"You and Georgina should take care to appreciate how her parents are feeling right now. Until you have a daughter yourself, it's hard to imagine."

"Oh, I know. You make a good point."

I hoped he would take my words to heart. "Keith, you know Dr. Bell pretty well, don't you? Does he ever talk to you about the death of his wife? I understand it happened earlier this year."

"He never mentions it. At the time, I know he was under suspicion, and the police were watching every move he made. I think he considered our lab a place of respite—the only place where he could get away from the police a-a-and the press. They were even worse."

"So you let him have a bit of peace? You didn't ask questions?" He nodded and I went on, "Did he know about you and Georgina?"

"Oh, no! We told no one."

"How often was she inside the room you share with Dr. Bell?"

"Never, that I know of. I can't recall her ever going in there, but I'm not sure."

"I see. One more question. Have you deleted Bram Fitzwaring from your study?"

"I told my assistant to do that. I assume she did."

"Have you ever known anyone to turn over furniture right before dying from hypoglycemia?"

Keith was sitting in his desk chair, his hand resting on its arm. At that question, his fingers clamped around the leather padding. It was a subtle reaction, but I caught it. "It would be rather unusual. Hypoglycemia tends to make them spacey and vague. If they get no help, they drift off into unconsciousness."

"That's been my experience as well."

"But one should never say 'never' in medicine. As soon as you say a particular thing can't happen, it happens."

"When I visited St. Giles this afternoon in your office, I couldn't help noticing the safe in the corner. He told me he keeps his dangerous chemicals, the saxitoxin he uses in his nerve studies, in there. Do you also keep things there?"

"It's St. Giles's safe. I don't know the combination."

St. Giles had told me the same thing.

TWENTY-TWO

I NEEDED TO pack everything except what I wanted to wear to the airport tomorrow, but I had no will to do so. I pulled out my large suitcase from the floor of my closet, set it on my bed, tossed in some lecture notes and underwear, then quit. I slid the suitcase onto the floor, lay down on the bed, and stared at the ceiling. Pale yellow light from the street lamps down Sycamore Lane crept through my tiny window past the decal warning me this was No Exit.

What was I to do? What would happen if I cancelled my plane ticket? My ticket, I recalled, was nonrefundable. I couldn't afford to waste it. I pulled myself to my feet, retrieved my blood glucose monitor from my purse, and checked. My blood sugar was okay.

I rounded up my shower things, slid my feet into my flip-flops, and flapped down the stairs to the bathroom. As I passed the window over the little refrigerator, I glimpsed a large shadow from the corner of my eye. Rising to tiptoes, I got a better look through the window. Since that first night when the same sort of shadow had spooked me, I had studied the lights on my side of the quad. A lantern-style lamp hung beside the entrance to Staircase Thirteen, and three low-wattage lights, stuck in the ground, were trained on the border plants. Only the lantern by the entrance would cast light across the quad, and the shadows produced by anything passing along this side appeared greatly magnified against the stone on the far side. Greatly magnified and moving faster than it actually was. It could be scary if you didn't know what you were seeing.

In this case, however, the shadow of the passing form was easily identified as Harold Wetmore. I saw the top of his head with its fringe of white hair as it passed beneath the window. I wondered where he was going alone and at this time of night.

Opening the refrigerator, I studied my insulin supply. It was too soon to remove it. I'd do that tomorrow just before leaving. But something was wrong. I stepped back and tried to figure what it was. I kept two kinds of insulin: one fast-acting and one slow. The slow-acting kind was in a squat vial and I had an extra one, still in the box. The fast-acting kind was in a longer, thinner vial. To save trips upstairs, I also kept some syringes in a box beside the medicine. What was wrong? It took a minute for the light to dawn, but when I saw it I wondered why it took me so long.

I always left the long, thin vial lying on its side because, upright, it was unstable. It fell over at the slightest disturbance. This vial was standing upright. I'd never have left it like that. I picked up the vial with the slow-acting insulin, the kind I use most often, and recalled that, this morning, it had been almost empty. The paper label kept me from seeing the liquid level inside, but, by turning it sideways, I could see through the space between the top of the label and the neck of the vial.

It was almost full.

I went cold all over. Not only was it almost full, the liquid within was the wrong color—a cloudy tan I didn't recognize. Steadying myself against the far wall, I pondered what to do next. I checked the top of the box on my extra vial and found it still securely sealed with the manufacturer's glue. So I did still have insulin for tomorrow morning, but if I'd used the open vial I was certain it would've killed me. Who would have access to this refrigerator? Anyone! This space was never locked and access from the quad was wide open.

Who did this?

I filled a new syringe from the tampered vial, wrapped it in my face cloth, carried it carefully up to my room, and placed it on the shelf above my clothes rack. Common sense told me that my would-be killer would check on me before dawn because they couldn't know exactly when I'd next take an injection and if I was still alive tomorrow morning, that wouldn't do. I'd be flying home with all the pieces I needed to solve two murders. I figured my killer was, at that moment, agonizing and wondering how long it would take me to sort it out. Wondering if I was already dead.

I set my chair as close as I could to the hinge side of my door, grabbed my tiny battery-operated book light and attached it to the Elizabeth Peters paperback I'd brought from home. Donning the same pants, shirt, and shoes I'd worn all day, I turned off the overhead light and sat, the only illumination now coming from the high, small window and from my book light. I did my best to concentrate on reading, but there was no way. I jumped at every noise. From the alley outside the window, from the water pipes beneath my basin, from places somewhere below. I couldn't tell if those sounds, like doors squeaking or floor boards groaning, came from the hall, from Lettie's room, or from Mignon's. What if Lettie or Mignon came up to visit? Of course they'd knock, wouldn't they? The person I was waiting for would not knock.

I looked at my watch every few minutes, tried not to, but failed. It seemed as if a building as old as this one should make more sounds. At times it felt as if I was inside a tomb and, in a way, I was. Around me, only stone that had long since settled into the earth beneath. No wooden rafters, no walls with aging insulation between dry wall and siding, nothing to pop or creak or go bump in the night except water pipes and late-night strollers outside, or someone coming up the stairs. Noises with actual causes.

Ten o'clock, ten thirty, eleven o'clock, eleven thirty, midnight. *I was so tired of sitting.* Twelve-o-five, twelve ten, twelve thirteen. *Noises.* I closed my book. False alarm. I decided it was Mignon returning to her room below. I could, of course, run down to Mignon's room and take refuge there, but that would ruin the trap I'd set. How terrifying it was to know someone wanted you dead. Someone wanted me to die! I realized that neither Bram nor Lindsey had prior warning of their attacks and would never have felt what I was feeling as I sat in the dark, waiting. Twelve twenty, twelve thirty, twelve thirty-four. Metal scratched against the keyhole in my door. Trembling, I switched off my book light. I almost dropped it.

The door eased open without a sound, and I stood. I brought the electric coffeepot down as hard as I could onto whatever it was coming through. A gun clanked to the floor. She had a gun! I never imagined she'd bring a gun, but I'd unwittingly disarmed her. Thank God!

I tossed the duvet from my bed over her head, wrapped my arms around the ghost-like form, and forced it to the floor. Screaming and kicking, my bundle struggled to

break free but it was no use because I was bigger. Daphne
Wetmore, tiny woman that she was, was no match for my
five-foot-five inches of aging sinew and muscle.

I hadn't previously considered what to do next, so I
sat on her until I figured it out. I set the chair across her
midsection and, with my knees on the chair seat, flipped
on the overhead light. The gun lay near my nightstand.
A bungee cord I'd brought with me to lash my luggage
together served as an arm restraint but only temporar-
ily. I knew she'd get out of it soon enough. I grabbed the
gun, closed the door, and called 911 on my cell phone.
What was wrong? Duh. In the UK, the emergency number is 999. I called it and told them to send police to St.
Ormond's, Staircase Thirteen, ASAP.

While I waited for the police, I looked at the gun in
my hand. It was obviously old. This was the gun that almost killed Lindsey Scoggin. I wondered how you fired
it. The trigger was obvious, but was it locked? I had no
idea how to tell except by actually squeezing the trigger, and I couldn't afford to let Daphne know I'd never
fired a gun in my life.

TWENTY-THREE

I MISSED MY PLANE, but it didn't matter. The next morning Chief Inspector Child said the police would need my help with their enquiries—I love that phrase—for a couple of days. I pled poverty, and he used the awesome power of the Crown Prosecution Service to arrange a Saturday flight on Virgin Atlantic for me.

I saw Larry Roberts off at the bus terminal as he scrambled to catch our previously scheduled flight. He wanted to stay behind and hear the whole story because he knew nothing about the night's events until I showed up at the terminal and told him I wasn't leaving with him. He had a million questions and, I suddenly realized, a bit of apprehension about flying home alone. His wife had put me in charge of keeping the absentminded professor from getting lost.

"Here are your car keys," I said, dropping them into his hand. "Here's the ticket for the long-term parking lot. You're in the green lot near shuttle stop eighteen. Here's the card I picked up to remind me where we were parked."

"Yeah, yeah. I got it. When will I see you again?"

I could tell he really didn't want to go now that things were getting interesting, but I left him there and took a cab back to college. En route, I called my son Brian and told him to keep my dog until I could pick her up on

Sunday. I called a neighbor and asked her to water my tomato plants and my houseplants for two more days.

Lettie was waiting for me in the quad. The news had got around somehow, in spite of police orders to keep a lid on it. I had said nothing to anyone but Larry, and he'd had no chance to blab because he'd been ready to board the bus when I told him. Lettie bounced from her seat on the bench—the same bench I'd shared with Bram Fitzwaring that first night—and ran to me.

I said, "It was Daphne. It was all Daphne."

"But why?"

"Long story. I've been at the police station all night. It feels like I've been wearing these same clothes for a week." I looked up at Keith Bunsen's window in the North Wing and saw the curtain pulled back, a face looking down. I waved to him and pointed toward the Middle Quad. If the Senior Common Room was open, I thought we could gather there. "If Mignon is still here, I think she should hear the story, too."

Lettie ran up to check on Mignon, and I waited for Keith, who lurched through the entrance to his staircase a minute later. He suggested we could get a scout to open the SCR for us, but when we arrived at the door we found the room already open, a scout inside vacuuming the rug. Lettie and Mignon joined us around the fireplace.

"It was all Daphne, all along," I began. "She killed Bram Fitzwaring with an injection of saxitoxin from St. Giles Bell's lab, and shot Lindsey with a gun from Lord and Lady Attwood's home."

"But why?" Lettie asked.

"Her inner audience," I said, recalling the phrase Claudia Moss had used. Looking at Keith, I said, "Have you ever noticed how often Daphne mentions her sister? Lady Attwood?"

Keith tilted his head to one side, and then nodded. "Yes, I have. And it's always a major event when her sister comes to visit."

I recalled the dressing down Daphne gave the poor gardeners on her sister's last visit. "Harold told me once that Daphne grew up in her beautiful, witty, sister's shadow. Daphne was the plain one, with no particular talents and a less-than-sparkling personality. Her big sister had all the boys. She had none. Her sister married a title and lived in a mansion. Daphne stayed home, destined for spinsterhood, or so she thought.

"When dowdy, fusty, old Harold Wetmore asked her to marry him—well, he wasn't Prince William, but he was a master of an Oxford College, and he was renowned as a scholar of early English history. That was good enough. Now she could claim some sort of parity with her sister."

"Like, okay, we're not so rich, but we *are* respected," Lettie said.

"Exactly. A few days ago Claudia Moss told me she couldn't help evaluating all her own actions through the eyes of a girl she'd roomed with in college. A girl who always seemed to outdo her in every way. It was as if Claudia went through her life seeking the approval of someone she hadn't seen in years. She called it her 'inner audience.' I started thinking about my own inner audience and how stupid the whole thing is."

"Who is it?" Lettie asked.

"I'd rather not say. Suffice it to say that Daphne's inner audience is her sister and, in everything she does, she strives to impress the woman who probably doesn't give Daphne's status a second thought. But what if someone is coming to destroy your husband's reputation? What if his standing among academics is about to go straight down the tubes? Harold Wetmore was an unabashed proponent of the idea that England languished helplessly, almost returning to the Stone Age when the Romans left, and offered no resistance when the Angles and the Saxons invaded."

Mignon snorted, but said nothing.

"How did Daphne know what Fitzwaring had in mind?" Keith asked.

I looked at Mignon. "Daphne knows the McAlisters, doesn't she? She, John Fish, and Bumps McAlister together planned the Grey Lady stunt for our entertainment. It's not inconceivable that the McAlisters knew Bram and Mignon were coming, and knew they had a bombshell to drop on our conference."

"They *did* know! Bumps and I talked about it," Mignon threw her pudgy hands to the sides of her face.

"Okay," I said. "Bear with me a minute. Here's where it gets complicated. Earlier this year, Dr. St. Giles Bell killed his wife. He probably injected her with saxitoxin, which he had handy. It wouldn't have shown up in autopsy because the medical examiner wouldn't have been looking for it. The lab may have tested her blood for alcohol or for the sort of drugs that often cause healthy people to fall down stairs, but not for a little-known shellfish toxin. I talked to Chief Inspector Child about this, but he's not willing to agree with me until they interview St. Giles again and check to see if the forensic lab still has fluid samples from the wife's autopsy. If not, they may have to get an order to exhume the body."

Lettie shivered.

I said, "Daphne discovered the truth but I don't know

how. Keith, did she ever come to your lab? This would have been about February."

"I—I—I don't remember, exactly, but I believe she did. I believe she was keen to know more about St. Giles's research, but I never wondered why."

"There you go!" I said. I was anxious to leave this speculation behind and go on to the parts I knew for sure. "Assuming she knew St. Giles had killed his wife and that the police weren't going to be able to prove it, she had information she could use for blackmail, but no reason to do so. Not until Bram Fitzwaring comes to the conference, ready to take on Harold Wetmore, *mano a mano*.

"I'll bet Daphne also managed to get into your records, Keith. She may have bribed or intimidated one of your assistants, but I'll bet she knew Bram Fitzwaring was diabetic and was in your study. If so, aha! Perfect. When Bram dies, it'll look like his condition killed him and if there's any reason to suspect his death wasn't natural, the most logical suspect would be Keith. The man who might have needed to lose a subject from his control group so his chi-square test will work out right."

Keith's ears reddened. "How the hell would she have known that?"

"I don't know. Maybe she didn't. But at least she'd know the police could connect him to you more easily than to her or to Harold."

"But now it's too late," Mignon said. "Bram's already been cremated."

"Right. I don't know if the police will be able to make the murder charge stick. But they have all they need to charge her with two counts of attempted murder."

"That's not good enough." Mignon's eyes narrowed in a serious scowl.

"I dare say, when Dr. Bell finds his own neck in the noose, he'll talk plenty. And he'll be able to tell the police exactly how Daphne did it."

"So then what?" Lettie nudged me back to the deed itself.

"Bram was scheduled to address the whole group on the first full day of the conference, so he had to die that first night. I think, rather than fill one of his insulin vials with poison, as she did with mine, she probably slipped into his room—she can get a key from the porter's station—and stuck the needle in him while he slept. Maybe the needle prick woke him up. Maybe he lunged at his attacker in the dark, missed, and began to lose control of his muscles due to the saxitoxin, thrashed around his room, turning everything over. Maybe Daphne was holding the door shut."

"Okay. Now what about Lindsey?" Lettie said. "Explain what she had against Lindsey."

"The police are probably talking to Lindsey right now, but here's what makes sense to me. St. Giles left something incriminating on his desk, maybe an email from Daphne left open on his computer. On Monday afternoon, I called Lindsey and questioned her about how St. Giles stores his saxitoxin. She was in the hospital cafeteria at the time.

"So Lindsey wants to tell St. Giles about my call and goes down to his lab. She looks in his office across the hall, opens his desk drawer, and sees, not the incriminating evidence, but a photograph of Georgina Wetmore signed, *All my love forever, Georgina.*"

A little smile crept to one corner of Keith Bunsen's mouth.

"Lindsey goes crazy. 'That rotten cheater!' Runs home

crying. St. Giles calls, and Lindsey tells him she never wants to see him again. St. Giles has spotted the incriminating email or whatever it was, and assumes that's what's eating Lindsey. She probably hangs up on him and doesn't answer if he calls back.

"St. Giles calls Daphne and says, 'I've got a problem and you need to fix it. Tit for tat. You killed a man with saxitoxin from my safe, and I can get you arrested for murder. Okay, we may both go down together, but maybe not. At least you'll go down, Daphne, unless you do what I want you to do. Kill Lindsey.'

"I need some water," I said. "My throat's dry."

Lettie ran to the sideboard where they kept mixers for drinks and poured me a glass of soda water. No ice.

"Lindsey had to be silenced quickly. There was no time to plan, so St. Giles dashed off to London to get himself an alibi, and Daphne dashed off to the Attwoods' mansion to swipe a gun. She couldn't use any of Harold's guns. Even if she tossed it in the Cherwell, the fact that a gun was missing from his case would be all too obvious. But a gun from Lord Attwood's huge collection would probably not be missed for a long time. Chief Inspector Child has already phoned, early this morning, and learned Daphne had actually practiced shooting clay pigeons with that very gun. Also, she knew where they kept the emergency key to a back door."

"Oh, dear, whatever will Lady Attwood say about this?" Mignon voice was full of irony.

"Next morning, first thing, Daphne drove out to Belle Glen. St. Giles had told her how to find Lindsey's house. She waited on a secluded path above the street of houses until Lindsey walked out and"—I looked at Lettie and lowered my voice—"shot her."

"How do you know all this?" Keith asked. "You haven't talked to Daphne, have you?"

"I went out to Lindsey's yesterday, remember?" I looked at Lettie again. She nodded. "After I took the children for a walk, I did some sleuthing on my own, trying to find out where the shooter would have stood. As I stood on the path I figured the shooter must have taken, I realized I was looking straight into Lindsey's yard. I could see her front door. It's wasn't that far away. I knew it was Lindsey's because, as the children and I walked along the street, I noticed her front door was the only one with an etched glass, Art Deco style window. The rest were mostly Georgian.

"Earlier yesterday I'd heard Daphne say, disparagingly, that she hated those new flats with their postage-stamp yards and their cheap little Art Deco doors. I stood there on the path and got a strange déjà vu feeling but I didn't consciously figure it out until late last night. I realized it must have been Daphne who was walking into Staircase Thirteen the night Bram died, simply because Daphne is so short she's one of the few people who could walk under that bathroom window without my seeing her, even when I stood on tiptoes. I started thinking about Daphne, about Claudia's 'inner audience' comment, and I wondered. That's when it hit me. The only person who'd call the front doors of Belle Glen 'cheap little Art Deco affairs' was someone who'd spent a good deal of time staring *at Lindsey's front door*, and who wouldn't have known it was the only one of that style on the whole street. So it had to be Daphne."

My cell phone rang. It was Chief Inspector Child and

they needed me back down at Thames Valley Police Station. No sleep for me yet, but what did I care?

When I closed my phone, Mignon said, "I don't suppose this is the most important thing, but what about Bram's thousand pounds? The money is still missing."

I said, "The police are questioning the scouts, especially Patricia, the woman who does the rooms on our staircase. They'll try to find out about the money, but honestly, I don't think they have any evidence to go on. They've no proof the money even existed."

Mignon bristled and I thought she was going to take exception to that statement, but she didn't.

"They're mainly interested in finding out how the bottle of syringes ended up in the dumpster on Sycamore Lane instead of the sharps container in the broom closet. Mishandling medical waste and dangerous objects is an offense for which someone could be charged or at least fired. As for the money, hey! Maybe you haven't looked in the right place yet. It could still be in the room."

"One more question," Keith said. "You asked if I got an upset tummy that night after the party. Did you think Bram had been poisoned by the food on Georgina's tray?"

"At first I did, but then I figured it would have been entirely too risky. How would Bram's killer know it would be he, and not someone else, who'd die? I think it's likely, though, that Daphne slipped a drop or two of very dilute saxitoxin on the mussels so some people would get sick. If they did, it would appear likely that the kitchen had purchased tainted mussels.

"By the way, Keith, I've been wondering how you've managed to attend our meals and parties? You weren't part of our conference at all."

"Georgina. She did the place cards and the name tags. Harold is too myopic to notice and Daphne was too hurried to care."

TWENTY-FOUR

HAROLD WETMORE SHAMBLED into the Senior Common Room a minute after Mignon had walked out. He greeted Lettie, Keith, and me, then took up a position directly in front of the hearth. Center stage. With his hands clasped behind his back, he cleared his throat and rocked up on the balls of his feet.

This was not going to be comfortable. I'd have given anything to be elsewhere. I didn't know whether to expect angry outrage that a guest, namely me, had dared accuse his wife of murder, or a tearful apology on her behalf. Either way I wished I'd left the room with Mignon.

"I've just been on the phone with Chris Burroughs. He's the director of the Thames Valley Radiocarbon Accelerator facility. They dated the bones Bram Fitzwaring brought them and found that they all date to about 450 ce, give or take fifty years or so."

"That's what Mignon told me," I said.

"And they are, indeed, human." Harold paused and a grin spread across his face "*Most* of them, that is. But did Mignon mention that the largest bone, the one that looks like a femur, is, in fact, the humerus of an aurochs?"

"An aurochs?"

"They were ancestors of today's cows but they didn't go completely extinct until the sixteen hundreds," Harold said. He pulled a handkerchief from his breast pocket, removed his glasses, fogged them with his breath, and used the handkerchief to polish them. "Not many people know that."

* * * * *

ABOUT THE AUTHOR

MARIA HUDGINS IS the author of four previous Dotsy Lamb Mysteries from Five Star and of two Lacy Glass Botanical Mysteries, available on Amazon Kindle. A former biology and oceanography teacher, she is an avid traveler. Having visited Oxford seven times, she considers it her favorite town on the globe.

A lifelong mystery lover, Hudgins writes the sort of books she likes to read. She's a member of Mystery Writers of America, International Thriller Writers, Sisters in Crime, and the International Association of Crime Writers. She lives in Hampton, Virginia, writes full-time, and travels all she can.